T0210128

Go Back With Me

A Nostalgic Recall of Early 1940 Life in West Virginia

NINA HOLLAND

WestBow Press books may be ordered through booksellers or by contacting:

WestBow Press
A Division of Thomas Nelson & Zondervan
1663 Liberty Drive
Bloomington, IN 47403
www.westbowpress.com
1 (866) 928-1240

ISBN: 978-1-9736-9170-9 (sc)
ISBN: 978-1-9736-9171-6 (e)

Print information available on the last page.

WestBow Press rev. date: 05/21/2020

Contents

Introduction

Maggie's People

I was born Magdalene Ella Snow, but I have forever been known as just Maggie. I've never had much in this life--never wanted much--and living here alone on this mountain is still enough to keep me content. Sometimes, though, I feel as old as these West Virginia hills, especially if I start thinking about my Aunt Phedelia's stories about the Civil War. But I was just a wee thing then--that eases my thinking a bit. Speaking about Auntie, I loved her stories, and never mind how often she reminisced about them times, her favorite story always had the family doubled over with laughter. It seems that a polecat had crawled into one of her pa's hen laying cages during the night and died. The next morning the henhouse still smelled to high heaven, so one of her brothers dumped the skunk into a big rusty lard can sitting nearby, thinking he would later haul the skunk, can and all, far out into the woods and dump them. But it so happened that a band of Yankee soldiers come rushing through Aunt Phedelia's little place that day and grabbed what chickens that were still left behind. Seeing the lard bucket sitting nearby, they asked what was in it. Aunt Phedelia said the first word that came out of her mouth was "tobacco." The corporal told one of his men to grab it and they took off. My aunt said she survived the war by imagining that man's reaction when he took off the lid for a chew. She was sure a sight.

Come to think of it, it was that same aunt that years later

pestered me to write down my memories of that place where I became so attached to, called Fancy Knoll. I thought about it for a good spell and the more I thought about it the more I put my mind to keeping those memories, as much as possible, from being lost and going to dust. At first that thought scared me, and I mulled it around in my mind for a good long spell. I knew it would take a lot of words to make a book, but I reasoned that since I'd never been short on words, I might as well take the bull by the horns and give it a try.

Anyway, those were stories and memories that had nagged at my own heart for years and wouldn't let go. Those eventful happenings and certain faces still haunt me today. Those people weren't my real family, mind you, but because we shared so much of our lives, and oh so much laughter, they became my family just by the living. There's no such place anymore, of course, but I don't want people to forget that one-time community called Fancy Knoll. By the way, I recently found out the place was named after the original Raleigh house which all the local folks' thought was fancy, because it had an indoor outhouse and store-bought window curtains. As time went on the name just stuck for the whole area.

I better explain first about my writing. I will just tell you that I ain't had much learning growing up, except what comes with plain everyday living; that's why I've had some help with these stories you're about to read. I wish I could write like I talk, but a well-meaning friend told me it would be better if I wrote using proper words. So, I own up to getting some help with my spelling and all, and I've never been much on commas and such things, either.

Now don't think the stories ain't true just because I got help in writing them down. No sirree! Every one of them happened just like they're written, and mostly told by good honest folks. I account for a lot of the details because for some reason people always liked to tell me about their feelings and all. I tucked those conversations away and later seemed to have a knack for putting all the pieces together in my mind. Some of these stories, though, I just heard from others--mostly from the Knoll women when we would have our get-togethers. It don't take much to get women to talk, you know.

Mind you, there's a lot of stories I could write about, but don't dare, since I would never want to cast a bad light on anyone. For example, a story about old Granny Moore just came to my thinking about one winter Sunday when she took it in her head to go to church. The problem with that notion was that she wasn't allowed to go out anymore, because she was a bit addle-minded. Her family tended to all her needs, so she wouldn't have to get out but, for whatever reason, she decided on that precise Sunday morning that she was going to church and that her big dog, Mutton, was going with her. The thought is that she knew it was Sunday because in her earlier years she had enjoyed the Sunday funny papers and on that particular morning some well-meaning person had left a paper at her door. At least that's what the family thought had triggered the visit to church.

Thankfully, Granny had dressed herself proper in a coat, gloves and a headscarf. Most likely being concerned that Mutton would get cold, she had tied a scarf around his head, also. The church folks thought it was hilarious that he also had a pair of gloves secured on his big paws with rubber bands, but it was soon obvious that it was to keep him from taking off his head covering.

I happened to be just ready to walk in the church door that Sunday morning when I looked to the right and saw Granny walking briskly down the road pulling Mutton along beside her while he was pawing like crazy at his head. I quickly called for Mr. Lantry to come and help get her into the church before she got frostbite. He got her inside and the unspoken question uppermost in the small group's minds was what in the world had brought her to church? Of course, Granny Moore seemed to think nothing was amiss, but the rest of us was trying hard to pretend it was perfectly normal for an old woman and a dog wearing a head scarf, and gloves, to be out walking in frigid temperatures.

The men folk tied Mutton in a storage room and got Granny to sit down long enough to get through the opening song and a prayer, but then she was ready to go back home. Of course, folks couldn't let her walk back, so Mr. Foster suggested he take her in his car, one of the very few around, and certainly the first one Granny had ever ridden in.

Folks just coming into worship reported that it was a sight to behold--Mr. Foster driving the car with one hand while the other one was locked around Granny Moore's shoulder. They reported Granny was sitting sideways, gripping the door frame with both hands looking like she was headed for the old folk's home. The cocker spaniel was sitting in the back seat with his head hanging over the front seat between the two, still in his head scarf. Mr. Foster reported later that he had no trouble getting Granny and the dog out of the car; both were gone like a shot and into the house before he could back up to turn around. She didn't even say goodbye. She could sure be a crosspatch at times.

As you can see, this is the kind of thing I couldn't write about when Granny was living, or for a long time afterward. It might have offended one of the Moore family and I would not want to be guilty of that. As I said before, I could write about a lot of other happenings, but I won't for fear of offending some of the family members that are still living.

It's best that I just get on with my stories. The Fancy Knoll people were some of the most obliging folks on earth and it gives me a lot of pleasure to relive some of the memories on that knoll, as well as up here on Birch Mountain where my little shack still sits. I hope these notions don't sound too prideful of me.

I'm going to start with how we got our church--I always thought that was the backbone of the community and it will also let you know something of the folks who first settled here back in the late 1800s--at least as it was told to me.

The Church on Huckleberry Road

The heading on the sign in front of the white structure on Huckleberry Road simply said, Church. A passerby could easily read the times for the Sunday and mid-week services underneath the words, but almost always a stranger passing through would ask someone about the nameless church. Surely, it had another name!

At least by that same visitor's second pass he, or she, would have looked more closely to see if erasure marks could be spotted, or perhaps peeled off paint on the church sign, or something that would indicate there was another name to go with the word, Church. But it had been painted that way by the area residents and they were totally comfortable with the one word. Those overly curious visitors to the community might be directed to Mr. Richter, who was now confined at the rest home over in Hankstown, for further clarification of the name.

Delbert Richter was now 95 years old, but was as sharp as a tack, according to most folks in Fancy Knoll. He had seen things that most others could only talk, or ask about, but he had experienced those times and was more than happy to share his knowledge with those curious about the earlier years. That was especially true for those wanting information about the seemingly nameless structure on Huckleberry Road.

Mr. Richter's memory had faded but little. He could still

remember watching from his granny's bedroom window as a ragtag group of confederate soldiers ran bent low through the back of their hay field. The soldiers had passed through in a few moments time and the young boy had wondered later if he had truly seen them. His grandma had assured him that for a fact he had seen them.

He could also remember the gas lanterns, the early cars, and the days before electricity. He loved to tell stories about a visit to New York as a young man and eating a strange new food that consisted of sausages sold on buns with sauerkraut piled on top. He never failed to remind folks that it was his German ancestors who were the first to bring hot dogs to our shores. Most of the kids made faces at the thought of sauerkraut on their hotdogs and furthermore could not imagine anyone old enough to have lived in the 1860s. Over the years, though, he had become a beloved member of the area.

His presence in the isolated community came about because he had inherited a piece of land just outside the area called Fancy Knoll. When he first came to the settlement, he brought with him a wife, a cow, a hen and rooster, a few household items, several types of seeds and his Lutheran faith--all the important things, according to him.

He proved to be right, and it did not take him long to increase his livestock and harvest a large amount of produce. Due to his bartering, he managed to have plenty of food and other goods for the two of them. He rented a furnished house, planted his fruit trees and with his wife by his side was ready to search for a place to practice his faith. It was well into the 1900s by then, and there still was no place for community worship.

There was also another old timer, Ola, who had come up from western Virginia many years ago to live with her daughter, Annie, and was concerned about a place to worship. She had balked at first about moving to the sticks, as she called Fancy Knoll, but like some others, had come to see the beauty of the area and decided to stay. The only problem for her was the absence of a good Methodist Church. Ola had lived a very sheltered life and had always worshipped with the Methodist folks. She was surprised to learn there were other branches of church.

However, Mr. Richter and Ola were not the only two who had preferences as to their previous denominations. The Lantrys were quick to own up to being Baptists, although Granny Dalton, Elsie's mother, had been brought up in the hard-shell branch and too was surprised by her daughter's brand of Baptist. That had been a bone of contention in the early marriage of the Lantry couple, but they soon learned that God deals with souls, not preferences.

It was only when the Thomas family moved into the community, inquiring about a Pentecostal church, that the possibility of a central place for worship came to the forefront. The Fancy Knoll community was growing, and the prospect of a church soon began to be seriously considered. Some of the more outspoken began to take steps to see what could be done about it.

One structure which had been around since the first family moved into the community was the schoolhouse. The first occupants of the area had been the John Raleigh family, who had bought large tracts of land in the mid-1800s. Along with John's family came several extended family members, and that necessitated the early building of a schoolhouse. It was told that his wife, Marie, had desperately prayed for a church to be built at the same time as the school, but for some reason it had never happened. She passed away in 1898, with her desire seemingly unfulfilled and forgotten.

However, God had not forgotten, for it was in that schoolhouse that a neighborhood meeting was called to consider the building of a church house for that little stretch of land called Fancy Knoll. Not surprisingly, almost every family in the community had a representative to attend the meeting, except for Mr. Giles, who lived on Crane's Creek. He sent word that he could care less if one were built, or not.

The appointed meeting began in a pleasurable way. After all, they were all feeling the same need as to the reason for the meeting. Tom Compton was quickly mentioned as a good spokesperson, since he was known as a good hand at talking. He good naturedly accepted and got up to speak. He decided to start simple and thought it best to make sure everyone was on the same page concerning the undertaking of a church. His first question was to ask if everyone agreed as to his or her need for a church. He got either a loud amen, a raised hand, or a nod from everyone in the group, including the women. He asked if all believed that by working together and pooling finances and volunteering physical labor it was possible to build a church. Again, he had the same response. He called for a hymn to give the gathering time to think about the reality of a church.

As the meeting progressed, excitement began to build, and most folks could already envision an impressive white church with a tall steeple sitting in a strategic place for all to see. Some even went so far as to wonder already who a possible preacher might be. However, Tom, and a few others had thought it through and knew it was not a simple matter of deciding yes and then starting services in a month or two. They were fully aware that it would take the whole community to build the church--and all that went with it.

Tom continued with the suggestion that maybe they should first discuss exactly where the church should be built, considering most of the area land was already taken. The room quieted down a bit with that question as minds turned more to individual preferences and ideas.

It took a while, but soon the suggestions for the reasons and the best spots for, started coming faster than Tom could possibly discuss. Everyone began talking at once, and Tom, seeing no hope of getting control of the meeting again, suggested they adjourn for another time to give the folks time to think over the suggestions. They all parted on good terms and with friendly goodnights, agreed on the next Friday night for another meeting.

News traveled fast and soon all the folks in the Fancy Knoll area were buzzing with excitement over a place to build their church. Ola was quick to suggest a corner of her daughter's two-acre lot since she had to use a walking stick to get around. She reasoned that if the church were next door, walking would be no trouble at all for her. Bill Webber, on the other hand, thought a meadow close to the foothills would offer a larger plot of ground in case expansion might someday be needed.

The Hackett and the Moffat families, who were related by marriage, made it known quickly that they couldn't give any of their land since they couldn't afford the land they already had. That caused some unkind words to be said. Others snickered behind their back saying that it was no wonder they couldn't afford the land they lived on, since it had already been given to them by their wives' father.

Some of the Raleigh family felt that everyone was pointing their fingers at them, since they already owned much of the area property, and they felt that was not fair. Why should they give up their land when Joe Compton, Tom's brother, now had almost as much land as they? That made Joe angry, and he and Hack Raleigh had exchanged some words at the gristmill on Saturday morning.

Seeing the possibility for some very unpleasant clashes among the men, Elsie Lantry felt in her spirit that some peace-making overtures needed to be made and they could best be made through the women. She and her husband, George, lived in the upper end of Fancy Knoll nearer to the foothills, and she had proved over the years to be a wise and resourceful lady and one that cared deeply about keeping harmony in the community. While praying on the matter, she felt she needed to address the situation in the ladies' weekly prayer group. From experience, she knew that discord in a community could get out of hand quickly and even though everyone in the community might want a church badly, disagreements could destroy all their plans before they got off the ground. And so, as she sought direction from the Lord, she felt a need to talk things over with Mr. Richter.

She made her way to her old friend's house that afternoon, hoping that one of the frequent thunderstorms might not catch her unawares. She did not want any delay in her meeting with her trustworthy neighbor. With that thought she hurried on, hoping that she might find him at home, which she did. Since the first settlers had moved into the community, these two had become fast friends and both had the welfare of the community at heart. As mentioned earlier, Mr. Richter had done so well as a wise businessman, he had been able to acquire extra land from neighboring farms and was now quite a wealthy man, according to some speculations. His desire for a place to worship, however, had remained top priority in his thoughts and now that others were thinking along the same lines, he realized he was in the position to help. The only problem was that his son, living just over on the Kentucky side, had partnered with him in purchasing a choice piece of land on Huckleberry road. It held a plot that would be perfect for the new church to be built and, although located a bit on the outskirts, it would still be accessible to each of the families.

Mr. Richter had written the son asking if he would be willing for the folks of Fancy Knoll to build a church on that piece of land. He was sure that his son would comply but needed to wait for a positive answer before the offer was made public. He had just placed the outgoing letter in the mailbox when Elsie Lantry came down the lane.

They greeted each other warmly, but Elsie didn't have a chance to mention the reason for her visit before Mr. Richter announced to her his intentions of donating the land. Her heart warmed immediately with a sense of knowing that this was an answer to their prayers. However, Mr. Richter cautioned her on the necessity of keeping quiet about the donor until he could receive word back from his son. The two spent a pleasant hour rejoicing over the possibility of a church in Fancy Knoll and took time to petition God further for His guidance on the many details. Foremost, though, relationships needed to be stable in the community as to have no further disagreements. In addition, the community needed to consider that not only was there a place needed to build the church, but the provision of all resources would be needed in the building of the church.

Elsie had sensed some unrest during the week among the men folks, nothing serious, just a bit of grumbling and side taking. She had also heard about the run-in between Joe and Hack, which could possibly accelerate if left unresolved. That being so, she decided to target the women. If the ladies could keep their attitudes encouraging and diplomatic, that would go a long way in keeping the men on good terms.

On Wednesday, the ladies' meeting was called to order at her house at one o'clock in the afternoon. She had made plans as to have the refreshments first to get everyone in a placid frame of mind. She had laughed earlier to herself as she took from the oven her blackberry and apple strudel. She thought that ought to put anybody in a good mood. The apples came from her own storage cellar, the walnuts from the big tree in the front yard and the blackberries had been picked early that morning. To top it all off she had a jug of fresh cream from her cow, Tulip, and a strong pot of coffee to go with it.

After the ladies were comfortable and full of strudel, she explained that they were going to deviate from the normal order of meeting, as they needed to talk about the proposed church building. They one and all came to attention immediately, since most had listened to their husbands grumbling in one form or the other for the previous two days.

In the meantime, Elsie pondered on how she should present Mr. Richter's generous offer of land without giving away his name. With elderly Miss Shinn's hearing loss in mind, Elsie spoke as loud and as clearly as was decent and presented the ladies with the good news that a donor had agreed to donate some land on which for them to build a church. The ladies could not contain their excitement and the meeting, in general, worked its way into a hubbub of voices.

Of course, they all wanted to know who the special person was who gave the land and where it was located. This was the awkward part, so Elsie carefully recited her prepared speech. "I am not allowed to disclose the source of this blessing now. However, I can tell you that he is a moneyed man with a heart made of gold and we know he will be greatly rewarded for his good deeds." She went on to explain that all would be told soon the name of the benefactor.

Elsie banged on her plate for their attention. "Ladies, there is an even more important announcement to be made so please listen carefully." She need not have worried because every woman's attention was now riveted to her every word. She continued her appeal, which only took about ten minutes, but she got her point across that although not everyone was able to give their land, they all certainly had something they could give for the actual building of the church. She reminded them that everyone's help was needed and that they and their husbands needed to get creative as to what they could give toward the actual building of the church. She also suggested to the ladies to be especially thoughtful to their husbands that week because a peaceful household could go a long way towards creating a united peaceful community. She also offered her apple blackberry strudel recipe to anyone interested.

Some of the ladies began to look a little doubtful at these words, whether it was due to the thought of being kind to their husbands, or being creative, Elsie was not sure. She knew they had misgivings about having anything to offer, so she began to ask about different things around their homes. Did anyone have any leftover lumber laying around, or what about extra paint? Any usable windows or doors? She further mentioned ways to make extra money by selling eggs, milk, or maybe a roadside produce stand as a possibility with all contributing. She even mentioned any heirlooms that might be sold, and the money given to the church. That was for Josie's benefit who Elsie knew owned an atrocious old spittoon handed down through the generations and Josie had been trying to sell it to every snuff and tobacco chewer in the community. It would surely be worth something to an antique store and a great idea for something for Josie to contribute.

The women got excited all over again and Helen Raleigh spoke up that her husband would probably be glad to donate a couple of pigs that could be sold, and the money given as a donation. As other ideas began to flow the Fancy Knoll ladies were good for another forty-five minutes of planning. What a fantastic response! Before the closing prayer, the subject came up as to how to let all the other ladies in the community know of the plans. Since the next day was the day for PTA, they needed someone not connected to the school. Why not Miss Shinn, suggested Nora Blandly. Although almost eighty years old, Miss Shinn still managed to walk her two miles a day, weather permitting, and she would be perfect to deliver the news to the other women around the area.

They all agreed, and Miss Shinn agreed. It was Nora's job then to repeat the message again to Miss Shinn to make sure she understood the instructions she was supposed to relay. They all listened again as Nora repeated to Miss Shinn in a loud voice that there had been a well-to-do man who was giving land for the church so all others would be expected to donate whatever they could toward the building of the church--and to speak to Mrs. Lantry for the details. Nora's voice got louder as she assured Miss Shinn for good measure that this was a project for the Lord and that they would certainly be rewarded for their efforts. Miss Shinn offended at being yelled at, nevertheless agreed to carry the news. The ladies left the meeting in high spirits.

Miss Shinn left early Thursday on her rounds and thoroughly enjoyed her assignment. She did not know when she had felt so important! At lunch, she stopped at the Hackett's for a tasty bowl of corn bread and beans and, in addition, had two snacks at other homes in the afternoon. She had repeated the message at each place, prompting a few raised eyebrows, but made sure each family understood the necessity of donating materials to help build their church. She also reminded them of their reward in the end. She cackled with laughter as she got to repeat to each lady that she was to be nice to her old man and, not being quite sure what a "moneyed" man was, said that it might be a rich old monkey for all she knew who was going to donate land for their church. They all knew Miss Shinn had hearing problems, so would find out clearer details later. She, in the meantime, had had a good day.

The Friday night meeting went off without a hitch, although the curiosity was high as to the identity of the donor. Also, when Tom asked for a list of their donations to help build the church there was an amazing amount of giving, or at least promises to give as soon as certain goods could be sold. It was a remarkable evening, which left the entire community with a downy feeling.

The group sang two verses of "Count Your Blessings," and they were dismissed until further notice. A few of the slower thinkers hung around as long as possible for their reward, but when there seemed to be no one left to present it to them made their way out of the schoolhouse, too embarrassed to ask about it.

A Community Builds a Church

The letter of permission from the son came back to Mr. Richter in speedy time and he liked to tell years later how he suddenly became the hero of the community. He felt ten feet tall when the thanks and congratulations began to come his way. It was Ola, however, who brought him back down to earth by reminding him that it did not matter who donated the land, it was God who owned the land in the first place. That admonition served him well and he never again would take any credit for the founding of the first church in Fancy Knoll.

The days and weeks following brought in all kinds of gifts. Nothing was turned down including used door hinges, scrap lumber, scrap roofing, a quart of linseed oil, even an ancient bell carried down into the area by the Thompson family. Local children spent hours retrieving nails from old buildings of days gone by.

Several offers of lumber were presented, with the Moffats and Hacketts offering pine and hickory lumber from their properties. Although they had not wanted to donate their land, they were more than happy to donate some fine lumber for the floors and pews. Everyone wanted to contribute. There were several men who had construction skills, with others having individual wood working skills. Granny Honaker and Nora, who loved needlework, began working on a beautiful snow-white altar cloth embroidered in pale blue lilies. They did not know it, but that altar cloth would last for many years to come. Lutie and Laura opted to sew a baptismal gown for the adult women which they hoped would get good use. In the meantime, the other ladies were content to wait and see what window dressings might be needed. There was not much fancy material around, or affordable, but it was well known what the ladies could do with a few feed sack prints.

With much of the canning done, foodstuffs stored, and the barns stocked with winter hay and grain, the people of Fancy Knoll went to work on a warm September day and prayed for good weather. Some started laying out the foundation, others worked on the studs and blocks, and several went back and forth hauling and unloading lumber from Joe Compton's makeshift sawmill on the Bluestone river. The women were kept busy providing food and snacks to the workers. The lovely feeling of harmony on that day would not soon be forgotten by the community.

The first order of the day had been, though, a short service of dedication and thanks for what was about to take place. The St. Clair sisters brought their guitar to the site and the beautiful old words of "How Firm a Foundation" rang out in the surrounding area. Mr. Richter gave a beautiful prayer for God's blessing on the building and there were few dry eyes in the crowd.

The weather held and by the end of October the final changes were being made on the newly built church. Many suggestions and personal preferences had gone into the building. Mr. Richter--reminiscent of his parent's Lutheran church from childhood--thought polished wood floors would be beautiful so pine lumber was donated, and the sanctuary floor was indeed a thing of beauty. The pews had been handcrafted by the local men with help from a cousin of Elsie. The local men did a fine job of putting together the 12-foot-long walnut benches, but Elsie having seen her cousin's work asked if he would be willing to carve the ends of the seats with a cross design, which he did. The podium had been handcrafted by the Raleigh family with the Raleigh name being carved in the corner of the raised stand where the Bible lay--in small letters, of course.

The Lantry family had furnished enough kerosene lamps to be used for the evening services when necessary, but the crowning touch was the installation of the 250-pound bell donated by the Thompson family. When the family had left Ohio, the bell had come with them on a whim. It had hung for years in their beloved Presbyterian Church and when it had been replaced by a much larger bronze one, the Thompson family had gladly paid the reasonable price that was asked for it and made sure it was brought with them into the state of West Virginia.

It was a memorable day in Fancy Knoll when the steel alloy bell was lifted to its wood frame tower. School had been dismissed and almost the entire community showed up for the bell raising. It took quite some time to get it into place, but it was finally done, and all the work ceased. The crowd became perfectly still as the bell pealed out for the first time, reaching throughout the community and a good way up the mountain rising behind the settlement. A place of worship had come to Fancy Knoll! Again, most all eyes were teary, and some were openly crying. No one would ever forget that day.

The next step to the establishment of their church would be the all-important choice for a speaker and a name for the church. This was not going to be an easy decision, particularly with such a diverse group of people. Up until this time, each family had been accustomed to private worship in which, for the most part, they followed the rule of worship they had been brought up in or felt comfortable with. Now the big question would be as to what set of guidelines, what doctrine, what order of service should their new church take so that everyone might be satisfied? Impossible? Some would think so, but one lady who seldom was seen about, and known well only by a few, sat in her small house high upon Birch Mountain listening to the bell with tears running down her face. Unknown to most others, Emeline Fox had been praying for 40 years for a church to be built on that very same spot.

In her early teens there had been an incident involving her father, which turned into a tragedy that she would never be able to forget. One afternoon a neighboring farmer's wife had been shot and killed while picking blackberries, and it happened that Emeline's father and brother had been out with their guns on that day. On questioning, her dad had explained that they were shooting in the area but that there also were another couple of men who were hunting. No one in the neighborhood would have thought it anything more than an accident, but the husband of the woman, who was known to be a hot-headed gentleman involved in liquor trafficking, begged to differ.

A terrible argument ensued between her father and the lady's husband, Abner, who happened to have several of his friends present who were urging the argument on. Emeline's father motioned for his son to go get help and then made the mistake of threatening to tell the revenuers about Abner's bootlegging business. That made the husband furious and, claiming to be acting on behalf of the law, easily incited his half-drunk friends that Emeline's father should be hanged for his crime. Before any outsiders could reach them, her father had been hung from a nearby oak tree. The hanging was carried out on the same property that later would be bought by Mr. Richter.

After her father's quick hanging the area was in shock, especially Emeline who was inconsolable. Abner only served a short term, but steps were taken to ensure that such an incident would never happen again. However, the damage had been done. The injustice of the act immobilized Emeline, and for weeks she mourned her pa. In time, she slowly began to heal but she was determined that his death would not be in vain. She began to pray for the message of a merciful and loving God to be preached on that very spot where her father had been hanged. She never lost her faith that it would happen. Mr. Richter had already been made privy to this information by a family member; in fact, it was a primary factor in his offering that piece of land for the church site. However, Emeline knew in her heart that it had been orchestrated by the Lord in answer to her prayer--a church would stand on Huckleberry Road. Thus, the sound of the bell was a sweet joyful sound in the ears of Emeline Cox.

Meanwhile, another meeting was called in Fancy Knoll to select a leader or a speaker for the community's new church. None had a clue as to who might be the best speaker for them. The best suggestion came from Elsie who mentioned a circuit riding Methodist preacher, named Robert Sheffey, who could possibly come. The problem was, however, that he rarely rode that far north in his travels, and they would need someone close by. Ola mentioned a nephew who was considering going into ministry, but he felt he needed some schooling before he could think of taking over a church.

The group finally arrived on an idea that the proper way to handle their dilemma was to go home and each family earnestly pray about who to call for their pastor. That was agreeable, and the meeting was cut short with everyone going his or her own way. They decided to pray for a week and seek the Lord's answer.

A small group met on Monday evening at the schoolhouse for a special called prayer meeting. They had issued an invitation to all but made it clear that fasting would be required during Monday before they met. They would be praying until they felt God had answered, so the folks should be prepared to stay for as long as it took.

Since the invitation was worded in such a manner, only a handful of people came to the meeting on Monday evening. None of the small group were offended at that, they only knew they had felt the call to be a part of this prayer meeting.

The Lantrys and Comptons were in the group as well as Ola, Mr. Richter, Annie Jones, and an unexpected visitor from up on the mountain, Emeline Fox. None were late for the meeting and after a few words from George Lantry the prayers began. A few left quietly at intervals, out of necessity, until around 11 pm when Emeline and Mr. Richter, the only ones remaining, got up from their knees. They felt a peace in their hearts, so the two sat quietly on the bench content in the silence.

After a time, Mr. Richter asked Emeline if she had received a word from the Lord. She shared with him that she felt they should call no one from the outside--the minister or leader for the church should be the people who lived there. Not surprisingly, Mr. Richter smiled and said he had received the same impression in his prayers.

Knowing they could not make the decision just between the two, they left the schoolhouse with the understanding that Mr. Richter would call another meeting for Friday evening to see what the other folks felt like God had spoken to them. It was a wonderful moment when almost all the prayers had concluded that the speakers should come from their own group. A two-hour long discussion brought some wonderful results. Not only would the speaker be from their community but also there would be several speakers from the various faiths, each taking turns on different Sundays.

This led to the idea of making a schedule for the different speakers to abide by, with the provision that all families would attend regardless of the church denomination of that Sunday. The response was amazing as each member thought of what that would entail. The excitement started building as they realized they would be worshiping, for at least part of the time, with others of a different church preference. Of course, there were some who were completely shocked by such a thing and Tom, knowing this, brought the meeting to a close to allow those people to get used to the idea. Of course, considering the nature of humans, there were quite a few with wait-and-see attitudes, and others totally against the idea.

Gradually the majority warmed to the idea, though, and individual speakers were being agreed upon by the various groups. George Lantry would hold a service in keeping with the Baptists, Mr. Richter for the Lutheran, Tom Compton for the Methodist, and Seth Thompson for the Presbyterian. The fifth Sunday caused a bit of haggling. Since only one family in the area held to the Pentecostal way and one to the Church of Christ persuasion, it was left to those two families to share the fifth Sunday--one in the Sunday morning service and the other in the Sunday evening service. Grant Moore would lead the morning, and someone from the Thomas family the evening service.

To complicate matters, though, Clara Thomas's husband had left the family and there was no man to take the service. After much discussion the group decided on asking Clara, despite the fact she had no husband to speak in the pulpit, if she would think about having her type of service on the fifth Sunday evening. She was delighted and accepted immediately ignoring the few raised eyebrows, due to her being a woman and all. However, the vote was cast, and the result was almost unanimous for Clara to conduct the service, an unheard thing for most.

With that settled, a name for the church was introduced into the meeting. It did not take long before Emeline asked to speak. The group fell silent as the quiet little lady stood and first gave her awe-inspiring testimony as to how God had answered her prayers for a house in which to worship. The group held onto her every word as she suggested they should simply call the place of worship, Church. That was a little hard for some to grasp at first, but after rolling it around on their tongue a few times, they began to see it might have a possibility. It might just work!

Mr. Richter also asked for the floor. Things got quiet again. His suggestion called for unity and tolerance in the dissimilar services and due to the assorted denominations present he suggested that the sermons, or talks if you will, would be limited to the basic beliefs which they all held in common--namely the gospel concerning the Lord Jesus Christ. Each and all would refrain from any controversial subject that might divide the congregation. Before he could stop speaking the congregation was on their feet with many hearty affirmations and support for his suggestions.

The spirit of the proceedings spread throughout the community as they prepared for the first service. On opening day, the pews were full and the people joyful. The fellowship, which began outside on the pathway to the church, was wonderful as neighbor greeted neighbor. There had been a lot drawn and the Presbyterians had the first service, led by Seth Thompson.

On November 20, 1902, the church bell rang for the first time to call the worshippers to the white steepled church on Huckleberry Road. They sang their first song as a united congregation with full and grateful hearts. The strains of "A Mighty Fortress Is our God" floated out through the open windows flooding Fancy Knoll with its message, thrilling the hearts of the people.

Seth was not a great speaker, but no one minded in the least. He chose for his text, Psalm 133:1. "Behold, how good and how pleasant [it is] for brethren to dwell together in unity!" Although he did his best, he soon ran out of words, so he sat down, and the short message ended. Emeline stood and requested everyone to stand and sing "Amazing Grace." A song had never sounded as beautiful to the folks of Fancy Knoll. The tears flowed, and voices and hands were raised in praise of the one God and Savior of the world, Jesus Christ. The people were as one.

Church became the heart of Fancy Knoll. People were drawn together as never before. They learned to worship collectively, leaving behind denominational lines. Each week brought a somewhat different type of service, which made going to church all the more exciting. All dressed conservatively wearing their best clothes, mostly overalls or homemade dresses. However, on the Lutheran Sunday, Mr. Richter usually sported a fedora with his white clerical collar in place.

Music became a favorite part of every service. Having a guitar, a fiddle, and a banjo player in the congregation, they never lacked for accompaniment. The congregational singing was awesome! Hymns on the Baptist Sunday were a favorite since Ma Lantry still enjoyed--and always led--the line singing method from her Primitive Baptist roots. One or two traditional songs would also be sung, of course, with "Sweet By and By" being the one most called for.

An interesting thing had happened concerning the singing. As time went on each group began to learn the other group's songs and, being a new church, with no rules except to respect God's house wholly and to respect each other's differences, the singing united the people faster than anything else could. Each church's favorite songs became all their favorites. My, how they did sing! Of course, there were other songs that they all had in common, but it seemed each group had a favorite.

The water baptisms were always held on the Church of Christ Sunday, since for them baptism was to be performed at conversion. The other groups simply waited for their baptisms to be performed on the same day as the Church of Christ folks and it worked out well. As for the Methodist, the entire congregation watched with great respect as they performed their baptisms by the sprinkling method on their appointed Sunday.

The most surprising service and the most rousing, though, came on the fifth Sunday evening service. Clara Thomas put some fears to rest by not attempting to speak or give a message. She simply opened the floor for testimonies from the congregation of what the Lord had done for them. Some folks said that anybody, or everybody, spoke on the Pentecostal Sunday. Indeed, they did and enjoyed it immensely. The meeting never failed to include a somewhat new song called "That Old Time Religion" which usually brought the congregation to its feet.

Some had said it couldn't happen. They said there was no way such a diverse group could worship together in harmony. The people of Church at Fancy Knoll proved them wrong when they fulfilled the words in Ephesians 4:5 which say, "One Lord, one faith, one baptism."

The Calling of Amos Buchanan

In 1938 if there had been such a thing as a contest for the meanest man in Fancy Knoll, Amos Buchanan would have won hands down, or if a contest for the most unpopular man had been held, Amos would again have won. He was unlikable, obnoxious, and certainly not invited to any affair ever held in the community. Even his dog, Rain Crow, knew to keep out of his way, especially when Amos was on one of his drinking binges.

That was why it was such a mystery as to who it was who invited him to Joe and Mandy Thompson's 15th wedding anniversary dinner. Amos and his wife, Cordelia, arrived at the affair a bit late and seated themselves at one of the back tables, seemingly to escape notice. However, they may as well have held up a big banner announcing that, "Amos Buchanan is in attendance!" All eyes were darting back and forth to the back table to observe the very uncomfortable and scruffy looking uninvited guest. His sweet wife, Cordelia, acted somewhat nonchalant as she smiled to everyone whose eyes she could catch and spoke a soft greeting.

The women smiled in return and Joe Compton walked over and greeted Amos, as well as Cordelia, hoping his surprise at seeing Amos was well hidden. Amos grunted in return and did manage to hold his hand out for the customary handshake. Soon the crowd turned back to their previous conversations before the arrival of the

Buchanans, and the dinner resumed. Cordelia filled two plates and it was noted that Amos soon had her fill a second plate for him, carefully keeping his eyes down on the table. Other than eating, his only other reaction to the dinner was to kick at Rain Crow who was under the table grabbing for the scraps.

After the meal, a couple of others went over and greeted Amos who only grunted and left hurriedly soon thereafter. Cordelia smiled apologetically to some of the women and then trailed along behind him. The two were the subject of conversation at most of the homes that evening. Just who was Amos Buchanan? Where had he come from? Why was he so unsociable? Little Clara Thompson innocently asked if his ma ever washed out his mouth with soap like her momma did for her one time. His bad language was one of the main reasons the community kept their children well away from his presence.

If truth were known, Amos had started drinking alcohol when he was only twelve years old. His pa had been an avid foxhunter when Amos was young, and it was well known that liquor was almost always present at their all-night fox hunts. The elder Mr. Buchanan had never treated Amos well. He had insisted his only son should accompany him wherever he happened to go, which sometimes included places that would take a young boy's mind and behavior far above where it should go. Thankfully, the mother of Amos was a godly woman who, although she could not control her husband's actions, she could pray for her son--which she did with all her heart. Unfortunately, in addition to her husband's ill treatment, she was also a sickly woman and many days she felt sustained only by God's promises to her for her boy's well-being.

There had been times that she felt hopeless, but one day she read in Psalms these words, "The Lord will perfect that which concerneth me." That one verse in the one hundred and thirty eighth chapter spoke volumes to her, giving her the faith to trust that someday the answer to her prayer would come. She passed away when Amos was seventeen without ever seeing her boy change his ways, but she never lost her faith that he would.

In the meantime, his drinking increased with the years. His behavior emulated his father's behavior more and more. He worked at meaningful labor rarely, but his making of illegal liquor was well known. In fact, he had made a name for himself due to his knack for producing high quality "hooch." He cooked his mash with birch bark at times, giving it a mint like flavor, which was a favorite with certain ones in the surrounding area, so he usually did not lack for customers.

That was how Cordelia came into the picture. Her pa happened to be a steady customer for Amos. Mr. Sanders had been drinking acquaintances with Amos's pa for several years and on one Tuesday morning, they both made one of their visits to the still in Swamp Hollow which would change all their lives forever. The two got into a conversation concerning the future of their offspring and in their drunken state, they decided it was time for them to be thinking of grandkids, since they were getting on in years. Mr. Sanders had a seventeen-year-old daughter whom he declared to be the best cook in seven states--he could not remember all the states he had traveled in, but he thought it was seven. He added, "She's fairly purty and a good hand at cutting up hog meat." That sounded like just the right girl for Amos, thought Mr. Buchanan.

That led to a more serious discussion of a possible union. Of course, the younger couple's preferences were not even considered, with both men being accustomed to making any decision needed for their households. As the conversation progressed, they felt the need to settle on a bride's price because according to Mr. Sanders, he was losing the best cook in seven states and he should be paid accordingly. Mr. Buchanan countered that in case of any desired grandkids from the union, his son would be the one responsible, therefore that would allow for quite a cut in the bride's price.

They haggled over money for a good hour while Amos half listened with a disgusted look on his face. He was almost twenty-four years old and had become more and more resentful of his pa's interference in his life. He had thought of leaving many times, but he had become accustomed to his easy lifestyle. He had all the white lightning he wanted to drink, and he felt no obligation to go anywhere, or to do anything he did not want to do--except to do whatever his pa told him to do. The need for a change, however, was becoming strong in his thinking.

In the meantime, the older men were getting nowhere with their trading. They had considered giving each other a prize cow, or possibly each paying fifty dollars for their part of the bargain, until it finally occurred to their foggy brains that they would each be getting the same thing they had already given and so dissolved into a bout of helpless laughter.

Amos was becoming more and more furious at the ridiculousness of the proposed marriage until he could hold his anger in no longer. He faced his pa shouting that the two men needed to shut up as he was not about to marry anybody. That brought Mr. Buchanan up short as his son had never dared to address him in that tone of voice, much less disobey him.

What happened next would end in tragedy as Mr. Buchanan grabbed his shotgun off the nearby table. What his intent had been, no one was ever sure, but Mr. Sanders grabbed the gun thinking, it was supposed, that his old friend was going to shoot his own boy. At any rate, the gun went off and caught Mr. Sanders full in the chest.

Mr. Buchanan dropped the gun and his face turned white, as Amos later described it, and sank down on the ground. He had killed his friend! With only a groan coming from his fogged brain, he staggered to his feet and walked away from the still and down the hill. That left Amos standing in shock, unable to call out to his pa. That was the last time he would ever lay eyes on his father.

There had been an investigation made, but with the reputation of Mr. Buchanan and the fact that no fingerprints were on the gun except his, Amos was dropped as a suspect. There was a posse sent out to find Mr. Buchanan, however, nothing more ever came of it and the case was later dismissed.

On the day of the killing, Amos had finally gone to the Sanders house and told Cordelia what had happened. She asked him if he would be kind enough to go get her Uncle John, her only other living relative. Amos found his way farther down the mountain to notify her uncle to take care of the burying, who immediately declared he did not know what would happen to seventeen-year-old Cordelia since he could not take care of her in addition to his own large family. Amos didn't care at that moment, went home, and drank himself into oblivion. Years later, he would tell Cordelia about what happened to him on the afternoon of the third day.

Amos had not been able to recall the time between his first drink of liquor after leaving John Sanders house and when something in the afternoon sun awakened him on Friday afternoon. He declared it to be the strangest thing that had ever happened to him. The warmth from the sun seemed to be speaking to him. He knew he had heard no audible words, but rather a sensation of words being spoken without sound. He remembered wondering if he had ever heard of such a thing as the sun talking. He would not relate the story to anyone for years because he was afraid people would think him crazy, but the strange words he felt spoken were, "I know your name!" The same words were being repeated over and over. He related that he was finally able to stand up and when he looked down at himself, he saw he was filthy dirty, and smelled horrible. He fully came to himself then and staggered down to the nearby creek and fell into the water with an intense craving to get the dirt from his body and clothes.

Now, lest the reader forget the mother's prayers, this experience will not seem so strange. In fact, for a short time Amos seemed to be changing for the better. The moonshine equipment remained inactive and Amos began fixing up his dad's place for the better. He had gone to see Cordelia and had a talk with her. He truly felt sorry for his and his pa's part in her father's death. He felt especially guilty since it had been his outburst that had started the argument. Cordelia listened to Amos's self-blame for a time but then began to encourage him to leave it be and get on with his life.

The thing that bothered him the most was the fact he couldn't do anything about Mr. Sander's death, his pa's departure, or the harm done to Cordelia. He had always been able to "fix" things, but these he could not. After a time, it came to him that he could marry Cordelia as the two men had suggested, and that might take away some of the guilt that Amos felt. It would certainly help her out as she had been mostly taking care of herself, while staying alone in the house. Her Uncle John did what he could, but it was a hardship for him to do so.

Ultimately, Amos and Cordelia had married, and he moved into her house in case his pa decided to return to the area. Amos vowed that if his pa did return to Fancy Knoll, he would never again have any more say so concerning Amos's life.

For a time, Cordelia was happier than at any time in her life. She shared with Amos that she too had a mother that lived by the Bible's principles and had tried to bring up Cordelia the same way. For a while it looked as if both mother's prayers were being answered through the marriage of her and Amos. As they shared their lives together, they were falling in love and for a few blessed months things indeed went smoothly for the young couple.

However, Amos's drinking returned when Cordelia lost her baby. He had been ecstatic when he learned he was going to be a father. From the first, he determined that he would never hold his son under his thumb as his pa had done him. He would teach his boy to hunt and fish and never allow him to have anything to do with liquor or the making of it. Cordelia lost her baby at four months, and Amos was inconsolable.

He had not thought of his prior experience with the voice calling him in months, and now his bitterness at losing the baby overcame any hopes of him thinking the voice had been nothing more than the effects of the hot sun and the hangover he had been experiencing that day. The next week he bought a pint of moonshine from an old buddy and that ended his sobriety. Shortly thereafter he returned to making the brew for himself and began spending long hours away from home.

The guilt of the killing returned full force and so did his anger at his pa. Nothing could be done about it, so he allowed the memories to slowly eat away at his sense of right and wrong and his happiness. Strangely, he never laid a hand on Cordelia. He left her alone much of the time, but his anger never turned toward her.

With both mothers gone it was up to Cordelia to keep pounding Heaven's door for help for Amos. She had seen his other side and she would stand by him as long as it took. After a time, however, things became so bad due to his drunkenness, his debts, and the community's mutual dislike of him, he and Cordelia packed up their few belongings and moved to an isolated place in West Virginia called Fancy Knoll. He turned to farming and with Cordelia's skills at homemaking, gardening and such, they were able to get along moderately well.

As would be expected, though, Amos's ill temper, bad language and love of drink caused him to be shunned by most of that community, also. Cordelia could have had solace from some of the women folk, but she chose to live out her lonely life at home and pray that the Lord would intervene soon in answer to her and Amos's ma's prayers.

She was beginning to see some small changes in his behavior, though. A lack of money had cut down considerably on his drinking and sometimes she detected the deep isolation in his demeanor and wondered if he was getting dissatisfied with his way of life. Even more than that, was the Lord dealing with him in ways she knew nothing about? That was why she had told him about the anniversary dinner for the Thompson's and pretended they both had received an invitation. She was delighted when he agreed to come, but he let her know he would not stay long and that he didn't want anyone talking to him.

That Monday after the anniversary dinner, Amos sat on the fence rail overlooking the lower end of Fancy Knoll. His head hurt from the last two day's bout of drinking and he felt miserable in body and soul. His thoughts turned to his ma for some reason. She had been gone for several years now, but on occasion she came into Amos's mind and he would find himself trying to remember the Bible verse she had spoken to him on the day she died when she told him about praying for him. A lot of good it did, he thought, as he hid his face in his arms. Surely, there was more to life than what he had experienced so far.

He left the fence and walked down by the water and sat staring at the water flow down the stream. He seemed to have become mesmerized. *Away, away, away! That's my life*, he thought, *always flowing away with nowhere to go.* Suddenly spoken words seemed to merge with the flow of water--words that he had heard before-words he did not like. "I know your name!"

"No!" He shouted. "how do you know my name?" He later related it was like a flashlight directed its beam right into his brain, and the memory of his mother's last day flashed across his mind. He began running and didn't stop until he entered the kitchen where Cordelia was preparing their noon day meal. She became quite alarmed thinking there had been an accident, but Amos could only blurt out that he thought he was losing his mind.

"Cordelia," he said, "get me your Bible." Those were words she had been waiting two years to hear and without asking questions handed him his ma's worn Bible. With frantic turning of the pages Amos went to the book of Revelation to the second chapter and fairly shouted at Cordelia, "That's it! That's it!"

"What's it? What is it Amos?"

"This is the verse that Ma spoke to me the day she died. Listen! 'To him that overcometh will I give to eat of the hidden manna and will give him a white stone and in the stone a *new name* written, which no man knoweth saving he that receiveth it.' Cordelia, them's the words my ma quoted to me on the day she died. I was so mad at my pa that day that I told her I wished I had some other name different from my pa's. She told me that the Lord would give me a new name if I would believe in Him. It must be God's voice that I heard. He was the only one who knew what my ma said to me that day!"

Amos fell to his knees and began to weep. Great convulsive crying came from the depths of his being. Cordelia could only stand by his side and weep her own tears. She knew whatever was going on with Amos was between him and God and she dare not interfere.

After a time, Amos arose from the floor and told Cordelia he would be back in a while. He went back to the creek and poured out his soul there on the creek bank with only himself and the One who knew his new name were in attendance. He let go of all the anger, the guilt, and the hurt he had carried for years. When he came back to the house, he was a different man, with peace and joy written all over his face. He simply held Cordelia and asked her forgiveness for all that had gone before in their marriage. There was a glorious celebration in their home that day.

A week later he and Cordelia made a trip back to their former home where Amos would make amends to several folks, as well as he could, with promises to others to repay them. He asked forgiveness of others, but before he left the area, he went to visit the gravesite of his dear ma. Although he knew she was not there he knelt by her grave and talked to her while Cordelia stood near the fence on the far side. It gave him a sense of joy to say the words to her that her prayers had been answered. He left the cemetery with a sense of closure and a great settled peace. He also asked around about his pa but still no one had heard anything of him.

Amos went back to Fancy Knoll a changed man. Even his dog Rain Crow seemed to note the change. He slipped a few times with the bad language, but he was so ashamed of himself that it usually took only one slip for him to let go of the words for good. Sunday found him at the church on Huckleberry Rd. This time he marched up to the front seat, holding tightly to Cordelia's hand. The opening song had been sung and now all eyes were focused on the front row pew. It was Presbyterian Sunday, so things were somewhat quieter than usual as the folks were still enjoying the same style of services as they had been doing since the church had been built in 1902.

Amos was the first one to stand up when the invitation came for a testimony from anyone in the congregation. The whole group seemed to be holding their breath. He started by apologizing to everyone in the sanctuary for any harm he might have done to them and then gave a full account of how God had saved him. At first there was total silence. It was at that moment, though, that outside the door, Rain Crow began to howl out his frustration at not being allowed inside. Miss Shinn with her impaired hearing thought the howling was the beginning of another hymn so with raised hands she began praising the Lord. Then Amos himself got so excited about his conversion that he did a little dance around the altar. That prompted the Pentecostal folks to join in and so began a victory march around the perimeter of the church. It was a glorious time, with everyone joining into, either the marching, or the singing, or the clapping of hands.

Amos didn't understand for a long time what prompted his next actions, but when everyone had sat down, and the sanctuary became quiet he walked up to the altar, turned to Revelations 2:17 and read the scripture concerning the believers having a new name. It seemed as if his face glowed as he began to explain in simple language what those words had meant to him there by Crane's Creek that day. Twenty minutes later he sat down on the front seat to a silent audience.

Mr. Richter, frail with age and soon to be transferred to a nursing home, made his way slowly to the front. He placed his hand on Amos's shoulder and with tears blinding his tired old eyes he spoke, "Amos Buchanan, God has not only saved you and knows your name--but He has called you. Beloved friends, I will have to leave you soon, but God has answered a prayer that I, and several others, have prayed for many years--that God would send us a permanent pastor for Church. God has spoken! This is the man!"

To Amos's astonishment, he felt the Holy Spirit witness to his own heart, also, that indeed, Mr. Richter was right. God had indeed called him!

He never learned what happened to his pa, although someone claimed to have seen him in another state. That was always a source of sorrow for Amos, but it was a burden he would have to carry--perhaps as a reminder of God's grace and forgiveness concerning his former life. In the meantime, he became the pastor of Fancy Knoll Church and was every bit as committed in his ministry for the Lord as he had been as a moonshiner--only now the results were very different. He never once doubted his calling.

Aunt Lucy Learns to Drive

There had been many anxious days in the history of Fancy Knoll and most with good reason. One, for example, was when Mr. Richter had emergency surgery and the whole community was on pins and needles awaiting the outcome. Or, in the late 1930s, when a killer hailstorm came through, and all the local farmers were waiting to see the extent of the damage. Those were normal things to be anxious about and all shared in the anxiety.

Just so, a new anxiety hit the community on the day that Aunt Lucy Cantrell decided she was going to learn to drive a car. Like an early frost warning, the news quickly spread around the neighborhood. At first it was passed off by most as gossip since Lucy was sixty-two years old and had hardly been in a car, much less driven one. In addition, doubts were raised after her driving skills were noted during her attempt at riding her nephew's bicycle. She had evidently wanted to "prove" her driving abilities, but it was broadcast that she had hit the family cat and ran into a ditch with her neighbor's freshly washed sheets still clinging to her. She later claimed she ran through the clothesline by accident, which blinded her, causing her to hit the cat and go in the ditch. That could have been true, but some folks were skeptical. It was days before the cat returned to the house and her neighbor, Mattie Raleigh, raised a ruckus concerning her clean wash for about that long.

However, Lucy was not to be swayed from her determination to drive a car. After watching Mr. Dalton for several weeks driving up and down the length of Fancy Knoll, it gave Aunt Lucy the idea that if a man could drive such a contraption, so could she.

It seems she had been raised in a household with six boys and being in the middle, as well as the only girl, she had to fight for her rightful place in the lineup. She balked at the unfairness of doing all the dishes and helping with all her younger siblings while the older boys got to work in the hayfields and go hunting and trapping. They then came home and, according to her, gobbled down every bite of food that she and her ma was able to put on the table. To make things worse she had to help wash and iron their clothes and according to her, there was nothing fair about that arrangement.

One day she took it into her head to learn to shoot as well as her older brothers. Her pa finally agreed to let her try out a few shots but had second thoughts after she managed to kill her ma's favorite rooster, and narrowly missed the family cow. She did learn, though, and noting a difference in her brothers' behavior towards her, she continued to learn to throw a lasso as well as her pa, could shoe the family's horse without help, and one day proudly announced to her ma that she had taken up "chewin."

That was the final straw for Ma Cantrell. She put her foot down and Lucy's hunting days were over, the tobacco was forbidden near the house and lassoing, and horseshoeing, were done only when Pa needed an extra hand and the other boys were busy.

The one good thing that came from her short rebellion was that Pa threatened the boys with their life if they teased her. They took it surprisingly well, but the fact that they couldn't continue their evening chew on the front porch after a hard day in the fields did cause some grumbling. One brother got in trouble when he told his sister that at least he would no longer need to dodge her bullets.

Lucy went back to her housekeeping duties, but never failed to at least try to outdo the boys when their pa's back was turned. The truth of the matter, though, was that her pa had a soft spot for his only girl and greatly admired her grit. However, he had to stay on

Ma's good side, so he usually concerned himself more with his boys' wellbeing and left Lucy to Ma.

Folks remembered one occasion, though, when Lucy outdid the boys and never let them forget it. Anybody that knows anything knows that West Virginia folk are masters at telling ghost tales--and a whole bunch of them not only tell them, but also believe them. It was a favorite past time back in the earlier years before cars, drive-in theaters and such. Many times, the younger folks would gather and repeat stories they had heard from the older generation and by the end of the evening be too scared to walk home by themselves. The storytelling was usually declared to be more enjoyable on stormy dark nights.

This was the scenario one evening when Lucy, her brothers and a group of other teens, were having one of their frequent wiener roasts. The roasts were usually held in the summer months in some secluded spot where, by word of mouth, the invitation had been given out to anyone interested. It was an innocent time of socializing, playing games and eating roasted wieners on a stick over an open fire. There was usually nothing to go with the hot dogs but perhaps a bottle of RC or Pepsi, brought individually. If truth were known, money was too scarce to bring much else.

On this night a group of the teens, due to the windy conditions, had gathered underneath a sheltered cliff for their roast. They decided to eat early in case it rained. As they were finishing up it did start to rain, and they had to be content with just waiting it out until they could return home.

The fire was being refurbished by the boys when Bob Henry asked if anyone had heard any good ghost stories recently. Considering the dark rainy night, it was a perfect suggestion and the telling began. Never mind that the story might be a rehashed one; it could be embellished a bit and still cause shivers down the backs of most.

Somehow, the conversation turned to the question of who was the bravest--the boys or the girls? That brought on a heated discussion and, of course, Lucy declared herself a much braver person than any of her brothers. Len Hackett suggested a contest to get to the truth of the matter. Then began a round of suggestions for an appropriate contest. Len was the one to think of a perfect plan, but to implement it they would need to wait for a burial in the Lankford Cemetery, which was located on the road to Kent. It was a larger area than their burial ground on Fancy Knoll and, therefore, had more frequent burials. Len suggested that at the next burial one of the boys would go alone at the midnight hour, choose a flower from the grave, and bring it back to the group. The girl would go and do the same. If they both succeeded, then it would prove the girls were just as brave as the boys.

They drew names and one of Lucy's brothers had drawn the boy's name. As for the girls, it was no contest--Lucy was the only girl brave enough to try. All agreed on the idea and the group soon disbanded declaring to meet on the next Friday, or Saturday night, that a burial had taken place in the cemetery.

It was the major topic of discussion among the young people for a couple of weeks, and their excitement reached major proportions when an elderly lady died and was to be buried in the Lankford Cemetery. The girls were quick to show their disdain at the boys proclaiming their bravery—especially, snickered Lucy, the ones "who didn't get their name drawed!" Her big brother, Hank, whose name had been drawn wasn't saying too much about it. If he was scared, he wasn't about to let her know it. It was agreed by all not to tell their parents for fear they would forbid them to carry out the dare.

Friday evening, they met at dark in front of the Jim Compton place and began the walk down the road toward Kent. There was a nice wooded area where they sometimes met for their wiener roasts, and that location just suited their plans. The played a few games and ate, but most of the talk concerned the trip to the cemetery. Hank and Lucy chose their straws, and Lucy was to go to the cemetery first. They decided on going at 10 pm instead of twelve, as it would make them too late getting home in the evening.

The appointed time came, and Lucy started out bravely towards the cemetery, which was about a tenth of a mile. She did fine until the sound of her peers' voices faded out and she realized she was all alone. She tried remembering words to her favorite songs, then she counted to 1,000 and as she neared the cemetery, she thought of singing loudly, but was too scared to hear her own voice. "*What if someone answers me?*" she thought. Instead, she kept as still as possible, rushed to the grave, grabbed a handful of flowers from the nearest wreath on the new grave, and ran out of the cemetery. She didn't stop until she heard the voices of her companions again. She quickly looked back and seeing nothing took time to catch up on her breathing and sauntered back towards the group. She managed to appear calm by the time she got to her companions and the other girls hurried to hug her. They all examined the flowers to make sure they had indeed come from the cemetery.

Then it came Hank's turn and he took off hurriedly as if he couldn't wait to get into the cemetery, whistling as he went. In truth, he was skittish about going also, but would not have let it show for the world. He walked bravely on singing to himself and as he approached the cemetery, he had to really concentrate on not getting spooked. He decided the best approach was to talk out loud as if there were someone with him as he neared the gravesite. He moved quickly to the flowered grave and as he reached down for the flowers a voice from a nearby grave growled, "Can't a body get any sleep around here without some big mouth waking him up?" Hank looked around just in time to see a figure rise to a sitting position and that did it!

He threw the flowers and hurled out of the cemetery before the voice finished speaking and he literally flew back towards the group waiting back at the road. He didn't even take time to stop and get his breath. He rushed into the group, pale as a sheet and gasping for breath, declared that a dead person spoke to him in the cemetery. That scared everyone else, and they one and all headed back down the road towards home, trying not to break into a run.

Hank had calmed down by the time they reached the Compton place, but he again solemnly swore that he had seen a ghost and it had spoken to him. Lucy was scared for his sake but that didn't stop her from declaring herself the bravest and the winner. For once, Hank was willing for her to have the title and she, of course, never let him forget it--even after they both grew old

It was several weeks later that the Lankford family built a fence around the cemetery. Several asked around as to why they were just now building the fence. Jeb Lankford explained that he was tired of Jake Lane stopping there on his way home and taking a snooze, every time he got drunk. He said Jeb kept breaking the flowers and leaving tracks on some of the graves. Lucy laughed till her side ached, and Hank finally had to join in. She would forever be thankful that for that one night she had sense enough to keep her mouth shut.

Time passed, and the kids grew up. Lucy never married but was a second mother to her many nieces and nephews. Most of them gradually left the area, but Hank's son, Teddy, remained in the area and had taken on the responsibility of watching after Aunt Lucy in her older years. Neither had many worldly goods, but Teddy did own an old Ford jalopy which was in poor shape. Since it was runnable, he kept it in Aunt Lucy's shed for use in emergency. Folks had almost forgotten Aunt Lucy's penchant for keeping up with the male population until the day she announced she was going to learn to drive.

Teddy begged her not to bother driving, or at least wait until he could afford a better car. However, Aunt Lucy had her mind set and Teddy went about warning the neighborhood that his aunt was going to be driving a car on the road. Most of the parents made sure their children were safe in the house during the driving lessons.

The first day out was a nightmare for Teddy, and none following were much better. On the first lesson, Teddy explained all the driving mechanisms, or at least tried to, despite his aunt's impatience. He then gave Aunt Lucy the key and instructed her to place it in the ignition switch. She, being nervous of course, tried to jam it into the opening at the wrong angle and quickly decided the key was too big for the car. She handed it back to him and suggested, perhaps, he needed to try another one. "No, Aunt Lucy. Straight in! Straight in!"

After a few times of getting the key straight in, he went on to the proper use of the clutch. He had her practice pushing in the clutch while changing the gearshift and letting the clutch slowly out again, emphasizing each time the "slowly" part. She finally indicated that she had it and was ready to try it out. After interchanging the gas-clutch-gear for a good three hundred yards, Teddy convinced her to leave the clutch alone and let the car roll on its own. He was already sweating, and it was only eight o'clock.

As Aunt Lucy began to get the feel of the car, she sped up to 15 miles an hour, a satisfied grin on her face. As they approached a cow in the distance, Teddy realized that he hadn't explained much about the brakes, so warned her well ahead of time that she would probably need to stop and let the cow pass by. Aunt Lucy continued at the same pace. Teddy warned a bit louder. She nodded her head okay, that she had heard. They were getting closer and Teddy's blood pressure was climbing. Finally, he yelled for her to stop. Aunt Lucy stopped--and Teddy almost went through the windshield. She simply turned to him with a stormy look and snapped, "Teddy, we ain't to the cow yet, why do I have to stop here?" Teddy whispered, "Can we go home now and go out again tomorrow?"

"Well, quit your whispering and show me how to turn this thing around!" Teddy wiped the sweat from his forehead and convinced her that since the road was narrow and hardly room to turn around maybe he should do it and she could drive home. Thankfully, she did, and they made it back safely. He left her on the porch with the order for him to be there about the same time the next morning, stating she wanted to drive before the traffic got heavy. Considering that only he and one other person owned a car, Teddy figured Aunt Lucy must have been talking about the cows and sheep that were known to be out at times.

Teddy became an expert in making up excuses not to have the

morning driving lesson with Aunt Lucy. Some days there was no getting around it, though, but it was obvious from the beginning that his aunt would be a mortal danger to society if she was allowed to drive a car. One day she turned sharply off the road, went into a nearby field, drove around a stand of trees and back on the road without a bat of the eye. Teddy, in near shock, gasped, "Aunt Lucy, what did you do that for?"

"Teddy, don't tell me you didn't see that snake crawling cross the road? For pity's sake if you don't need some glasses! And stop holding your hands over your eyes. I need you to look for cows crossing the road!"

"Aunt Lucy, we really need to get back. I heard my neighbor was bad off and they need me to take him to the hospital!"

"Well, why didn't you say so sooner, for crying out loud?" Lucy shoved the car in reverse and jerked the car around as Teddy yelled, "Aunt Lucy, they think he'll live."

"Slow down!" Teddy hid his face in his hands for the umpteenth time

The inevitable happened, though, soon enough when Aunt Lucy informed Teddy she would need to be taken over to Kent the following week to get her a driving license. She stated she was anxious to drive on a hard surface road. He first told her it would cost her fifty cents for the license thinking that would discourage her from going any farther. She complained a bit but decided it would be worth it to be able to drive over to Kent any time she wanted. Teddy then told her she would have to take a driving test with a county sheriff sitting right beside her, thinking that would certainly detain her. "Fine," she said. "I just hope he's that nice cousin of yours and I won't have a bit of a problem!"

Aunt Lucy would never know it, but she had just given her nephew an answer that would make sure she didn't get a driver's license. His cousin, Dudley, on his ma's side, was indeed a county sheriff who happened to owe him a favor and Teddy would ask him to at least ride with Aunt Lucy, and then use his authority to block her from getting a license. Teddy was just that sure that if Sheriff Dudley rode with Aunt Lucy there would be no further talk of a license to drive a car.

The sheriff balked, as Teddy predicted, stating that was not his job and no way could he pretend to be giving a driving test. Teddy reminded him that he owed him a favor and explained to him that he only wanted him to ride with Aunt Lucy and surely, in such an important office as his, he could influence the outcome of the test. That mellowed Dudley a bit, but he protested that no way would Teddy's aunt let him in her car if she knew what he was up to.

Teddy was ready for that response also and proceeded to tell the sheriff of his plan. The sheriff in turn thought the whole idea a bit drastic but finally agreed since the election was coming up in the fall.

Monday morning came-the day Aunt Lucy had chosen to go to Kent for the test. She was ready at 6 am. She usually wore a clean apron on going out, but on this important day, she wore a nice dress and her hat. She got out her pocketbook since she had three dollars, plus the license fee, and planned to look at some dry goods before coming home.

By eight o'clock, she was a bundle of nerves and highly upset with Teddy who still had not made an appearance, even though he had told her he would be there at eight thirty.

At eight fifteen, a neighbor came down the hill from Teddy's house and gave Aunt Lucy the news that Teddy wasn't at all well, and that Aunt Lucy would need to wait another day since she should never drive that far without a man going along with her. That did it! Having a man along was something she could most certainly do without in which case she would just drive herself and show that bumbling nephew of hers what she was made of.

Teddy's neighbor hurried back to his house up on the hill and signaled to Teddy and the sheriff who were waiting a good way down the road that Aunt Lucy was getting into her car. The sheriff got out of his patrol car, dressed in plain clothes and minus his badge, and reluctantly watched Teddy turn down a back road towards Kent.

Teddy did park a way down long enough to see if Aunt Lucy would stop to pick up the sheriff. Everything depended on that and she did not let them down.

Lucy would never admit it, but she was relieved when she saw the hitchhiker. It was common to hitch a ride since there were few cars, so she thought nothing of riding in a car with a strange man. Of course, she would never let Teddy know that she indeed had company on the way to Kent.

She managed to slow and stop smartly in response to the sheriff's thumb being raised. She noted his pleasant smile and greeted him cordially, asking where he was going. On learning it was Kent she assured him she would take him right to the place he wanted to go.

The starter hesitated a bit so with the use of the choke they jumped a few feet and then were on their way. Although still very perplexed by her long wait and Teddy not showing up, Aunt Lucy tried her best to appear relaxed and confident. However, as they moved along, the presence of her rather large purse with her license fee and her three dollars inside sitting between her and this stranger started to intrude into her thinking. What if he were a highway robber she had heard about? After all he was a big man and could easily overcome her and get her money.

Aunt Lucy was no small woman herself and between the two of them, there was not much room left for her purse, so she knew he must be very aware of it brushing against his side. The more she thought about it, she decided she should move the purse to her other side but wasn't quite sure how to accomplish that without him becoming suspicious that she was suspicious. After fidgeting a few minutes, she just out and told him she would move her purse to her other side to make more room for him. She reached down for it with her right hand while keeping her left hand firmly on the steering wheel. He in turn wondered how there could possibly be any room on her left side.

To her aggravation the sheriff was sitting on the purse straps and as she gave a tug it caused the car to veer some. He quickly obliged by shifting his weight and she straightened the car back on the road. However, due to the small amount of slack he could give her, she had to tug rather hard again to free the straps. Thankfully, the purse came loose but caused her right hand to hit the steering wheel causing the car to veer off the road again. The sheriff grabbed the wheel at that point quickly bringing them back onto the road. Aunt Lucy responded by slapping his hands smartly, telling him in no uncertain terms that she was driving the car and to keep his hands to himself.

"Sorry," he mumbled, as he began to re-think exactly all that Teddy had mentioned about his aunt's driving skills. At that point Aunt Lucy asked rather crossly, "What's that up ahead in the road?"

"I believe, Ma'am that's a flock of sheep. Maybe you better slow down cause if it's sheep they ain't going to go nowhere fast!"

"Well, I beg your pardon, but they have no business being on the road." and Aunt Lucy lay on the horn keeping the same speed.

"Ma'am, you really need to slow down…."Stop!" He threw out his foot but since there was no place to put it, he simply leaned over and pushed down on the brake with his hand. That resulted in his head being jammed between the windshield and Aunt Lucy, who was pushing against him as hard as she could. With his nose pressed against the windshield, he thankfully realized the car had skidded to a stop a few feet from the sheep.

Aunt Lucy reacted by grabbing the sheriff's shoulders and shoving him back to his side, snapped her head towards him and said icily, "I don't know what you think you're doing, but do you think that you can keep your hands--and your feet--to yourself long enough for us to make it to Kent?"

Sheriff Dudley was sweating profusely and for once was completely without words. He thought about getting out of the car until he realized they were still two miles from Kent. He just leaned back on the seat with his arms crossed on his chest. It looked as if he was praying. His reprieve was short, however, when about a mile from Kent he spotted a crane sitting beside the road where some county men were working on light poles. Aunt Lucy stopped the car. "What's wrong?" asked Dudley.

"Well, don't you see that thing up there? It's liable to fall right on us."

"No Ma'am, it won't fall on us!" His voice rose a bit, "It's a crane and it's supposed to be up there."

"Well, tell them to please lower it till we can get past!"

"Ma'am…forget it!" The sheriff slammed the door on his way out and walked toward the group. Since most knew the sheriff, they exchanged pleasantries and the sheriff told them he had a crazy lady in the car who wanted them to lower the crane, so she could drive by."

"Well, where's she going in such a hurry?"

"You wouldn't believe it if I told you," the sheriff snapped.

One and all turned their backs in order that the woman could not see them laughing as they told the sheriff they were not about to lower the crane. If she was in that big of a hurry, she could take the side road. However, she should proceed at her own risk. They warned she would need to take it slow since the road had been used by cattle and there were several holes.

"Okay," said the sheriff, "but she ain't gonna like it!"

Aunt Lucy did not like it and proved it by jerking the car in reverse and heading down the side road without so much as a wave goodbye. Sheriff Dudley's words of caution were still on his lips when she hit the first hole. The linemen told the sheriff later that they could hear him hollowing over the noise of their machinery for her to slow down.

Lucy hit at least three more holes and sideswiped a tree before the rear tire gave a sharp pop and with Lucy still gunning it, the car sputtered and died on the spot.

The car was towed into town a half hour later with the sheriff's face white and Aunt Lucy's just as red. Sheriff Dudley passed Teddy, who was hiding in the jailhouse, and said simply, "Get her home and I don't want to ever see her face in Kent again!"

It was left to the justice of the peace to tell Aunt Lucy that she would not be getting a driver's license anytime soon and a neighbor took her back to Fancy Knoll on a horse. The car was later quietly sold, and the money put into Aunt Lucy's bank account.

Aunt Lucy was not an unreasonable person and on thinking things over decided she would stay put in her own little house and wait until her nephew got him a better car before she tried again. In the meantime, she heard that they were putting in a small airport nearby and were going to give flying lessons. Teddy told her to quit listening to rumors, that it would never happen in Fancy Knoll. It did happen later, but Aunt Lucy was gone by then. Teddy was hard put whether to feel sad or glad.

A Time to be Angry

As soon as Lutie opened her eyes that Saturday morning, she had a strong feeling that she needed to be on her guard. Due to that sensation, she decided an extra quiet time with her Bible would be needful. Her mind had been centered on her good friend, Laura, all week or at least whom she had considered to be her friend for the past ten years. Laura and her family had moved one April day in 1930, up from their home place in Arkansas and settled on the back forty of Hezekiah's property. The two women had quickly become fast friends and sometimes visited back and forth several times a week. There was always a recipe to be shared, an item to borrow, or just time to sit down and chat. Neither ever lacked for something to say. Lutie wasn't sure how she would have survived her own move, if not for Laura.

She had left her own parents and friends in Tennessee the year before. The first year had been hard on her, money got scarce, and Hezekiah had rented the four-room house which stood empty in their back field. That was when Lutie Lantry got her new neighbor and friend, named Laura.

There were predictably going to be some difficult times of adjustment for these two women on arriving in Fancy Knoll. Since both women were transplants into a community of people who had lived on the same land for a hundred years, there were naturally going to be differences in their lifestyles. That included differences in the way they cooked, cleaned and not least of all how they canned their summer fruits and vegetables.

From the first time that Lutie's new Presto canner was put to use, she and Laura both realized that the ladies of the community were not going to think much of their canning methods. After all, those women's mothers, and grandmothers had used a hot water bath for canning all their lives and how could anyone possibly put up a better batch of Kentucky Wonders than they could. To complicate matters, Lutie's mother-in-law always won a blue ribbon for her canned beans at the county fair.

Perhaps it wasn't so, but somehow Lutie and Laura were made to feel that the local families held it against their husbands for going off to "who knows where" to find a wife. Hezekiah had reassured Lutie numerous times that she was wrong, but it fell on deaf ears. She saw several pretty young women around the community and wondered herself why the men would go outside their state to get a wife. Hezekiah explained to her that if he saw the prettiest Jersey cow of his life pastured over in the next state, he would certainly consider going after her. Lutie blushed and decided to wait until later to figure out if she had been given a compliment, or an insult.

Lutie had been so proud of her new pressure canner when she had first arrived in Fancy Knoll. Her friends and family in Tennessee had been puzzling for a month after the wedding, to think of a going away gift that would be both useful and last for years to come. Several had contributed money for the gift, so her mom had daringly ordered the new craze from the National Pressure Cooker Company. The Presto canner was new on the market and the community thought it would be just perfect for a wedding gift. After all, they didn't want the Fancy Knoll folks to think they were a stingy lot. As for Lutie, she could hardly wait to get started housekeeping in her new husband's home and put her canning skills to use. She was sure they would be duly impressed.

It wasn't going to happen. Mrs. Lantry had taken one look at the strange contraption, declared the thing dangerous and the canner was put back in its box. It stayed there until Lutie's newly acquired friend, Laura, came from Arkansas and moved onto their property.

Things worked out, though, since Lutie now had someone to boost her courage. Come canning time she proudly brought out the Presto and proceeded to ready her beans for canning. The community duly took notice. In fact, she and Laura thoroughly enjoyed the reaction of the community to Lutie's new canner. Some of the neighbors would not come into the kitchen when the cooker was going--they were afraid it would explode. Laura had even heard of people thinking pressure cookers were the result of witchcraft because of their continued hissing. A few others took a wait-and-see attitude.

As time went on, however, things settled down and gradually Lutie and Laura became accepted in the community. Hezekiah was patient with Lutie, and Lutie was patient with Ma Lantry. It took the entire canning season, though, for Ma Lantry to admit that Lutie's funny looking pot did the job just as well as the huge pot she water bathed her fruits and vegetables in. With both methods getting a good workout, the canning season was declared to be a successful one.

During the next several years, Lutie and her mother-in-law became close friends. The grandchildren had naturally formed a great bond between them, but also the families were together much of the time due to their being in church for frequent meetings. Worship was an important segment of everyone's life in Fancy Knoll. Almost someone in every household attended the little church on Huckleberry road. There they shared their joys and their sorrows and learned to lean on each other for almost every part of their lives.

That was one reason Lutie was so upset with Laura. Every woman in the community knew that gossiping was detrimental to the peace which they enjoyed among themselves. Theirs was a small cluster of people and it was imperative to maintain a respectful and a kind relationship with one another. They drew strength from each other and could not afford for gossip to circulate. They also took seriously the Bible's admonition against it.

In the ladies monthly missionary meeting, each member was very careful to stay away from any conversation that might hint of gossip. Sometimes that was very hard on the ladies, of course, but they would be the first to admit that it had gone a long way in keeping a peaceful loving spirit in the neighborhood.

Once, the ladies' efforts to refrain from gossip was taken a little too far when a visiting lady from a close-by town came for a visit. The lady stated that her church was considering starting a ladies' group and thought she might get some ideas from the Fancy Knoll ladies. She was treated very cordially by the women who were present, but soon she began to ask questions about a certain woman of questionable behavior in the community. What the missionary ladies didn't know was that she was the woman's sister and was trying to find out if her sister was in any trouble. What the visiting lady didn't know was that her sister had indeed been acting in an untimely manner, but no one was willing to talk about the matter. That was due to the agreement among them that there would be no more talk concerning her, so as not to be guilty of gossiping.

It might be said that some of the ladies in the room would have liked to glean some information on the said woman, but they didn't dare go against their decision concerning gossip. Consequently, they all clammed up to the visitor and some even moved to a different side of the room to avoid the temptation. The lady left shortly after dessert, and never came back. Neither was anything more heard about a women's group being started in the Lawson Church area.

Agreeing strongly with the no gossiping rule was one reason Lutie could hardly believe that Laura had told something about her that she had specifically asked her not to tell. It had initially begun with one of the family's rare visits to the town of Tazewell to pick up supplies from the Farm Bureau. There, Lutie and Hezekiah had run into his distant cousin, Ruby, who was a favorite among their Virginia side cousins. Lutie had been drawn to her from the first time they met. Hezekiah went inside to conduct farm business and left Lutie and Ruby to catch up on family news. Somewhere during the conversation, the subject got around to teeth. As a child Lutie had suffered with gum problems and consequently had dentures early in her life. Over the years there had never seemed to be enough money to buy new ones, although hers had become chipped and somewhat ill fitting. The cousin, on the other hand, had not only one pair, but had recently purchased two new beautiful sets of shiny white dentures. Although normally folks don't stand on a public street discussing and admiring dentures, Lutie and Ruby did and had quite a pleasant conversation between them. Lutie was disappointed when Hezekiah announced he was ready to go.

A couple of months passed, and they happened to meet the same cousin again--again in Tazewell. Lutie was pleased to see Ruby and again they engaged in an enjoyable conversation. To Lutie's surprise, Ruby pulled her over to the sidewalk and spoke in a soft voice, "Lutie, you don't need to tell this to a soul, and it's nobody's business anyway, but I want to buy you a new set of dentures."

Now Lutie had been hit with a lot of things, but never had anything come close to this offer. Her mouth dropped open, and her eyes got big as Ruby explained that she knew of a place where if one could get there early, she could get her teeth the same day-and best of all the teeth were very inexpensive. Not thinking of anything else to say Lutie sputtered that she would pray about it.

After being quiet most of the way home she finally told Hezekiah about Ruby's offer and waited to see what he thought about it. Surprisingly, he thought it was a wonderful offer and commented on what a great lady he thought his cousin to be. He had known her to be a very generous person who had always seemed to enjoy helping others. Lutie could hardly believe he was so willing since he usually thought things over carefully before accepting help from others.

"But," she sputtered, "It's so expensive!" "Now Lutie," he said, "If she hadn't been able to afford the dentures, she would never have brought it up." Lutie chewed on that a while and looking into the rear-view mirror began to imagine what she would look like with a new set of teeth.

Later she couldn't remember if she ever got around to praying about it, but she had decided she would indeed take Ruby's amazing offer. She called Ruby, thanking her profusely and a time had been set for Lutie to go by for the money. Ruby, having just purchased her own teeth, knew the exact amount and gave Lutie a money order already made out to the clinic.

Hezekiah had Lutie at the dental clinic before seven on Monday morning and read a magazine while she waited in line for some twenty minutes. She soon was in the chair with her old teeth removed, the impressions made, and she was instructed to come back at eleven to get her new teeth. It was so easy!

The only drawback was in having to leave her old teeth, as she had never allowed anyone to see her without her teeth. On coming out of the treatment room, she suddenly realized she must pass through an office full of people. She almost panicked, but instead ducked her head down and whispered to Hezekiah to get her out of that room fast. Although not understanding why, Hezekiah turned her rather sharply toward the door, resulting in Lutie colliding with a gentleman who had just entered. Lutie was horrified when she recognized the man as her son, Tag's, previous schoolteacher. She slapped her hand over her mouth, left Hezekiah to apologize and ran out to the truck. She was somewhat mollified later when Hezekiah told her that Mr. Karnes had told him he was there for the same reason as Lutie.

They returned at eleven, as instructed, and they were shortly on their way back home. They marveled how quickly everything was done and Lutie couldn't help glancing in the mirror every few minutes. My, how pretty they were! She couldn't wait to get home where she locked herself in the back bedroom, got out the hand mirror and proceeded to smile at several different angles to examine her new teeth.

In her excitement she needed to show someone her new look and who other than her good friend, Laura, who predictably went on about how nice she looked. Lutie gave her a hug before she started home to get supper. She turned back and said to her friend. "Laura, don't you dare tell anyone about how I got my new teeth, in case they notice, of course. Look me in the eyes and promise!" Laura made a sign of zipping her mouth and Lutie went down the path humming a tune while running her tongue across her white even teeth.

At Bible study the next day she smiled more than usual, but no one seemed to notice until Granny Honaker started to take the prayer requests. It was then that Sadie, never known to be one to speak softly, pointed out Lutie's new teeth and asked pointedly who the benefactor was who had given her such a nice gift. Lutie was furious! It took all the grace she could muster to answer Sadie. She couldn't wait to get out of the church and go home. She glared darts at Laura who had the nerve to duck her head down and set there as if nothing was amiss. Lutie went home blind to the compliments of her friends. Her best friend had slandered her.

By Friday, Lutie knew something needed to be done soon or her problem was going to escalate much too far for anyone's good. "Lord," she whispered, "show me what I should do about these bad feelings." She re-read Psalm 32, especially the verse about God's promise to lead and guide. Surely Laura was in the wrong for telling people about her new teeth even if Lutie had smiled several times hoping someone would notice. Realizing time was passing and baking needed to be done, Lutie went into the kitchen to finish breakfast.

As she walked from the bedroom, she paused in the living room to inspect the floor. Had it been a month already since she had waxed the floor? The morning sunlight sifting through the window told her it had indeed been a while. The skid marks of brogan shoes were in abundance when she looked at the floor at just the right angle. "Well," she thought, "nothing to do but get busy after breakfast and get it done!"

The morning continued and Lutie finished putting a thick coat of wax on the living room floor. Thankful for a quiet moment, she poured herself a cup of strong coffee and set quietly, not liking the unrest returning to her heart. If only this feeling of betrayal by Laura would go away! "Lord," she prayed, "You know Laura is my dearest friend and I can't bear these negative feelings against her. Show me what to do."

Making her way to the kitchen, she re-checked the water level of the pot of beans bubbling on her ancient wood stove. A beep of the clock told her it would soon be lunch time and she needed to finish the preparation for their noon time meal. She quickly finished mixing the cornbread batter and placed it in the bacon greased iron skillet. She knew by the heat which poured out of the oven door that no more wood would be needed to sufficiently bake the bread, so it was not until ten minutes later that she spied the baking soda sitting on the back of the cabinet board, unopened. *Oh, for crying out loud,* she thought, *maybe Pa won't notice I forgot the soda.*

"I really need to keep my mind on my dinner," she whispered to no one in particular. She knew the importance of keeping her mind focused on the present activity. She was well known by her family for getting completely engrossed in some new plan or project, completely forgetting her present task. Such as the time Hezekiah had asked her to cut the price tags from his new suit jacket before wearing it to the Easter service at church. She went for the scissors which she was sure were in the second drawer down in the washroom, but found instead a roll of scotch tape which prompted her to remember she had promised to bring wrapping paper to the children's Sunday school class for a special project. It was only from the startled looks of some of the congregation as her husband usher passed the offering plate that gave the first clue that something was amiss. The $10 dollar sale tag managed to drop down from underneath his sleeve each time he reached the basket along to another participant. Luckily Tag was sitting in the third row back, saving his dad from further embarrassment, but also by whispering rather loudly, "Pa, your tag is showing!" It took a while for Hezekiah to forgive Lutie for that one.

Lutie proceeded to pull out the cabinet board, getting out the flour bowl and other ingredients she needed for the sweets her family loved to eat. She sifted the flour under the cabinet bin and proceeded to mix and roll dough, all the time quoting the verses from Psalm 91 that she had been trying to memorize for the last two days. She scraped the excess flour off the board and proceeded to clean up her mess she had made.

It was just at that moment that Tag came bounding upon the back porch in a full chase of Tom, the dominecker rooster, who was squawking loud enough to wake the dead. For the hundredth time Lutie wished for a screen door which Hezekiah had promised her an equal number of times.

Unhappily, the rooster came straight through the hallway to the kitchen just as she was emptying the excess flour into the trash can. In that split second, she had to decide whether to hang on to the flour bowl and the trash can or try to grab the rooster before he headed for the freshly waxed living room floor. She chose the latter and in doing so collided with Tag who unfortunately had two freshly laid duck eggs in the front pockets of his overalls. Tag, of course, didn't stop but kept close on the tail of the rooster.

Tag rounded the dining room door which led into the newly waxed living room the same time as he grabbed the tail feathers of the illusive rooster and held on with all his might. Then began a chain reaction which was to furnish a lesson, and laughter, in the Lantry household for days to come. The table on which Grandmother Stella's lamp stood also was placed just around the corner into the living room, on which also held the full cup of coffee left by Lutie a few minutes before. The rooster, Tad, lamp, table and coffee all went down together on the gooey sticky waxed floor. The squawking of the dominecker and the high-pitched yells of Lutie and Tag served to suggest to Hezekiah, who was out in the barn, that a gruesome assault on his family must be in progress; that resulted in his running into the fray fresh from cleaning manure out of Bessie's stall to save his family from a tragedy. In his hurry to get around the dining room door and unable to slow his momentum, he thankfully skidded over to the side of Tad and Lutie, but sadly nailed Tom to the floor who had just broken loose from Tag's death grip on his tail feathers.

The room became frightfully quiet as each stared at the other in total disbelief. Hezekiah on seeing that his family was safe, Lutie's flour covered face looking mournfully at her freshly waxed floor and Tag at the large number of feathers held tightly in his hand with broken eggshells covering his bibbed overalls. Had not the kitchen alarm clock announced the bread was done, they would have probably taken a while longer to extract themselves from the flour, eggs, wax, and feathers. As it was, Lutie rose carefully from her awkward position, dusted herself off and spoke, "Well, it could have been worse. It could have been one of the good layers." She flicked a bit of cow manure from her apron and proceeded into the kitchen.

Poor Tom lay still, conquered at last, with only his sparse remaining feathers needing to be plucked before being placed in the big pot hanging on the wall behind the stove. Hezekiah left Tag to fend for himself as he hurried back out to the barn where he howled in laughter with only Bessie's mournful gaze watching him in wonderment.

The evening devotional time was more subdued than usual as Hezekiah pondered possible lessons to be learned from the day's adventures. Short Bible phrases came to mind such as 'thou shalt not go out in haste," which he certainly had done when he heard the caterwauling coming from the house and "thou shalt not kill" as he thought of poor Tom lying quiet and featherless on the living room floor in the wax. Instead he thumbed through the Old Testament calling out the books to himself, "Joel--Amos--Obadiah--yup, Jonah!"

"Good," said Tag, "I love the part about the whale puking Jonah out on the shore!" Hezekiah flipped a couple more pages. "Ah! Here it is," he said, "Chapter 4, verse one. Nope," he said thoughtfully. "Let's start in the last verse of chapter 3."

"Here it comes," groaned Tag. "I have a feeling Jonah has done puked and now he's sitting under that tree where that worm eats up all the leaves." Tag wanted to plug his ears, but he knew that would never do, so he tried to focus on how big the worm must have been. His pa started to read.

"And God saw their works that they turned from their evil way; and God repented of the evil that He said He would do unto them, and He did not do it."

"Now," Pa said, "verse one of chapter 4, 'But, it displeased Jonah exceedingly, and he was very angry." Hezekiah skipped down a couple of verses, adjusted his glasses and then quoted verse 4. "Then the Lord said, 'Doest thou well to be angry?"

Hezekiah turned his head and looked directly at Tag.

"Tag, when you became so angry at old Tom what would you have answered God if He had asked you that question at that moment?"

It became very quiet as Tag thought over the situation. "Well, Pa, I reckon I had a right to get mad. That rooster was hurting that hen and she was already hurting enough!"

"Well now, let's think about that. Just maybe Tom was protecting his family."

"What!" squeaked Tag? "But Pa, that chicken was his family!"

Pap scratched his head for some example to clarify the matter and remembering an earlier conversation between Tag and his ma while doing Tag's homework, Hezekiah said, "Tag, chew on this a bit. What if your friend, Buff, came to my door, and asked if you could come out and play catch. Now, it just happened that I had just received a note from your teacher telling me to keep you away from Buff at all cost, because some earlier tests had come back positive and Buff has the Yellow Fever!"

Now, Pa really had Tag's attention because they had just finished studying about Africa in their geography class and he had just learned about that dreaded Yellow Fever! "Whatcha gonna tell him, Pa?"

"Well," Pa continued, "I'm in a dilemma, Tag. Buff is a little boy just like you and I know you really like each other. But should

I let him come in because of that or should I take steps to keep you away from him?"

Pa sat quietly for a few minutes knowing from Tag's expression that he was slowly getting the connection. "Now Tag," he said, "Sometimes, roosters are very protective of their flock. He knew that hen was sick and even though he had earlier liked that chicken, he was now trying to protect the rest of the flock from any further harm to them. Does this make you feel any forgiveness in your heart for the rooster?"

Tag looked up at Pa defiantly. "Nope! Pa, he wouldn't even stop after I yelled at him and even hit him with a stick?"

"Now, that's another matter, Tag. Why are you so angry that he wouldn't stop when you told him to?"

"Cause…cause…just cause!" sputtered Tag.

"Is it fair to say that you were now mad at him, not because he had earlier hurt the hen, but that he didn't obey you?"

"Well, yes. And you would be too, Pa. He stood there glaring at me like he owned the chickens."

Pap allowed a small grin as he hugged Tag to his big chest.

"Tag," he explained, "Sometimes we have every right to be angry, although we need to honestly examine the reason for our anger. I like to think of it as worthy, or unworthy anger. You were mad because Tom was, in your opinion, hurting the defenseless and sick chicken, at least as much as you understood about the situation. That was good! You tried to help. That was also good!"

"The problem came when you continued to hang on to your anger. If you think carefully about your feelings, you will come to see that the reason you were then so angry is simply because you could not make Tom do what you thought he should. You probably wanted him to run away from you, squawking in fear. Tom thought otherwise and so you two clashed."

"Tag, most all anger in us humans come because we either lose control of a situation, or maybe never had any. Misunderstanding a situation also is a major cause of anger. We can be angry at pain in a loved one because we can't make it stop. We get angry at the bank when we forget to pay on time, and they charge us a late fee. Our anger usually comes down to us not getting our own way or something we took the wrong way. Of course, it's good to be angry at injustice or hurt brought to another person, but we need to be careful that our resentment is not directed toward someone because of our own ego or selfishness."

At that remark, Lutie sat up a bit straighter. Hezekiah's words had hit home! "Lord, is this what you have been trying to tell me all day? Have I been mad at Laura just because she did something that hurt my ego or my pride? Did I really see things as they actually were last Tuesday?" Lutie didn't know if that was the case, or not, but she knew one thing. She had to find out!

With her bonnet in place and a resolve to get to the bottom of things, the next morning Lutie walked the half mile to the farmhouse of the widow, Sadie. After the pleasantries and a cup of Sadie's peppermint tea, Lutie mentioned the comment made at Bible study and came right out and asked Sadie how she knew someone, other than Hezekiah, had paid for her new teeth.

"Well," said Sadie innocently, "You know my Aunt Hattie who lives over on Possum Creek, well she happened to be getting her false teeth re-lined at that same tooth clinic as you and was standing right behind you when you got up to the desk--my what a line she said they had that day--anyway when you went to pay for your teeth--and mind you she wasn't listening on purpose--but she heard you telling that secretary lady that someone had given you the most wonderful gift and that was why someone else's name was on the money order and then Aunt Hattie told her daughter-in-law Lucy and when Lucy came to borrow my sausage grinder she told me." By this time, Lutie was winded just from listening, when Sadie slapped her hand over her mouth and said, "Mercy, you don't think I was gossiping at Bible study do you?"

Lutie didn't know what to do with Sadie's explanation. She was terribly afraid she was going to burst into a giggling fit but being so happy to learn that Laura had not been the guilty one just assured Sadie that all was well. She soon made her exit and went straight to Laura's house and gave her a big hug. Laura, a bit surprised, hugged her tightly, but before Lutie could explain the reason, Laura, blurted out, "Can you believe what that Sadie said in Bible study? I wonder how in the world she knew about your teeth?" "I know, dear friend," said Lutie, "and after I can forgive myself, I will tell you all about it."

Momma slept well that night and even made blueberry pancakes for breakfast the next morning. Hezekiah questioned her good mood but chalked it up to the cup of sassafras tea that she had first thing.

Curtain stretchers

In Fancy Knoll, everyone watched out for each other. They shared, and borrowed, without giving it a second thought. For example, each summer the big apple butter kettle made its rounds and after each batch, the kettle would be carried by one of the stronger boys or men and moved to its next location. Sometimes a team of horses would be borrowed to plow new ground for spring planting. Also, the location of the best blackberry and huckleberry patches were passed from neighbor to neighbor and a special time came in early winter when select cuts of pork would be shared with neighbors at hog killing time. The sharing and borrowing were a great way of helping each other and enabled some to accomplish chores that they could not have done otherwise.

On one occasion, Granny Shinn borrowed Granny Honaker's tomcat, Rouser, to get rid of the annual influx of field mice which had invaded her house. That almost ended their friendship though, when the cat took a liking to Granny Shinn's pet canary and spent most of its time peering into the cage, keeping the canary in a state of shock, as well as Granny Shinn. Seeing her mother was in a state of panic, the daughter took Rouser back to Granny Honaker and bought a bunch of mousetraps instead.

The first time Granny Shinn opened her kitchen cabinet and saw a tiny dead mouse with only its tail caught in the trap, she almost fainted and immediately sent for her daughter to remove "that torture machine" from her house. The traps were dutifully taken out and rat poison was purchased and put into places where Granny Shinn could not have access. It worked except that neither could Granny excess the dead mice and sent for her daughter every couple of days to come and find the dead mice because her house "smelled worse than three dead polecats!"

The search for dead mice kept the daughter in a tizzy and Granny Shinn further upset, so that it was finally decided to move the canary to the daughter's house and bring Rouser back to Granny Shinn's. That worked well and after a time the cat was taken back home to Granny Honaker. However, another upheaval came when they discovered Rouser had evidently developed a fondness for the taste of mice and the attention, he had received in the Shinn household. He finally had to be fastened on Granny Honaker's back porch to keep him home. Thankfully, the break-up of a long friendship was averted, when Rouser again got accustomed to the comfy blanket and rich cream, he began receiving on Granny Honaker's porch.

Another popular item that was borrowed by all the neighbor women was a pair of curtain stretchers owned by the Rudd sisters, Josie and Rosie. The 83-year-old twins lived in an old farmhouse near the base of Birch Mountain. Their family had lived there almost as long as the Raleigh's, but all had died except for the two sisters. Although they lived in the same house, the rivalry between the two was well known and forever a source of amusement in the community. They were well liked and got along well with everyone else, but not with each other. They had spent most of their lives, seemingly, trying to outdo the other.

As to the curtain stretchers, no one was sure exactly which daughter owned them, as both had desired them, and both had asked their mother to leave the stretchers to herself after Ma was gone. To the dismay of both girls when the will was read, there were some blotches on the paper, perhaps caused by water, or something of that nature and the first letter of the daughter's name was obliterated. The daughters thought it might have been caused by their mother's tears, but it was thought by others that it was probably done on purpose since their ma, knowing of the rivalry, did not want to cause further conflict between the two. The water blotch, or whatever it was, resulted in the clause being read as, "I bequeath my curtain stretchers to my beloved daughter, osie." That was enough of a blow to them that they had asked around about the possibility of contesting the will.

The result was that they were forced to share ownership and the women in the community who wanted to borrow the stretchers were hard put to ask to do so, without causing a brawl between the sisters. It was usually resolved by one of the area women addressing the request in the presence of both sisters and asking something to the effect, "I would like to borrow your curtain stretchers this week, if possible." Of course, she asked with lowered eyes, and both sisters usually answered in the affirmative.

For the benefit of the reader who is not familiar with curtain stretchers, they were one of the handiest methods of shaping or freshening up old curtains that anyone could imagine. The adjustable contraption consisted of a large wooden frame with tiny pins around the edges on which the lace curtains or table clothes were attached after washing and starching. The homemade starch was usually made from either cornstarch or flour and after being mixed with water, made a very stiff concoction. The freshly washed curtains, after being dipped in the starch mixture, were attached quickly to the pins on the stretcher and allowed to dry. The results were beautiful fresh-looking curtains, which were carefully removed from the pins and then hung on the windows. They looked as bright as if they were new. Mrs. Rudd's curtain stretchers had been purchased in the early 1900s for $2.50 and had serviced the family, plus the community, for the past 40 years. They had been well worth the money.

The ownership of the stretchers wasn't the only thing about which the two women differed. Josie sided with the Baptist, Rosie with the Methodist. Josie used Rinso powder to do her laundry, Rosie used Duz. Josie washed her hair in creek water, Rosie with rainwater--it seemed they could not agree on anything. Yet it would be unheard of to separate the two sisters. Granny Honaker suggested one day that one of them move over to the next farmhouse that happened to be empty and Josie snorted that that was "stuff and nonsense" and asked if Granny had forgotten they were flesh and blood. Besides that, Rosie added, they got along fine together. Thereafter, the community had left them alone realizing they would not be satisfied in any other situation.

One day the sisters announced that they wanted to have the Ladies Aid meeting at their house for that month. The others were a little doubtful and wondered if the two could agree long enough for them to have a meaningful meeting. However, they could hardly refuse and were pleasantly surprised on arrival to find the sisters were evidently having one of their more amiable days. The house looked immaculate with the curtains looking freshly stretched. The table was laid out with china cups and saucers for the usual tea, and glasses were also present for a cold beverage. Rosie and Josie both were known for their cake baking skills, so the women knew they had something to look forward to at refreshment time.

Lutie did a fine job of bringing out their Bible lesson for the day. It was taken from Titus 2:3-5 and focused on Christian women and their role as teachers. She read, "The aged women likewise, that they be in behavior as becometh holiness, not false accusers, not given to much wine, teachers of good things."

It was their practice at each meeting for a different lady to read and discuss a few short verses from the Bible, with all joining in the discussion. This group of women was not all "aged women," but they agreed that the verses could certainly pertain to any one of them--at least the part about not being false accusers and being teachers of good things. They also agreed that "not given to wine" was thankfully not relevant for any of them. That declaration would be on most of their minds for days to come.

When they were ready for their refreshments, finger sandwiches were brought out and two different kinds of cake. Josie was a chocolate lover and Rosie preferred the vanilla flavored ones. In addition, two pitchers of fruit juice were placed on the table. Josie proudly announced that she thought hers was the best grape juice she had ever before put up. Rosie, in turn, placed her pitcher on the table with the comment that she was very certain that her blackberry juice was tasty enough to win at the county fair.

Several glances were exchanged between the other ladies, sending the message that they needed to try both or there would be a problem. They then dutifully bragged on both the blackberry and the grape, declaring they were going to need two glasses, while the makers of the juice stood beaming on the sidelines.

Having two glasses of juice, plus a cup of tea, caused the ladies to linger a bit longer than usual. The conversation turned serious when it was mentioned that Mr. Foster had an accident mowing his grass which led to a visit to the doctor in Tazewell. It seemed he had been mowing on a steep hill and the mower got away from him. As he vaulted down the hill to catch it, he grabbed the mower in the wrong place which made a deep gash on his hand. Annie Johnson spoke up and said it was a mercy he hadn't bled to death.

At that point in the story, Lutie noticed that Grandma Lantry was bent over with her head in her lap seemingly sobbing into her apron. Lutie, thinking she was feeling bad for Mr. Foster, patted her on her back and whispered, "There now, Ma, don't worry! He wasn't hurt badly!" Imagine her amazement when Granny rose up with tears streaming down her face from laughter.

Lutie, feeling ashamed of her mother-in-law, reprimanded her, "Ma, what are you laughing at? That thing drug him right through a bunch of rose bushes."

Granny responded by squealing with laughter. Laura took one look at her and began giggling as well. That started Jessie and Cordelia, and from then on it was useless to try and stop. The whole group, along with Lutie, got involved and in the end the only ones not laughing were Josie and Rosie who stood wide-eyed not knowing what in the world was happening.

The happy bunch of ladies did quiet down but seemed to be

having such a good time that in a short time both pitchers of juice were emptied and declared the juices was delicious and each lady would love to have the recipes.

The women got up to leave and since some had to help the others to their feet, they went into gales of laughter. The twin sisters stood horrified as they realized what had happened. The women were drunk, and it was their juice that did it! However, which one? Neither was going to admit it was hers, so they ushered the ladies out the door as soon as they could get them moving, quickly offering up a prayer that they would make it home safely.

It was a merry bunch of women who made their way down the road that afternoon. Thankfully, no revenuers were in sight. On arriving home, most had to take a nap before they could start supper, and it was not until the next day before they gathered at Laura's house that they discussed their adventure. Of course, by then all of them knew what had happened and were thankful Pastor Amos had only his wife Cordelia to confront. It was bad enough having their husbands howling with laughter at their episode, much less their pastor seeing them in an inebriated state.

At church on Sunday, Rosie and Josie were subdued and for once did not try to best the other one in anything. The men folks of the community teased their wives unmercifully, asking every few days when the recipes were coming for the juice making.

The twin sisters lived a few years longer, but when Rosie died of respiratory problems, Josie followed her in death a month later. It was thought they could not bear to be apart for long. The curtain stretchers were kept in the church closet and were available to any women in the community. The juice incident was referred to for many years as the day the Ladies Aid was "given to wine."

Hog Killing Time

One of Tag's least liked, but sometimes also the best liked, day of the year came on the fourth Thursday of November. That was the wonderful day of Thanksgiving. A day of family, of the aroma of pumpkin pie, and of family games in the afternoon. In addition, there was always the excitement of a Christmas to come. Of such were the normal things that excited Tag about Thanksgiving, but in the winter of 1940, he was having trouble getting excited about the holiday.

For most rural homes Thanksgiving had somehow evolved into being not only a day of thanksgiving, but also a perfect day for killing hogs. Ordinarily this would not have put a damper on the day's pleasure for Tag and his group of friends, since they were exempt from any chores and free for the day. The menfolk and women folk would be doing all the work.

However, this Thanksgiving Day was going to be different, and especially hard on Tag. His Pa had announced the week before that of the three possible hogs slated for butchering this year, one of them was to be Tag's favorite pet, Blessing. Tag could not bear the thought that Blessing might die in pain during the killing process.

In past years, Pa had allowed the boys to come to the pens only after the slaughter of the hogs. That was okay with them because sometimes the hogs would squeal while being butchered, and so the kids wanted to avoid that part of hog killing day. Each year during the early part of the butchering, they never failed to hold their hands tightly over their ears in case of squealing. It would thankfully be over quickly, though, and then Tag and company could enjoy the rest of the day, especially knowing they would be given the hog bladders. Those would make dandy balloons, or they would fill them with water and use them to play their version of volleyball. That was something they always looked forward to.

This November, however, the hog slated for the butcher was one that had become a family pet over the years, most especially for Tag. He had been giving her extra treats in her slop bucket for several years now, and in return she had provided the family with multiple litters of piglets. To him, she was a family pet just as much as his dog, Bandit.

Years later, no one could recall just what started the notion of Blessing being the offering for this Thanksgiving. The family decided perhaps the hog was just getting too old, and she needed butchering while there was still plenty of belly fat to furnish them with a good amount of lard for the coming year. Others thought, though, it was Grandma Liza's constant nagging to phase out the raising of hogs, that might have prompted it. She had already been on to grandpa about his diet. Tag did have to admit that Grandpa loved his pork, as well as his salt, and that could have been the deciding factor.

Another theory was that, perhaps, it was simply because Blessing was already 16 years old and she had contributed enough to the family's welfare over the years. She had indeed lived up to her name and needed a long rest. However, none of the reasoning made sense to Tag. Years later, he still resented the fact that the slaughter of Blessing had even been a consideration.

It was this sentiment that triggered an elaborate plan by Tag and his friends, and his cousin Jackson, to save Blessing from such an unsure conclusion to her life. They had all helped feed her at some point, so she had become a familiar and predictable fixture in their happy carefree days of boyhood. They could not bear to think that she would suffer any pain on her demise.

Pa was always in a good mood on Sunday, so Tag approached

him in the living room with the most downcast saddest look on his face that he could possibly muster and pleaded with Pa again to spare Blessing. He even carried one of Pa's white handkerchiefs to wipe the tears from his face and to blow his nose if it became necessary. It was hard for Pa to keep a straight face, especially since Tag had never carried one before.

Although Pa was touched, he remained firm on his choice to slaughter Blessing. He explained to Tag just how important it was this year to slaughter the fattest, best fed of the hogs. He was well aware of the extra food Blessing received at times, from some well-known benefactors, had contributed to her large size. Although he did not want to make Tag feel guilty, he explained that they had used up their supply of lard last year too quickly, so as it was predicted to be a lean year, the fattest hog needed to be butchered.

His heart ached for his son, but he also knew how soon boys could forget such dramatic events, due to their desire for further adventure. Perhaps he would take the boy deer hunting over in McDowell County before Christmas. He surmised that if he could make sure Tag bagged a deer that it would go a long way in his forgetting about his hog. In case Tag did get a deer, Pa would just have to put up with bragging the following weeks. The excitement and bliss on Tag's face would be worth it all.

In the meantime, Tag called an emergency meeting with his group of friends and they gathered at Joe's house on the last Friday before Thanksgiving to discuss the dilemma. All the boys were highly respectful of Pa's decisions usually, but this time he had gone over the edge as far as they were concerned. They desperately needed to come up with some plan to either delay Blessing's slaughter until another year, or if not, to somehow devise a plan to keep her from suffering during the process. They gathered around the hog pens on that frosty evening to discuss the matter, as the three hefty Berkshires watched them mournfully through the wooden fence rails.

Cecil spoke up, "We just gotta do something! I have never liked a hog better than I do Blessing!" The boys mulled it over for a few minutes and decided it was necessary to come up with a plan. After several minutes of discussing ways of easing the hog's pain, they gradually got around to thoughts of sedating the pig by some method. If they could think of something that would both relax her and work as a painkiller, her passing would be made much easier, hence no squealing before her demise. That would be the best thing they could do for her if they could just manage to give her something moments before she was to be slaughtered. Therefore, they kicked around a few ideas.

Charlie mentioned giving her a big dose of stanbacks right before the men gathered to start the butchering. A few smiles lit up as they realized that might have possibilities. Jackson, the youngest of the group, spoke up and suggested castor oil, since his mamma used it as a cure-all for "anything and everything". Maybe it might help deaden the pain. On seeing the disgusted looks on the others, he decided it might not be such a good idea, after all.

"Hey," Cecil said, "What about giving her some ether." That got all the boy's attention as they began to discuss exactly what ether was supposed to be, and to do. Cecil did not quite know either, but he loved the attention he was getting, so he shared with them his experience the previous month when he had his tonsils out. Making sure they were all listening, he began to relate how the doctor had laid him on a table "right in the doctor's office and all he had to do was take his shirt off." He told how the nurse in a white uniform had held an awful smelling handkerchief--that was the ether--over his nose. He had not had time to even count to ten, and he was fast asleep.

"Wow," said Tag, "that sounds like just the thing for Blessing! But where are we going to get any ether?" Their faces fell as they all realized the futility of finding someone to give them ether. Most of the boys never remembered even being in a doctor's office, and the only reason Cecil had was because of his diseased tonsils.

They continued discussing ways to help Blessing to pass to the other side in comfort. Charlie thought whiskey might work well as it had put his dad to sleep enough times. "Are you kidding," said Tag. "If Ma would get a whiff of whiskey on Blessing, she'd never rest till she knew why and where it came from. I'd have to wash the supper dishes for the next year."

It was Joe who finally mentioned the suggestion of giving the hog a big dose of Chamomile tea. The others howled with laughter. "Laugh all you want to," he said, "but that stuff really works. Ma gets cranky as all get out sometimes and doubles over with stomach cramps and Pa always says, 'Joe, make your momma a cup of Chamomile tea!" Joe explained that it was no time before his ma settled down and got all quiet and sleepy like. "I tell you guys, it works!"

"Well," said Tag, "maybe we better think about this. Your ma is what--about 140 pounds--and that sow is about 500. It'll take a lot of tea to do her any good!"

"Let's do some figuring," Joe said, as he began drumming his fingers against his forehead. "Ma only takes one tea bag to calm her down and a box of tea has about 50 bags. Now, if my 'rithmetic is right, that oughta be more than enough to calm Blessing down. Should even put her right to sleep." The others looked admiringly at Joe's mathematical skills and decided they just might have hit on a great plan to help Blessing over to the other side.

They talked on for another good hour about the particulars. Surely that amount of tea would be enough that she would not mind what was being done to her. Cecil suggested adding a few doses of stanbacks into the tea, which would further ease the pain.

The boys all began to feel much better about the fate of Blessing and began to make plans as to how early, and how to go about giving Blessing the dose before the men arrived for the hog killing. It would have to be timed just right to be the most effective to ease her suffering--in case there was any.

That week all the farmers in the neighborhood anxiously listened to the weatherman to give his predictions. Sure enough, Thursday was supposed to be a cold crisp day--just right for hog killing! An enormous flurry of activity by the boys was noted by the older family members, but it certainly wasn't that unusual. The kids always managed to get crazy excited at just about any happening in the area that was somewhat out of the norm. However, this time serious business was in the making, and there wasn't much time to get all the things together that was needed to carry out their plans.

Since the boys Sunday school lesson, the previous Sunday, had been all about speaking falsehoods, it was agreed by the group that it was okay to keep their plans a secret, but they absolutely must not lie in case they got caught. They weren't quite sure how big of a sin lying was, but they didn't want to take a chance. Therefore, the boys stood solemnly in a circle, stacked their hands one on top of the other, and in one voice they repeated the ninth commandment. Then a loud "Amen" was heard from each boy. The agreement was sealed!

If one of them were indeed found out, they would just have to shuck the whole chamomile plan, fall on their knees, and beg Pa in one accord to spare Blessing from a painful death. They even went so far as to practice the falling on their knee's ritual a few times. Jackson was to be sure and look upward into Pa's eyes and if he possibly could, he was to try to cry some real tears. Therefore, with that settled, they somehow managed to get through the weekend, using every spare minute in finalizing their plans.

Tag was back and forth to his friend's houses a dozen times a day, or so it seemed. Youngsters staying at each other's homes overnight was not at all uncommon for those living in the community, so the boys managed to be together an unusual amount of time without causing too much suspicion from their parents.

It would also be necessary for them to be under one roof on Thanksgiving morning to carry out their plans. Mrs. Lantry readily gave permission for the boys to stay overnight with Tag on Wednesday evening. They would then offer to "help out" with gathering wood, and such, so that no one would be suspicious of their early presence at the slaughter.

A Remedy for Blessing

Due to the boy's finagling, they managed to finalize their plans at Tag's house on Wednesday evening, which included Cecil, Joe, Jackson, Charlie and Tag. The tea had been purchased while on their way home from school on Tuesday. Tag and Joe had pooled their money that they had earned from digging potatoes and apples on Joe's pa's farm that fall. They felt it was a small sacrifice to make in exchange for Blessing's wellbeing,

Jackson had managed to get four packets of his mom's stanback powder, a popular analgesic, from the box on the top shelf of their kitchen cabinet. Of all the boys, Jackson was feeling the most pangs of remorse concerning their plans. He was not sure why, but since the boys had made a pact about not lying, and keeping things secret from their parents, he had felt guilty. He thought it had something to do with Preacher Hanshew's sermon the Sunday before about being a deceitful person.

Was doing something in secret, in order not to get caught, the same as being deceitful, he wondered? Was it as bad as lying? The preacher's main message had been from a verse in Jeremiah that said our hearts are deceitful and desperately wicked. The reason Jackson remembered the sermon so well was because his most recent archenemy happened to be named Jeremiah and Jackson couldn't wait to point that verse out to him. He figured Jeremiah really needed to hear it. The slam of the screen door put to rest any more theological debate over the matter, and Jackson was gone out the door in a matter of seconds.

It would be Joe's chore to mix the chamomile and bring the concoction to the pigpen. They decided it would be best to put the analgesic in at the last minute. They also needed to make sure the mixture was still comfortably warm. They couldn't risk Blessing not appreciating iced tea on such a cold morning.

By Wednesday evening, the boys were wildly excited. Charlie, always the more practical one, decided they needed a pep talk or the whole plan might get blown sky high. Therefore, it was that Tag's dad had much to ponder as he passed by and observed the group of boys huddled in a chilly semicircle with only one solemn voice intruding in the still night air. "Hmmm," he thought, "that's unusual," but as he counted five heads, and none seemed to be in pain, he passed on by never realizing what an exciting agonizing ordeal the boys were planning on the following morning.

"Bzzzz!" Jackson jumped straight up as the alarm buzzer went off. Quickly fighting his way from under the heavy quilts, he began shaking the other boys. The other four had not been able to sleep until well after midnight so it took a moment to focus their minds on what morning it was. None had bothered getting undressed the night before, so they only had to slip into their brogans, tie the laces and head out into the dark night. They grabbed some slices of light bread and a poke of apples and slipped out the bedroom door. Cecil's watch showed it was a bit after 5 am.

The need to hurry grabbed all five boys' attentions as Tag reminded them that the helpers would be there at 6 am. Joe grabbed the gallon of water, which he had filled the night before. To keep it warm the boys had sealed it tightly, tied it in a thick towel, and then put the jug near their feet hoping it would stay reasonably warm for a few hours. Cecil had the stanbacks secure in his overall pocket and Tag had a coffee can of chop to add to Blessing's tea breakfast. Sneaking out the back-bedroom door, Tag could hear his mom moving around and already the smell of coffee was permeating the crisp morning air. A visit to the outhouse and a quick walk down the hill brought them to the pig pens tucked away on a flat area near the bottom of the hill.

The boys were glad that Blessing was isolated in her own pen. It would make it easier to deal with the preparations. There was not a sound of anyone approaching yet, as the boys began to get frantic wondering if there would be a hitch in the plans. What if Blessing didn't like the chamomile tea and what if the dose wouldn't be timed right to get the desired effect? A dozen doubts were being stammered out with everyone trying to get everyone else to talk quieter.

It had taken Joe only a few minutes to add the tea and stanbacks to the gallon of water, since they had dumped all the tea bags the night before. With everyone's nerves near breaking point, Tag suddenly remembered they needed to say a proper goodbye to his favorite hog. What would be a nice ceremony? A few weeks back a dedication service had been held at the church and Tag had watched fascinated as several men had laid hands on the outgoing missionary and prayed for him. Tag had thought that was a wonderful way to say goodbye, so maybe Blessing would benefit from such a sendoff. Therefore, hopping into the pen, and with the other boys leaning over the rail fence, they all managed to touch Blessing on some part of her body. A passing traveler could not have made out any actual words the boys were saying, but they would have certainly recognized the seriousness of the mumblings. Tag also felt a need to ask Blessing's forgiveness in case things didn't work out.

The dedication over, they huddled together and kept their eyes and ears open for any sign of the men's arrival. They knew that things moved fast once the men came. The fire had been made ready the night before waiting only for a spark on a bit of kerosene to quickly send the dry hickory wood into a roaring blaze. In the meantime, they munched on bread and apples.

Straining themselves to listen carefully for movement, or voices, the boys forced themselves to wait until the watch showed 25 minutes to 6. "Let's do it," whispered, Tag. Into the trough went the gallon of tea after another hardy shaking by Joe to make sure the stanbacks mixed with the tepid tea. Tag, not real sure if Blessing would take to the tea, sprinkled a liberal amount of chop on top of the tea mixture.

They all held their breath, anxiety oozing from their very pores as Blessing began to gobble down the mixture. Literally holding their mouths to keep from shouting they jumped around like they had just spotted the winning marble. Blessing did indeed like chamomile tea! After a moment of wild glee, they managed to quiet themselves down to a whisper. The other two hogs looked pensively through the rails of the wooden fence, as the first sounds of the men's laughter sounded in the morning air.

The area came alive with Pap arriving first and several neighbors close behind. Tag was right about the fire. Shortly after Pap arrived, the fire was lit, and the men were gathered around to have the usual morning greetings and a sharing of the latest weather predictions.

Pa had noted the early presence of the youngsters but chalked it up to their natural excitement of the day. After a time with everyone agreeing it was a fine day to kill hogs Pap hollered, "Boys, Let's get at it! We ain't got all day."

Now Pap knew the sentiments of the boys and knew it would be especially hard on Tag who had fed Blessing ever since he was old enough to carry a slop bucket. Unable to read his son's eyes, he gently asked Tag if he wanted to take himself and his friends up to Ma's warm kitchen for some of their favorite pancakes and maple syrup.

In response the boys did move back away from the group of men. To be honest Tag would have liked to get away as fast as he could, but his level of curiosity was beyond high and he had to see if their plan had worked well enough to spare Blessing in her final hours. He would hurry to the house as soon as he found out how things went.

The men approached Blessing's pen. She lay seemingly unconcerned on the far side. "Strange," said Pap, "she usually has her snout hanging through the fence at the first footstep on the path."

Mr. Bennett, the next-door neighbor said, "It is kind of early, maybe we got her confused as to her breakfast time." He then proceeded to pour some of the slop intended for the other two hogs into her trough calling, "Soooi! Soooi!" One of her ears twitched. The men and boys waited.

Pa banged on the slop bucket with his gun. A full minute passed before Blessing began to rise in what seemed like slow motion, almost gracefully, and came ambling over to the group. The entire group of men and boys stood captivated. In later discussions, some declared she looked as if she had a smile on her face.

She came straight toward them, unafraid and a little unsteady, but if hogs could manage a queenly entrance, Blessing managed. She walked right up to the mesmerized group of men, and with nothing but the rail of the fence between them, held her head high and proceeded to demonstrate projectile vomiting as it had never been seen before.

Jumping back as one man, the amazed group, unable to say a word watched as the puking went on several minutes. Blessing then slowly walked back to her corner, lay down leisurely and went back to sleep.

The group of boys could not contain their joy. They forgot all restraints and began pounding each other on the back, Pap turned just in time to see the faces of his son and his friends. A light turned on as he thought of the mysterious behavior of the boys in the previous days. Pap never batted an eye, never hesitated in his speech, but said only, "Men, get the other hogs ready to butcher. If Blessing is sick, we don't dare butcher her today."

Only a dad who loves his son very much could appreciate the ecstasy on his son's face as the group of boys realized for the first time that not only was Blessing in a comfortable state, but she had just been given a stay of execution. Their joy and relief were a thing to behold! In fact, Blessing never was butchered for family meat. She would live a few more years and remained a special friend of Tag and his buddies.

There were to be repercussions, however, as Pap couldn't dare let the boy's manipulations go undealt with. As always, he knew the benefits of lessons learned in the minds of young boys. God had given him a very wise father and he had long ago decreed he would to be the same for his son.

His dilemma came from not knowing the boy's entire role in the behavior of Blessing that Thanksgiving morning. He guessed something had been given orally to the hog and that it could possibly have been something dangerous. Therefore, after the replacement hogs had been cut into portions, ground up, salted down and shared, the tired neighbors and family members went their respective ways still discussing the strange behavior of Blessing. Soon after supper, Pap called a meeting for the five young boys in the family kitchen far from the ears of all others.

With the smell of fresh fried pork and a stomach topped off with Ma's pumpkin pie, Pa just simply looked at the small group. Knowing the ways of boys, he gave them a few minutes of squirming to contemplate the events of the day. "I know," he began, "that our hog, Blessing, was given something this morning that would cause her to act in such a way as she did. Thankfully there have been no ill effects as I can see, but she might have died-- not from being butchered to supply meat for the family, but because she was given something deadly by a group of certain young boys."

All eyes were suddenly drawn to the clean red checked tablecloth that Ma had put on earlier for their supper. "To clear up this matter," Pa continued, "I very much need to know what you boys gave that hog to eat or drink early this morning. I'm not so much interested in how, or even when, but what I do need to know, Tag, is what you gave Blessing for her to act that way?"

Pa crossed his arms across his stomach, leaned back in his chair, and waited. A pen could have been heard dropping as the boys each examined their actions. Their oath to be truthful lay heavy on each one, but it was left to Tag to be put to the test. With a soft voice, but still audible by everyone, he spoke the truth, "Chamomile tea," he whispered. Pa's chair hit the floor. "What did you say?" "And stanback powder," spoke the timid voice of Jackson from across the table. Another pin could have dropped, "But why?" sputtered Pa.

Freed at last from their shady secrets, all the boys began to talk at once. Tag managed to get across that he could not bear to hear Blessing's squeal in case the bullet didn't hit just right, and chamomile tea had been recommended by Charlie, because it always settled his momma's nerves and crankiness. Cecil wanted to get his word in as to how he was able to buy the tea and Joe, not to be out done, proudly told of his role in mixing the tea just right to make it more palatable for Blessing. Pa stood up suddenly, "Hold it! Hold it!" Pa just pointed to the back bedroom, his words muffled, and said, "Go to bed! "Now!"

The boys went. They didn't take time to wonder why Pa was so abrupt but being exhausted they quickly climbed into bed. It had been a great eventful day and their sleep was sure to be sweet knowing that Blessing was still in her pen down the hill. It had been one of them "great" Thanksgivings.

Behind the closed door of Pa and Ma's room, it was quite another story. Pa was doubled over, howling with silent laughter with his head jammed into the pillow. Ma thought he was chilling since he was shaking so hard, but she couldn't persuade him to stay still enough to tell her what was wrong. Getting really concerned she bent down to his ear and asked him loudly if he needed a stanback, or something stronger. He shook harder. She finally realized he was laughing. She begged him to stop, but he could no longer control his hilarity. That triggered her funny bone and she started laughing just as hard as he, with the exception that she didn't know why she was laughing.

It was a while into the night before the bedroom became quiet again as Pa told her the full story of the chamomile tea and the stanbacks. The two were able to fill in most of the rest of the story themselves when they compared notes on the boys' behavior for the last week. Pa loved the boy's ingenuity but knew he had to figure out a teaching lesson for them which could benefit down the road. However, he would worry about that tomorrow. It had been a long day.

That next evening Pa sat with the boys as they played their usual round of dominos. Ma was making a pan of fudge and all were enjoying the pleasantry of the warm friendly kitchen. "Mr. Lantry," Jackson spoke up, "Which do you think is worse, telling an outright lie or not telling all the truth?" Pa looked at the little boy's troubled face and recognized the opportunity to get across the needed lesson that he had been mulling over all day. The other three boys squirmed. Cecil was the only one missing since he had to keep his colicky little brother while his Ma and Pa went to the weekly prayer meeting.

"Now Jackson," Pa spoke as if Jackson was the only little boy that could possibly be guilty of such a quandary, "let's look in the dictionary and see just exactly what a lie is."

Jackson took a moment to find the word and silently moved his lips while screwing up his eyebrows. "Well! Read it out loud," said Pa. Jackson fumbled a bit and then spoke, "lying is to tell something that is not true, in, in…"

"In what?" asked Pa. Jackson continued, "in a conscious effort to deceive somebody." Jackson had provided just the springboard that Pa needed to teach a necessary lesson to the group of youngsters. He spoke of the insincerity of lying outright or telling the truth only if you get caught. He noted the interest in the faces of the other boys who had pretended disinterest only moments before. "Charlie, look up the word, deceit, and tell us what that says." Charlie was in a grade higher than Jackson, so it took him only a moment to find the word and began to read, "To mislead, or deliberately hide the truth from someone."

Ouch! Pa didn't say anything for a few moments. With sudden insight written all over his face, Jackson blurted out, "but that means that we told a lie without telling a lie!'

"Exactly!" grinned Pa. "That sounds a bit complicated, but

Jackson hit up on a great truth. Lying and deceit are basically the very same thing!"

Now having the exclusive attention of every boy in the group Pa went on to illustrate the point that had just been made. "Let me tell you about an experience to demonstrate my point. Tag, do you remember when you were trapping for muskrats last winter and someone took your trap. Do you remember that?" Tag sat up straighter realizing Pa was telling a story about him and, like most kids, loved to hear stories about himself.

"Well," Pa went on, "if you recall as we were asking around about the trap, a certain someone suggested that maybe some other wild animal could have caught itself in it and drug it off to where you couldn't find it." Tag thought back and remembered that that was exactly what had been said and that he had come to believe the trap had been drug off. He hadn't even questioned any other possibility; he just moped around a couple of days over his lost trap.

"I've never told you this, Tag, but I found later that the trap had been taken on purpose by the man. Now, remember that the man had said that "maybe" another animal had taken it. He didn't say he did or did not take it himself. What do you think?"

"He told a lie!" shouted Jackson who was quickly rewarded with a punch to his shoulder by Tag.

Pa went on talking not seeming to notice. "Okay, Tag, was he lying, or not lying, or just down right being deceitful?

Pa watched as the light came on in Tag's expression as he looked over Charlie's shoulder and re-read that deceit was to mislead someone or deliberately hide the truth from them. Pa watched Tag's mind connect to the past few days, the excuses made to the parents to cover up their hush-hush meetings, the secret purchase of the chamomile tea, secretly taking the stanbacks, the whole episode. He had to face the truth. They may not have lied outright, but they sure were guilty of deceiving everyone. Pa further drove the lesson home by reminding them of the Bible passages about the Lord's dislike for lying and deceitfulness.

With a sniffle or two in evidence, each of the four boys, including Tag, asked forgiveness from Pa for "deceiving" him. Tag's friends declared they would confess to their parents, and if they got grounded for the rest of the year, they would try to send word. Pa didn't let on that the parents already knew and had been furnished with several days of delight and laughter.

A Child Named Blue

The arrival of Maggie Snow on Birch Mountain was a puzzle to most people in the community. Children were afraid of her and the adult women couldn't think of a way to get a good look at her. Usually a walk-by would bring some results, but a walk up a mountain path was just not feasible. Soon, however, an even greater mystery came to light concerning the seemingly disappearance of her husband and children. What had happened to them? Where had they all come from? After a few months of speculation as to her entrance into the community, the interest in Maggie waned and if anything, she was completely ignored. At times a rumor would spread that Maggie was on a rampage. At those times people tended to stay clear of the area where she lived.

Maggie carried a gun and did not hesitate to brandish it in case anyone got too near to her, or her property. She had been known to shoot at passers-by that she felt threatened by, although no one had ever reported any bullets coming near them. Still no one wanted to push their luck, so usually a wide path was made around her place. That did not stop, however, the many prayers that were said by some on her behalf.

Her place was simply referred to as the Snow house. She had moved into the vicinity in the early 1940s with a husband and two children and had rented the four-room house about half-way up Birch Mountain. At first, overtures had been made by the local women to get acquainted, but after being told several times that she wanted to be left alone, the attempts became less and less. She and her husband had been spotted a few times, but as time went on there were less and less sightings of the Snow family.

Once, someone reported seeing Maggie sitting on an old car seat underneath an apple tree, alone with her head down. For once, she did not challenge a passerby as to their intent of being near her property. That added more speculations, making her even more of a mystery as time went on. The community continued to be puzzled as to the whereabouts of her children. They seemed to have vanished along with her husband.

There was, however, one person who was persistently interested in Mrs. Maggie Snow and that was a curious little girl named, Blue. One summer day found the determined little five-year-old going down the pathway leading to the Snow house. Maggie tried to shoo her away and began throwing rocks at her, telling her to get back home where she belonged. For whatever the reason the child seemed unafraid of Maggie, and she later told her ma, Nettie, that none of the rocks came near her. Blue had not gone any nearer but did call goodbye to Maggie as she went back up the path.

In the meantime, the folks at Fancy Knoll took a renewed interest in Maggie Snow. Although she had ceased to be a frequent topic of conversation, on hearing Nettie's story about Blue visiting Maggie, curiosity levels were once again elevated. Of course, Blue was admonished sternly to stay clear of the Snow place, but unknown to the community the stage was being set for the redemption of Maggie Snow. God had heard the prayers of the faithful few who had continued praying for her.

Blue had lived all her short life with her ma, Nettie, and her Grandpa Hack Raleigh, about a quarter mile from the Snow place, but a bit farther up on Birch Mountain. Grandpa's wife, Helen, had died in a house fire in late 1920 down on the Knoll and, seeking solitude from his sorrow, Grandpa Hack had bought the old home place of Emeline Fox upon the mountain. Emeline had been a beloved and stalwart member of the Fancy Knoll area for years but had been found dead one day sitting peacefully in her rocker on her front porch.

To further his sorrow, Grandpa Hack's son, Joseph, had also died the next year from a bout of pneumonia. That resulted in Joseph's young wife, Nettie, and her new baby daughter, Blue, being left alone with no place to go. After some thought, Grandpa Hack had invited them to move in with him, and though the house was small, it had worked out well for them all. It was a lonely life, however, with Grandpa Hack still grieving for Helen and Nettie struggling with depression. Consequently, Blue was left to herself much of the time.

It would be hard for some children to be left to entertain themselves, but not Blue. She seemed quite content to roam and explore the area around Birch Mountain. She would spend hours in the woods, especially in the spring where she could make elaborate playhouses out of the dark green moss, which grew in abundance a short distance from her house. The moss provided the floors for her several roomed house and berries and plants were the decorations. Sticks and stones were used both to separate the rooms and to provide material for her furniture, which she loved to change around. Sometimes she would spend hours erecting a new bed from forest sticks and twigs, using stacked leaves or feathers from Ma's hens for mattresses.

Her voice was sweet and melodious and sometimes she could be heard singing much as if she were standing in a church choir. The birds and the wood animals were her audience as well as her dog, Stout, who usually went to sleep during her performances. One day someone caught a glimpse of her with her body twirling in dance underneath a tall pine tree with its soft bed of needles as her dance floor. When seeing she was being observed, she ran like the wind and disappeared into the underbrush.

Not much happened on the mountain, or in the foothills, that Blue didn't know about. She was quick to see strangers and friends alike before anyone else did. Although she never yet attended the church on Fancy Knoll, she was able to watch every baptizing that had taken place on Crane Creek as the creek ran along the foot of the mountain. She always stayed out of sight, but loved to watch the ceremony, which she found fascinating. She also had learned the songs well enough to sing along, although quietly.

Consequently, she had watched the Snow family move into the cabin below her own house and had observed most of the activity around the place. That's how she knew that the speculation of Mrs. Snow possibly harming her children was pure gossip, since Blue had seen the husband leave the area one day with the two children and coming back alone on another day. She faithfully reported all her sightings to her Grandpa Hack who was almost as curious as Blue about the Snow family.

Mr. Snow usually came back carrying several bags. Occasionally Mrs. Snow would leave with him and return late in the day. Eventually Blue's curiosity got the best of her and she knew she would have to find out more of what was going on. She could stand it no longer. The mystery just had to be solved!

One day Blue had finally worked up enough courage to approach Maggie Snow's house. She reasoned that although Maggie threw rocks at her, she had missed her on purpose. That gave Blue enough encouragement to try again.

On the next Tuesday Blue felt it was time to try again to talk to Maggie. She thought for a good long while and finally came up with a plan. This time she called out a good way from the house and was careful to address Maggie as, "Mrs. Snow." Maggie was busy making dinner and on hearing her name, was not at all happy at being interrupted. She came through the screen door, flour and all, and told Blue in no uncertain terms to get back home where she belonged.

"But, Mrs. Snow, I need to ask a favor," Blue called.

"Well, go ask your Ma, for pity's sake," hollowed back Maggie.

"Can't!" replied Blue,

"And why in the world why not?" said Maggie

"Cause she don't know the answer," said Blue.

"What do you think I am--a dictionary?" Blue was silent.

"Well, spit it out", said Maggie, "what's the question?"

"My dog, Stout, has got a tick in his ear. How do I get it out? He's suffering something awful."

"Oh, for crying out loud, tell your Ma to just pull it out slowly as close to its head as possible and don't squish it."

"She won't cause she's afraid it will get on her."

Now Maggie Snow was in a dilemma, and she did not like it one bit. She had created purposely an image of hostility in the area to be left alone and here was this child wanting her help. She had grown accustomed to being thought of as a grouch, and preferred to stay that way, but this child didn't seem to pay any attention to that.

Blue waited quietly with her saddest look possible for Maggie to make up her mind. Finally, Maggie gave in and told the little girl to stop dawdling and bring the hound up on the porch.

Blue was ecstatic. She hurried down the path trying to look as concerned as possible but being the child, she was, she could not totally conceal her joy at being invited up on Maggie Snow's porch.

Maggie looked at her a little suspiciously, but then disappeared in the house and came back a few minutes later with a pair of tweezers. Stout stood very still as she proceeded to grab the tick up close to its head with the tweezers and slowly pulled it out of Stout's ear. Blue sat very close to Maggie with a look of adoration.

"Mrs. Snow, you're one of the smartest women I have ever met. Me and Stout sure thank you." Stout even looked a bit grateful.

"Cat hairs," said Maggie, "Now get along with you before your ma starts thinking I done something to you."

And Blue went. It was years later that she confided in Maggie that she had already gotten many ticks from Stout's ears; she had only used that for an excuse to get to know Maggie. Maggie replied she knew all along that Blue was up to something.

After that day Blue made sure she stopped by Maggie's house about two, or three, times a week, always staying a respectful distance from the porch, calling out pleasantly. Sometimes she told Maggie about finding some mountain tea berries, or a baby rabbit hidden in the leaves. Finally, one day Maggie, with her hands on her hips, made claim that she was tired of seeing Blue hanging around like a leech and told her to come on up on the porch like a decent person ought to.

That was just what Blue had been waiting for and before you could say, Jack Frost, she was seated comfortably on the top step. "Thank you, Mrs. Snow, can Stout come up to--since you saved his life and all?"

"Good lands," said Maggie snappishly, "I hardly saved his life by getting a tick out of his ear," but Stout was already bounding up the steps and plopped down beside Blue.

Blue sat quietly for a few moments and when she could hold it no longer, she said, "Mrs. Snow, we need to talk if you don't mind."

"Well," said Maggie, "and just what if I do mind?" But seeing Blue's hurt look, she snorted, "Oh, go ahead and spit it out!" The following conversation would have been extremely interesting to the population of Fancy Knoll.

"Mrs. Snow I do hate to be the one to carry such bad news to you, but I thought you might want to know. Some people, whom I shall not name, are talking about you behind your back."

"Well, do tell," said Maggie, "and just what might they be saying?"

"Well, I truly don't like to gossip--Grandpa Hack says it's wrong--but....well, I'll just say it. They think you might have killed your husband and done away with your two kids."

Maggie's mouth flew open, almost losing her dentures and sputtered in a loud voice. "They what?" Blue hurried on, "But, don't think that I think that of you Mrs. Snow. If I did, I sure wouldn't be sitting here!"

Maggie was stunned, to say the least. The implication of that kept her speechless for a few minutes. No wonder the people had steered clear of her! "Child," she managed, "that wasn't my husband. My old man has done gone on to his reward, if you must know.

So, you can tell them nosey people in Fancy Knoll that man they have seen around is my brother, Buddy, and not my old man! And Buddy and his two kids are very much alive over in Stewartsville. And besides that, it is none of their business and I should think they would have something better to do than gossip about me!"

On hearing that Blue shot up, "Oh glory, Mrs. Snow, they don't mean no harm, they just don't know what a nice person you are. And I am so happy to hear that you are not a murderer," and Blue proceeded to clap her hands in joy, jumping up and down on the steps, before hugging Maggie tightly.

"Sit down before you fall off the steps and for crying out loud, stop calling me Mrs. Snow."

Blue sat down in a hurry, "Well, what can I call you?"

"Just Maggie!"

"Oh no, that wouldn't be polite. Besides my ma would tan my hide if I called you by your given name."

"Well, I don't care. Call me what you want."

Blue studied it a while and then asked timidly, "Can I call you Aunt Maggie?"

That jolted Maggie a bit. She didn't know if she liked that title, but had a feeling she was going to be called Aunt Maggie, whether she liked it or not. Besides, it sounded kind of nice to her ears.

And, so it was, that the door was opened to a friendship that would last the rest of Maggie's life. Before sprinting back up the path towards home, Blue reassured Aunt Maggie that even if she had shot her old man, Blue knew she must have had a good reason because she was too nice to do it on purpose.

As the reader may have guessed, Maggie became accustomed to the visits from Blue, indeed if Blue did not come for three, or four days Maggie would become anxious and catch herself looking up the mountain path frequently. In the meantime, she learned all about Blue's family and her Ma's depression and her Grandpa's sorrow at losing Grandma Helen. She learned Ma Nettie liked to sew, but not to cook. Neither was Nettie overly fond of animals.

She allowed Stout to sleep on the porch but never to come into the house. Grandpa, of course, didn't do much--him being old, and all, but he liked to reminisce about the old days. Blue didn't mind that, as she loved to hear his stories.

One day while visiting Maggie, Blue announced, "Now, Aunt Maggie you know a lot about me, but I don't know much about you, so go ahead and tell me about yourself. I won't mind." *"My, that child does have a way to get a body talking about herself,"* smiled Maggie to herself. And so, she told Blue about her life before Birch Mountain. Blue hung on every word, sometimes with a tear slipping down her cheek. Maggie related how she had married young and thought she was going to be the happiest woman alive, but it had not worked that way. Her husband or, "old man," as she called him had begun to mistreat her soon after her marriage. Maggie never knew why but he seemed to make her the brunt of his anger and at times became violent in his treatment of her. She had become devastated as he became more aggressive. One day her brother, Buddy, came and told her he was taking her away where she would be safe. And that place would be on Birch Mountain.

Buddy had heard first about Fancy Knoll while at a Charleston hospital where he had met Hezekiah Lantry. Hezekiah had brought his ma in for tests, and Buddy had taken his wife there also, following surgery complications. As the two women were in the same ward, the two men had hit it off well, and began sharing information about themselves, Hezekiah had talked fondly of his home place in a small community called Fancy Knoll. He explained that it sat in the foothills of a beautiful mountain called Birch Mountain. He also talked of their close-knit community where people had great respect for each other and lived peaceful simple lives. Buddy had voiced wistfully that he would sure like to find such a place to live. Hezekiah invited him to come up any time and he would even help him find a place around the area which he could rent reasonably.

And so, it happened that after Maggie's husband once tried to kill her, Buddy immediately thought of Hezekiah's offer, and before her husband could return to the house took Maggie and as much of her belongings as possible and left for Fancy Knoll. He shared her predicament with Hezekiah who immediately saw to the renting of a small house on the mountain and Maggie was installed in it with instructions to stay away from people for a while. Hezekiah assured Buddy that he would keep quiet about Maggie's reason for moving into the area.

Maggie's husband had been furious at her disappearance and sent word to Buddy that he would track her down even if he had to hire a detective. And furthermore, she would be sorry when he did find her.

Maggie had been terrified and decided not to trust anyone for fear her whereabouts would be leaked back to her husband. Consequently, she had led a lonely life. She seldom ventured beyond the mountain, her brother brought her a good amount of groceries once a month, or he came and accompanied her to a nearby town for what she needed. Besides that, she had a flourishing garden, a goat and a cat named Juniper. Gradually Buddy's visits were needed less and less.

One day Buddy had come with the news that Maggie's husband had been killed in a farming accident. She felt relief at the news, but found she had no desire to return to the place that had brought her so much unhappiness. She hesitated to leave the place where she had found such safety. All in all, she was very content with her living arrangement, albeit lonely at times. "And so, here I am!" she said to Blue.

Maggie finished her story and Blue took Maggie's big hand in hers and said, "Aunt Maggie, I'm so glad you're safe. Do you mind if I pray? I just have to thank Jesus because He made you a place here on the mountain to live." And Blue proceeded to do so, then she hugged Aunt Maggie and after asking if Maggie had baked any more fried apple pies, excused herself to go home. She just had to somehow think of a way to get her ma and Aunt Maggie on the same porch.

She began to search her mind for a plan. The next week she

finally got an idea from Aunt Maggie herself. Maggie had confided in Blue as to how much her visits cheered her up--and that included Stout. Maggie was quite fond of the dog and unlike Ma Nettie, he could not only come up on the porch but could also sniff around inside if he so chose.

On this day before Blue left for home Maggie had told her to come back soon or she would be worried about her. *"That's it!"* thought Blue. *"If I don't come down here for a few days, Aunt Maggie will come up there to see about me!"* Blue now knew what she could do to coax Aunt Maggie up to their cabin.

Blue had to devise a plan to stay at home. She played out in the rain all one afternoon hoping she could catch a cold, but with not even a sniffle showing itself, she had to come up with something else. Then she hit on a brilliant plan-or least she thought so.

She never went over three days without visiting Aunt Maggie, so for three days she played in the woods and went roaming on the far side of Aunt Maggie's house. During that time, she began collecting extra food from the table and slipping it into a poke under the table, until Ma commented on how much she was eating. She just replied that she was a "growing girl." Then she snitched several scraps from their pig's supper, apologizing to Lulu for her smaller amount of hog slop and she even shorted Stout on some of his food and squirreled it away. By the fourth day she had quite a cache of food hidden in her secret hiding place in the woods beneath a dead oak tree.

It was her chore, usually, to feed Stout morning and evening, but many times she was off chasing butterflies or what not, and at those times Ma fed him. But early on the fourth morning Blue got up right at the breaking of dawn and took Stout out the trail a distance. There she fed him a large bowl full of the scraps she had been hiding away, then she hurried back home quickly, hopped into bed, and waited for Ma to call her to breakfast. After eating, Ma gave her the usual scraps for Stout. Blue took them obediently outside and offered the food, but old Stout was ready for a long snooze after his earlier breakfast and refused to eat. Blue went straight to her ma and told her that Stout wouldn't eat his breakfast.

"Well that sure is strange," said Ma. He usually gobbles it down before you can get it in his bowl. Do you think he's sick?"

"Let's wait till supper. He'll surely eat by then--but I better stay around the house just in case," said Blue. By evening Aunt Maggie hadn't shown up so Blue took Stout off in the woods and again loaded him up on a bowl full of scraps. In addition to that, he had caught a squirrel earlier, so he was full as a tick.

After supper Ma went out to feed him and he just looked at the food mournfully and lay down again. Being truly worried, she talked with Grandpa about what to do. "Ah, Nettie, quit your fretting. He'll come around!"

On the fifth morning Blue repeated a heavy feeding before the others got up and again Ma tried to get him to eat. Again, he went around back to sleep it off. She told Grandpa that something was going to have to be done. Blue herself was getting a bit worried, but not about Stout. *What if Aunt Maggie didn't care enough to come and see about her?*

The next day she made sure she kept a close eye on the trail below the house and she was greatly relieved when she spotted a bit of blue through the trees and rightly guessed that it was Aunt Maggie. She hurried quickly out back to where Stout was having his third nap of the day. Soon she heard, "Yahoo! Up in the house. Anyone home?"

Nettie peeped out the door, "Mercy, Grandpa, it's that Mrs. Snow, what shall I do?"

"Well, I spect the sensible thing is to go see what she wants!"

Ma anxiously went out on the porch. "Yes, Mrs. Snow. Did you want something?"

"Well yes," said Maggie worriedly, "I haven't seen Blue for a few days and wondered if something was the matter. Is she sick?"

"No, she ain't sick, but something's wrong with Stout and she's been really worried about him."

"You don't say! Well, what kind of symptoms has he got?" asked Maggie.

"Well, he won't eat, and he just acts puny. I'm worried about him too, but don't know what I should do for him."

Maggie hesitated, then finally said, "Well, if you don't mind can I take a look at him?"

"Well, of course, come on up on the porch. I'll have Blue bring him around."

Blue was beside herself with glee, but she really tried to look worried as she led Stout around the house and up on the porch. Of course, Stout was beside himself also, and if Blue hadn't had a tight close reign, he would have jumped all over Aunt Maggie for sure. Blue had to speak harshly to him to get him to lie down so Maggie could have a look.

Ma Nettie wondered if a dose of castor oil might be needed to fix his problem and Blue nearly fainted. She sent up a quick prayer on Stout's behalf. She hadn't counted on that as a possible outcome. Aunt Maggie saved the day, however, by mentioning they should wait at least one more day. Otherwise Stout looked fine to her and maybe he just had an upset stomach from eating something wild out in the woods.

Agreeing to do just that, Blue took him back pulling him all the way. He wanted to stay with her, but she tied him up again and gave him a bit of sausage she had hid in her overalls. Blue stayed out back as long as she thought decent, to give her ma and Aunt Maggie time to start talking, and they did not disappoint her. By the time she got back to the porch. Ma Nettie was showing Aunt Maggie the new quilt she was working on and Grandpa was grinning from ear to ear. He winked at Blue when she came up on the porch and Blue knew her dear Grandpa had figured out her scheme to get the two women together,

After an hour Maggie left, but only after inviting Nettie down to see her morning glories, which were in full bloom, and promising to give Nettie her pickled bean recipe. After she left, Nettie just could not stop talking about how nice Maggie was and "nothing like she had imagined," And to Nettie's surprise Stout ate his whole bowl of scraps for supper and begged for more. She commented, "It's a good thing we didn't give him that castor oil!" *"Ain't that the truth!"* thought Blue.

Predictably, Maggie and Nettie became good friends and it seemed like it was just what Nettie needed to climb out of her depression. She began to take more interest in Blue and her well-being and she and Maggie together had a good time making Blue a new wardrobe from the pretty prints from their combined feed sacks. Blue couldn't have been happier, but decided she needed to talk with Aunt Maggie about a few things more.

The Baptism of Maggie Snow

One day the conversation between Maggie Snow and Blue Raleigh turned to spiritual things. "Aunt Maggie," Blue began, "Where do you think you will go if you die--mind you I hope that won't be for a good long while yet, but I just wanted to know."

Maggie wondered where this was going, "Well, I suppose out here in the backyard--it don't make no difference to me."

"No, Aunt Maggie, where is the real place you are going? Do you think you'll make it to Heaven?"

The question made Maggie uncomfortable and she did not like the feeling. "Well, where do you think you will go, little Miss know it all?"

"That's easy, Aunt Maggie, because I'm going to Heaven!"

"Well, Miss Smarty Pants, how do you know you're going to Heaven?"

"Because I'm a believer!"

"What's a believer?"

That's just the question that Blue wanted to hear, as she settled herself into the old rocking chair. She knew Aunt Maggie wasn't being mean to her so didn't take offense at all to her remarks.

"Well," she began, "This may take a while, but a believer is someone who believes in Jesus--you can't see Him, but He's God's Son, you know--and He was so good that He never did anything wrong. But everybody else does do wrong things--even me--and God can't look at me when I do wrong. Sooooooo," said Blue as she strung out the so for emphasis, "God made Jesus into a little baby--you do know what Christmas is all about don't you--and then when Jesus grew up He did all kinds of good things and then some mean men killed Him and they hung Him on a cross and He died and all His blood ran out--and that was because everybody's sins was put on Him and when His blood was all gone, all our sins were gone too."

Blue leaned in closer as if she needed to speak quietly, and said, "And Aunt Maggie, Jesus is coming back again. Ain't that great! Some people don't believe that, but one day they will and let's pray for them that they will have another chance to believe like me, cause now I get to go to Heaven. I'm a believer and that's all there is to it!"

Blue never realized what an impact her words made, but Maggie being Maggie, tried to make light of it by saying, "Well, it sure took you long enough to spit all that out. Who told you all that stuff?"

"Grandpa Hack. He heard it from Miss Emeline--she used to live in our house before she died. She wanted Grandpa to become a believer and he did. And after that he got my ma to be a believer and now, I'm a believer." Blue looked earnestly in Aunt Maggie's face and said soft like, "Aunt Maggie I want more than anything for you to become a believer too."

Maggie choked back her tears, and said testily, "Well, Miss Believer, I expect you better run home before your ma comes looking for you, so git!"

Maggie sat thinking a long time after Blue had disappeared up the trail. What she hadn't told Blue was that she had heard of the Way a long time before, although never quite like Blue had explained it. Her dear mother had talked to her in much the same way in earlier years, but she had never made the decision to become a believer herself. Her miserable marriage had taken much of her energy and time. If truth be known the bitterness left over from the marriage had stolen away any thoughts that had been put into her heart in prior years. Blue's words had brought it all back.

Consequently, because of Blue's words, Maggie was once again faced with the truth of the Gospel. She had turned away once but felt in her heart that she must now decide once for all. So, with tears falling freely she went into her bedroom, knelt by her bed and asked God's forgiveness. She poured out her soul to Him in repentance and soon arose from her knees with a great settled peace within her, as God's indwelling presence filled her heart. Maggie truly became a believer that night and fell into a deep restful sleep. Her last thought had been on Blue's delight at hearing what had happened.

As Maggie predicted, Blue was ecstatic and could not stop dancing while chattering like a magpie. "Let's sing," said Blue, and without waiting for Maggie, began singing as loud as possible the hymn she had heard from the Fancy Knoll folks, "When the Roll is Called Up Yonder, I'll be There!" Maggie just couldn't help but join in and sang every bit as loud as Blue. Further up, Grandpa Hack and Nettie were so happy, they began singing to. Hack said later that even the birds were quiet that day, so as not to miss the joy being felt on Birch Mountain.

On Blue's next visit she announced to Maggie that the next step, now that she was a believer, was to be baptized. Maggie turned pale and told Blue that she couldn't possibly do that. "I'm not gonna let that preacher take me down in the water. I can't stand the thoughts of it."

"But why, Aunt Maggie, don't you want everybody to know that your sins are washed away"? Blue thought for a moment, "Aunt Maggie, are you afraid of the water?"

Blue had hit the nail on the head. Maggie was afraid of water. She started to deny it, but remembered she was a different person now, and just told Blue the truth. She explained how she had come near drowning as a child and had never got over her fear of water.

"It's okay, Aunt Maggie," comforted blue, "I have an idea that might help you. Me and Stout will show you just how it's done so there won't be any surprises."

A while later, Maggie, Blue and Stout made their way down to the creek and to a pond where the water was deepest. Blue instructed Maggie to set on a nice smooth rock and watch the ceremony. She assured Maggie that there was absolutely nothing to be afraid of and she and Stout would show her, step by step, how the baptism would proceed.

First Blue stood on the bank and solemnly sang a few lines of "On Jordan's Stormy Banks I stand," just like she had heard the folks of Fancy Knoll sing at their baptisms. She then proceeded to put a white dish towel around Stout's neck using a safety pin to fasten it with. She explained to Maggie that some of the folks wore a long white robe to be baptized in, which she herself preferred. The large handmade dish towel almost covered Stout and would work as a robe. Stout was excited about the affair and gave Blue some problems holding him still, but he did allow her to lead him out into the water. To be safe she held him tightly by his makeshift collar. He had been used to playing along the edge of the creek with Blue, so went happily, although rather hesitantly.

Blue talked soothingly to him about what she was going to do and assured him she would not let him drown. She had him stand up with his front paws on her chest, just like he always did. She had to dodge his wet kisses, so knew she had better hurry and dunk him. Since she had never been able to hear the few words the preacher man spoke just before taking the person under, she just laid her hand on Stout's head and began to lower him backwards--and that was her undoing. Stout went wild! He must have realized what was about to happen because he lunged sideways taking Blue with him dunking her under instead. He then heaved himself out of the water, stopping only long enough to shake the water out of his heavy fur right beside Maggie, who was crawling backwards trying to get herself out of range. He shot past her and was out of sight before Blue could upright herself out of the water.

An angler further down the creek related the story later that he had heard a loud howling laughter and had hurried to see where it was coming from. There was Maggie Snow sitting on a rock, wet from head to foot laughing uncontrollably. She was trying to get to her feet but looking at Blue so increased her laughter that she just gave up and sat. Blue was sitting high on the bank looking like a drowned rat just watching her with eyes as big as saucers. Blue herself had never heard Maggie laugh before and if the truth be known Maggie Snow had not laughed that hard in years. She didn't know when she had felt so good!

Finally, Blue returned home to find Stout lying far back against the wall behind the rocking chair. Nothing could coax him out. She apologized profusely, but Stout wasn't budging from his spot. Finally, to show her remorse she gave him a biscuit covered with gravy and a big piece of fat back bacon on top and left it by the chair. The house fell quiet before Stout hesitantly crawled from under the rocker and gobbled down his peace offering. His baptismal gown got in his way a bit, but he managed, before he snuggled back beneath the chair.

Poor Blue was convinced that her bungled baptism attempt would really discourage Aunt Maggie from considering her own baptism, but Aunt Maggie assured her the next day that she would indeed like to be baptized and asked Blue to ask the preacher if he would come to visit her.

Two days later Maggie heard a dog barking and looked out her cabin to see Pastor Buchanan coming up the path from the Fancy Knoll direction. This woman, who previously would have shot at this intruder approaching her cottage, now met him with a glass of lemonade, made from the cold spring water from above her cabin. Preacher Amos later declared that was the best lemonade he had ever tasted.

Their talk lasted about an hour and no one ever knew the content, but no one could doubt that Maggie's heart had indeed been changed and she was ready for baptism. The day was set for the following Sunday and she felt a great feeling of satisfaction settle into her heart.

The news spread like wildfire that Maggie Snow was going to be baptized in Crane's Creek on Sunday next. The day turned out to be beautiful and warm and the biggest crowd that had ever been known to attend a baptism began to arrive an hour before the set time. All eyes were on the wooded area where the pathway ended for the mountain folks coming down to Fancy Knoll. Many were there because they had prayed for a long time for Maggie. Others came more out of curiosity and just wanted to see what Maggie looked like.

They were not disappointed. Maggie exited the woods barefoot, dressed in a long white robe with a rope belt tied around her waist. It had been Blue who had suggested the robe, so Maggie and her ma had made one from some bleached feed sacks. Blue also had entwined some clematis vines around the rope belt. Aunt Maggie looked beautiful! She walked tall and dignified to the water edge as she greeted Pastor Buchanan.

Most significant, however, was the expression on her face--it had nothing of the anger or fear that people had seen before. She kept her eyes down, for the most part, as she waited for Pastor Buchanan to lead her out into the water. Blue had stayed right at her heels not wanting to miss a thing. She especially wanted to hear the words the preacher said right before he baptized her. She had waited a long time to hear them. Stout had followed Blue but stayed well up the path away from the water.

The people began to sing the words of the old hymn, "Yes, we'll gather at the river, the beautiful, the beautiful river, gather with the saints at the river that flows from the throne of God." Oh, such singing! It brought tears to many eyes. The preacher prayed a prayer of praise for Maggie's decision as the congregation became so quiet you could hear the ripple of the water flowing over the rocks near the creek bank. Blue stood rapt as Preacher Buchanan intoned the words, "I now baptize you in the name of the Father, the Son, and the Holy Spirit." And then he lay Maggie down in the water as gentle as a lamb and swiftly up again. Maggie's face shone as she raised her face and hands in thanksgiving. The crowd broke out in singing "Amazing Grace" so loud that the words drifted all the way up the mountain to Grandpa Hack's rocking chair. The tears rolled down his face as he joined in the song with his own thanksgiving.

From that day forward, Maggie was friends with the community and even hosted the Ladies' Bible study on occasion. Because of the walking distance, Maggie did not attend Church regularly, but was faithful to pray for the folks of Fancy Knoll. Blue, Nettie and Grandpa Hack remained her closest friends and that closeness continued for the rest of their lives.

One morning in late summer, Blue came down the path looking like she had lost her best friend. Maggie questioned her as to what was bothering her. Blue sighed as she settled herself on the lower step and told Maggie she had been thinking about her future. Maggie waited as Blue put her elbows on her knees and held her chin in her hands and seemed to be deep in thought.

"Well," said Maggie, "Spit it out. What's on your mind?"

Another big sigh from Blue, and then, "Aunt Maggie, I've been thinking about my future. I thought I might want to get married someday--after I learn to read and write- but I've been having second thoughts."

"Well, child, that's a long way off--a marriage I mean--and you just told me the other day you were looking forward to having a family. What in the world has changed your mind?" By now Maggie was surprised at nothing that Blue came up with, so she just waited patiently for Blue to reveal the reason for her gloominess.

"The truth is, Aunt Maggie, you changed my mind. I've heard your stories about your old man, and I don't want to marry an old man. I think you could have been so much happier if you had married someone young."

Oh dear, thought Maggie, I better set the record straight, so she patiently explained that "old man" was just a figure of speech and that her husband had been young when they married.

Blue thought for a minute, "But, if he was young like you, why did you let him treat you that way!"

"Well, Blue, sometimes there are mean people in this world

that become mean often because of things that have happened in their life. Maybe they were treated mean by another person, I don't know. And sometimes when they are mean they will hurt others. My husband became mean soon after we married and though I tried to do everything nice, so he wouldn't get angry, there was just something about him that made him want to hurt me. Maybe I was his scapegoat. Do you understand..."

"What's a scapegoat?" interrupted Blue before Maggie could finish.

"Well, it's like when someone else takes the blame, or punishment, in place of another person's wrongdoing."

A light came on in Blue's heart as it dawned on her that it was just like Jesus being punished because of the things we do wrong, when it is really us who should be punished.

"Oh, Aunt Maggie!" she cried, "it's just like Jesus, He was our scapegoat. Don't you see? He died for our wrongs and we don't have to be punished. That's what I've been trying to explain to you! Don't you see it?"

And indeed, Maggie did see it. She had heard about a scapegoat all her life but had never thought about it in that light. "Yes, yes, child I do see." They both got very still as each realized what an awesome thing redemption was, and it was all because of Jesus taking the blame instead of them. There were tears in each of their eyes as they thought about just what that meant.

After a time, Blue spoke, "Aunt Maggie. I've decided I will marry, but you know what? I'm going to make sure he knows who the real Scapegoat is before I ever promise to love and obey him. Don't you think that would be a good idea?"

Maggie held the precious little girl close and assured Blue that she had found out a great truth and that she believed that God would send her a good man to share her life with--and that he would be a young one, of course.

Blue and Maggie had many such talks with Maggie being the learner as often as the teacher. She never ceased to be amazed at Blue's insight into the spiritual side of things. Years later, Blue would indeed have a wonderful husband and four inquisitive, well brought-up children and she would be known by many as the "Believer." Many women on Fancy Knoll would talk of a visit from Blue and how much better they felt after her visit.

Moonshiners in Swamp Hollow

School started in Fancy Knoll the first week of September and ended in the middle of May. For most, school opening was an exciting time. Who would be the schoolteacher, and with whom would she or he board? Were there any new pupils? These questions would start in August as parents scrambled to get new bib overalls for the boys and new dresses-mostly homemade--for the girls. Usually a new pair of sturdy shoes and winter underwear would also be required for the new school year. Although Tag, his cousins, and their friends were reluctant to give up their fishing days, they too were curious about the new teacher.

There had been three different teachers the previous year due to various circumstances--their location being one of the main reasons. Either the teacher had to travel a long distance, by whatever means of transportation she or he could find, or they would need to board with someone. In addition, being in an outlying area, Fancy Knoll School usually got a young inexperienced teacher just fresh out of the teaching college in Athens, or it could be an older weathered one who sometimes could be tough on kids. The children usually hoped for the younger teachers.

On opening day in 1940, all eight grades arrived at the one room school, excited to see what Miss Sally Lester looked like and they were not disappointed. She was young and pretty, and most of the younger pupils fell in love with her from the first day. The older students took a wait-and-see attitude. Tag, Joe and Charlie were in the fourth grade and would reserve their estimation of Miss Sallie after a week or two. Jackson and Cecil liked her right off.

Almost every student knew each other, but this year there were a few new additions, and among them a first grader, five-year-old Blue Raleigh, from far up on Birch Mountain. Her Uncle Willard, who lived near the school, had offered to go to the foot of the mountain and meet Blue. It would be easy for her to walk down to the foot of the mountain, hop on the horse behind Uncle Willard and ride the mile and half to the Fancy Knoll School. On bad weather days, she would remain overnight with her Uncle Willard's family.

It had earlier been thought by Blue's Ma, Nettie, that Blue would be unable to go for another year, but being five- and one-half years old, and with Uncle Willard's offer, she could begin in September. She had been wild with excitement almost the entire month of August. She was by nature a very inquisitive child and one that loved learning new things. Her favorite thing to wish for was to be able to read and write. Her Grandpa Hack had taught her as much as he could, but there were few books, or other helps, around that he could use. What he could do was to help Nettie purchase the few needed supplies to start her first year, which he did. The State Board furnished the books, her Ma or Aunt Maggie furnished a good lunch every day, and so she was all set.

The first day did not go too well for Blue and she was disappointed. For one thing, she felt different from the other girls. They all wore hair ribbons, with most matching their dresses. Some of the girls had store bought dresses, or at least store-bought material made into dresses, however, Blue's were made from cow feed sacks. They had seemed pretty on the mountain, but on Fancy Knoll they looked like just what they were--feed sacks. Then too, Blue's hair was not tied back in a pretty ribbon, hers was short like a boy and straight as a stick. For the first time in her young life, she wished for curls.

They did not even talk the same, Blue thought. She chatted like a magpie, while most of the girls seemed to draw out their words, and besides, as she later told her ma that, "they kept looking at me like I was a mountain goat!" She decided she was not going to like school very much.

Of course, as it always happens, Blue and the Fancy Knoll kids would learn to like each other and soon forgot all about their differences. Tag Lantry decided the first day that he liked Blue and since she was so little that he was going to watch out for her. Neither would have dreamed that his notion to watch after Blue would last all their lives, through their children and grandchildren.

Blue, in the meantime, decided she was not going to like Miss Sally, either. From the first, the new teacher let her know that she must not bring Stout to school with her after that day. Since he had always gone with Blue before, that was going to be easier said than done. Therefore, the next day Stout came along again, but Blue tied him a short way from school telling him she would be back at lunchtime to check on him. Things went well for a while since Stout was about as curious as Blue and he had a lot of sniffing around to do. However, after a time he began looking towards the direction Blue had gone. Soon he set up a howl heard clearly in the classroom and continued to howl until the teacher asked about the owner of the dog. Again, Blue was told that she absolutely must leave him at home. The third day Blue tied him farther back in a little cove where he could not be heard. She stayed with him a while explaining to him the situation. He seemed to understand--at least to her--and Blue went on to school. At about 10 am Stout came bounding through the open door to the schoolhouse with the rope dragging along behind him. That prompted a visit from Miss Sally to the home of Nettie and Grandpa Hack.

Aunt Maggie, seeing them go by her house, became worried and wondered why a visit was necessary already. Knowing Blue, she could not help but feel anxious. Maggie had already spent time worrying if Blue could adapt to being closed in a one room for an entire six hours.

However, it turned out to be a nice visit, with Miss Sally realizing the attachment that Blue and Stout had for each other. She then suggested that if Blue would tie Stout close by the schoolhouse--and if he didn't howl--she could bring him with her. But if he caused any distraction at all, Blue would have to make sure he was left tied at home. That overjoyed Blue and she decided she rather liked Miss Sally after all. The next day Blue took him with her and tied him to the oak tree near the school where he could see her from the window. He was content, and all the kids had a great time with him at recess.

In the meantime, Blue took to her lessons quickly. She was a very intelligent little girl and soaked up learning like a sponge. She found pleasure in learning big words like "unfortunate" and "continental." Miss Sally was astounded at a first grader's thirst for learning and knew she would have to keep on her toes with Blue. She realized Blue was not only taking in her first-grade lessons but also the lessons of the higher grades.

Blue found a new joy in the bright colored crayons, which she had never had before. In fact, she won a box of them by being the first one to learn her alphabet. She was delighted and drew constantly. She drew pumpkins and black cats for Halloween, although she declared she did not like that holiday. She said some ornery boys once had tried to turn over their outhouse and Grandpa had to shoot buckshot over their heads. She thought that was so "uncouth" of them--one of her newly learned words.

She did enjoy learning about the pilgrims and the first Thanksgiving, though. Her family had never done much to celebrate that holiday, except for maybe a pumpkin or a mincemeat pie for supper. Blue immensely enjoyed the stories that Tag told about the hog-killing episode at his house. In fact, his Pa had sent some shoulder meat and ground sausage, up to Blue's family as a neighborly gift.

What Blue looked forward to most of all, however, were the activities associated with Christmas. By the end of October, Miss Lester had announced a campaign for raising money for a Christmas party. They were encouraged to work as a group to find any possible means to contribute to the fund. While teaching the children to be resourceful, Miss Sally hoped it would also teach them about the advantages of teamwork. The kids on the north end of Fancy Knoll included Blue, Tag and friends, and Clara Blandly. What fun they would have!

By the end of October, Grandpa and Nettie were worried. There were rumors circulating that there was a moonshine still being operated in Swamp Hollow. Ordinarily this would not have caused concern but in this case, to reach that vicinity, one would need to go straight up and over from their place, which happened to be one of Blue's favorite hiking trails. Swamp Hollow was a private area and in earlier days had been a favorite place to picnic, or a good place to go hiking for school children and adults alike. After a while, though, the moonshiners had taken over the vicinity as it had provided a hidden haven for men to make their illegal liquor.

Grandpa and Nettie's concern was that Blue might wander too close to the still and be put into danger. They knew very well that her travels sometimes took her a good distance from the house. They never feared her getting lost, however, because of the tall pine tree that stood directly above them on the mountaintop. When in doubt about her location she only needed to look up at the pine and immediately, she would know where she was.

The older folks were especially concerned when Blue and her friends from Fancy Knoll were together on the mountain. The kids' natural curiosity seemed to get them into all kind of situations and they never failed to come home with different adventures. Grandpa, of course, delighted in listening to their tales of the day's doings.

One day, Blue's friends, Clara, Tag, and Charlie came to visit. They informed Ma Nettie that they were just going up the mountain and assured her they would not go any distance down the other side. They took along Stout and Tag's dog, Bandit, and were ready for some serious ginseng hunting. They had decided on that for their money-raising project for their Christmas party. If they could find some of the elusive ginseng roots, they could be sold for a good amount of money at the pharmacy in Tazewell.

Near noon they had almost reached the top of the mountain when they still had not found any ginseng plants, so Tag called for Bandit and Stout as they prepared to go back down to Blue's house. When the dogs didn't come immediately, they looked around for them and spotted Stout a bit farther up standing near a pot like container. Thinking it was probably water, and since the dogs had been running quite a bit, they thought nothing of it and called them to go home.

The kids began singing their favorite song "She'll be Coming Round the Mountain" as they began skipping down the path. Charlie was the first one to notice the dog's strange behavior. Bandit was trailing behind Stout who seemed to be wobbling. Becoming alarmed, Tag ran back up to see what was going on and then noticed Bandit also was weaving from side to side with a rather glazed look on his face. He couldn't seem to focus on the pathway and kept going off on the side. The kids became truly frightened as they began to check the dogs over--for what they did not know. It was then that they noticed a strange smell. "Phew! These dogs have got into something awful. What if it is poison!" wailed Blue. At that possibility, all began to run, half dragging the two dogs down to the house.

Nettie was greatly alarmed at seeing the kids fright and told Blue to run and get Aunt Maggie to come quickly. In the meantime, Stout and Bandit lay down, and as Blue related later that they became "unconscious." Tag was frantically begging Grandpa to do something. "Do you think we should take them to the hospital?" Grandpa, on hearing the dog's soft snores, and recognizing the smell of alcohol, became suspicious but held his tongue. Maggie and Blue then came running in the door.

Aunt Maggie immediately knelt close to the animals, and never one to mince words snapped, "These dogs are drunk as a skunk!"

"What!" sputtered Blue? "How do you know?" Maggie spat out,

"Can't you smell them, child?" Of course, she then realized that none of the children had probably ever smelled alcohol.

Between Blue and Clara's sniffling and Grandpa's snickers, the story finally was told of seeing the dogs drink from some type of a container. Then the truth dawned on the three adults as they realized where it probably came from. They didn't know how the container got there but they felt it was somehow connected to the moonshiners. Something had to be done to make sure the kids were kept safe!

After Blue was tucked in bed and Stout was back on his feet, the three adults sat at Grandpa's kitchen table to plan what they could do to keep Blue and her friends from the top of the mountain. They surmised that the still wasn't there, but for some reason a sample of its output had been left by the wayside on this side of the mountain.

They knew it would be almost impossible to keep the kids from the woods, so the problem was how to keep them from going up to the top. They felt the kids were safe if they kept on the family's side, as far away from Swamp Hollow as possible.

Aunt Maggie had an idea that she shared with the others, "I bet if we could give those kids a good scare, without hurting them of course, we wouldn't have to remind them to stay away from the other side of the mountain."

"How are we going to do that," said Nettie. "I don't want them having nightmares, or anything!" "Let me think on it," said Maggie, "and I'll come up with something."

And something she did! She shared her plan with Nettie and Grandpa the very next day while Blue was away at school. Maggie would be on the lookout the next time the kids came up to visit Blue and be ready to put her plan into action. Nettie's part was to stall the kids while Maggie would go out her back way and circle around, to keep out of sight. She then would go up as high as she could get, without going all the way to the top, and find a hiding place. When the kids got close, she would moan out something scary and hopefully the kids would think it might be a ghost. Nettie brought up the fact that they would recognize Maggie's voice; however, Maggie explained that she was going to put a few marbles in her cheeks so that her voice would be unrecognizable. She was sure her knack for sounding like a wandering spirit should easily scare them, although she admitted she wasn't convinced it would actually work. However, anything was worth a try!

Nettie and Grandpa agreed that if it didn't work, they would have to seek outside help, although they did not want to do that. They knew the moonshiners were probably local people and would not hurt the children, but they could not be sure. It would be best for everyone if the kids would just avoid the top of the mountain, and beyond.

Maggie's chance came sooner than expected. Blue announced on Friday that her friends were coming up to visit on Saturday and they were planning to go looking for ginseng again. Maggie prepared during the day while school was in session. She had a long white apron she could use to help cover herself, in case she couldn't hide herself well enough. She washed the marbles and practiced her "whoooooos," until she was hoarse. All that was needed now was for the kids to climb up the mountain, instead of out to the sides.

A little before 9 o'clock on Saturday morning, the kids' noisy banter could be heard from a quarter mile down. That gave Maggie time to scoot out the back way and climb up to find her a good spot to observe the kids' movements. If they didn't climb up the mountain, she would need to try it again on another day.

She needn't have worried. The curious kids headed straight up since they were anxious to see exactly what kind of container the dogs had drank from. Their curiosity now was stirred up concerning the bootleggers and they hoped they might find more evidence to share with Grandpa.

Maggie was ready for them. She placed the marbles in her cheeks and waited until the kids got about 500 yards below her and she began her moaning sounds. She started with a long sigh. The kids listened. Was it the wind? They looked at each other. Soon there came a moan, then a whispery voice, *"whoooooooooo! whoooooooooo!"*

What Maggie didn't know was that there were two men stationed a little above her who were returning for the container that one of them had dropped the day before when a swarm of bees had threatened him. Now the two men watched Maggie's antics with great curiosity. Once they saw her wrap her apron around herself, nothing could have got them away from their hiding place. What was she up too? They then saw the kids climbing up and realized something was up. Once the sighing and moaning began, they realized what was probably going on. That woman was trying to scare those kids!

A great idea came into one of the men's minds. In his pocket was a whistle that sounded exactly like the screaming of a mountain lion. The moonshiners had used it on occasion when outsiders got too close to their still. When Maggie's wailing words were being spoken, the man blew his whistle as loudly as possible. Being only about 300 yards behind Maggie, it immobilized her a few seconds, but then her feet took wings and she was gone! She screeched, Blue screamed, and the boys slammed into each other, in an effort to find the path. Ultimately, the entire group, including the dogs, began running down the mountain as fast as they could possibly go.

Being en masse, as they were, they wondered later how they managed to get down the narrow path so quickly. Even more puzzling was how Aunt Maggie managed to pass them up to get in front of them. Maggie herself could not imagine how she could have passed and left those kids behind. The evidence of her reaching the porch before them said otherwise, a fact that Grandpa would tease her about for a long time to come.

Tag declared that just before Aunt Maggie passed them that a bullet zoomed by his head and he swore it was as big as a marble. Nettie started to remind him not to swear but figured that this time it might be okay, him being terrorized and all.

Grandpa knew he had better not laugh openly, or it would undo all of Maggie's work, but he knew he had to get out to the outhouse fast. He made it to the outside before he collapsed on the ground laughing so hard the tears were streaming down his face. With all the commotion going on inside the house, only Stout and Bandit were left to wonder at his strange behavior.

The two moonshiners on the mountain had well split their sides laughing as they made their way down the other side towards Swamp Hollow. In the meantime, neither the kids nor Aunt Maggie ever wandered up the mountain again unless well chaperoned.

Christmas on Birch Mountain

The month of December was a flurry of activity for the community. It was Blue's first Christmas as a school pupil, and she was wild with excitement. The school play practice was in full swing and she was busy memorizing all the necessary songs. The words of "Oh Little Town of Bethlehem" sounded throughout the Raleigh house from morning to night. Grandpa declared that he could sing it as well as the school kids--without ever looking at a songbook. Homemade Christmas cards were agonized over as Blue kept changing the words on the cards. She and her friends were busy gathering pinecones and cedar branches to decorate the school. Blue learned all kinds of new things about Christmas. Since Grandpa Hack and Ma Nettie lived rather isolated lives, they were truly enjoying Blue's stories and new ideas for celebrating Christmas.

One day Blue came bursting through the door with a page from a Sears catalogue that one of the girls had brought to school. On it was a picture of a doll in a pink dress and bonnet. Blue had never owned a store-bought doll and she was ecstatic. Her brown eyes pleaded with Grandpa to get her that doll. It was priced at $2 dollars but had been reduced to $1.89 cents. "Please, oh please she begged. I will do all the house-work every day and wash all the clothes, and slop the pigs--and feed Stout every day..."

Nettie stopped her and explained for the umpteenth time that money was scarce, and they would have to wait and see, but Blue must absolutely stop talking about the doll before they all went crazy.

One evening at supper, Blue voiced her regret that Grandpa and her ma were not able to join into any of the Christmas activities at Fancy Knoll. They didn't own a horse and so had to have someone bring their food staples, usually Uncle Willard. However, that did not happen often since their store-bought goods were at a minimum, due to all the canning and drying of foods.

Grandpa sounded rather wistful when Blue explained about the special church services and school play, as well as the community get-together at the St. Clair place. "Oh, I wish you could go to something," said Blue, "Christmas is so wonderful! Isn't there some way you could go down to the church?" Grandpa Hack replied that he hadn't been off the mountain for years and now he was just too old to make the trip.

The next day a sad-faced Blue visited Aunt Maggie and told her about her concern. She knew Aunt Maggie could always think of something. Maggie chewed on it a while and Blue knew exactly when the idea hit her, "Well, why don't we bring Christmas to the mountain!"

"What a glorious amazing idea!" squealed Blue, "would that be possible?"

"Well, why not, we could invite several of our friends to come up here and we could have a Christmas party."

"A real live party," said Blue, "but where?"

"Well, what about your Grandpa's barn? It's big enough, it's dry, and it could be cleaned up--and there's that old wood stove of Emeline's still out there. We could get some of the men to get it set up and we could have a nice warm fire."

"Oh mercy!" Blue ran home as fast as she could and with her eyes shining like the moonlight on Cranes Creek she burst in the door.

"Aunt Maggie says we can have a Christmas party right here on the mountain in our barn and invite all our friends. Won't that be stupendous? Can we Grandpa, can we?"

It took a few minutes for the idea to soak in. In the meantime,

Nettie said, "Go get your Aunt Maggie. Let's talk this over before you split your mouth from grinning."

Grandpa did love to have people around and He wondered, *"well, why not?"* Ma was more cautious and not sure at all that it would work. *"What would we feed them? What should be done at a party?"* she fussed to herself.

Blue went bounding back to Aunt Maggie's and practically pulled her back up to the house. "Ma's scared, Aunt Maggie, about having a party. You've just got to talk her into it."

After Ma had poured Maggie a cup of coffee, they all sat around the table and talked about the party. Aunt Maggie, never one to dawdle, wanted to know right off just why they couldn't have a party. In the short time it had taken Blue to run back to her house she had decided she could send word to her brother, Buddy, to bring his wife, Jolene, and their two kids, Rink and Jenny, to spend Christmas with her on the mountain. Of course, she would subtly mention that their help would be greatly appreciated in preparing for the party. "Nettie, it would be a wonderful time for you and Grandpa Hack to see old friends and for me to visit with my family," said Maggie.

Of course, Blue couldn't stop dancing as she realized how much fun a party would be. "But what can we do to entertain so many people, and what about refreshments or where can we probably seat that many people?" Nettie was worried, but Maggie could tell she was warming to the idea from her tone of voice. "We'll just plan." said Aunt Maggie, "where there's a will, there's a way!" And so, plans for a Christmas party on Birch Mountain were put into motion with ideas coming from all directions.

As to food, Maggie loved to cook so she would be responsible to fry a couple of chickens and announced that Nettie could make the potato salad but seeing Nettie's frown Maggie changed it to pie making--baking being the one part of cooking that Ma did enjoy doing. Later, when she got into it, Ma discovered she was enjoying making the pies so much that she also made a large batch of walnut fudge. The ideas began to flow! Grandpa wanted to get involved also, so he declared that if one of the men would bring a couple of squirrels, he would clean them and cut them up. Aunt Maggie would just need to pop them in a frying pan. That prompted Nettie to offer to make a big pan of biscuits that would "melt in your mouth." Maggie would have to see to the rest, they declared. By this time, the entire family was hungry, and they stopped planning until after supper.

Later they discussed other aspects of a party. There would be music, of course. Mr. Cantrell would bring his fiddle and Preacher Buchanan would be glad to play his French harp for a sing along. Joe Thompson's wife, Mandy, could sing like an angel so they would invite her to sing. Grandpa mentioned that several of them liked doing the "flat foot," and they were sure Mr. Cantrell could come up with a few dance tunes.

"And, Ma" broke in Blue, "us kids can put on a play for you all. Can we please?" Before Nettie could answer Grandpa chimed in, "Well, of course you can!" He knew that if the kids got involved there was certain to be plenty of entertainment.

So, the plans were put into action. A letter was written to Buddy, and family, inviting them to Birch Mountain for Christmas, along with a plea for help with the preparations. It would be a wonderful thing for Aunt Maggie to have a family member present for Christmas. It had never happened since she moved to the mountain. Besides Buddy was right handy with a rifle so he might be able to bag some extra meat for the party.

Invitations were written out by Nettie and Blue, and Blue was responsible for handing them out at school the next day. Grandpa had to be content to wait for Buddy and then he could at least have a hand in getting the barn in order. He could oversee the cleaning and the stove preparation.

Nettie and Maggie started planning the food and a grocery list was made out for such things as sugar and flour to be given to Uncle Willard. Walnuts, dried apples, canned peaches and cherries were gathered to be made into cobblers and pies. A plentiful supply of potatoes would be brought in from the cellar for a big pot of stew. Maggie had talked Grandpa into a squirrel stew instead of fried, since there would already be fried chicken. Canned green beans, sauerkraut, pickled eggs, homemade cottage cheese and canned pickles of several varieties were put on the menu. And so, it was that a full dinner was planned instead of just the normal refreshments. "Well," commented Grandpa, "we may as well go whole hog!"

Blue became a very busy little girl. In addition to all the Fancy Knoll activities, she now had to plan a Christmas play for her and her group of friends. She already knew that she would play the part of Mary. Tag would be Joseph, Charlie and Cecil were the two shepherds, and Rink, Joe and Jackson would be the wise men. Clara and Jenny would be the angels. As to their costumes, some nice blue feed sacks would do for the wise men and head scarves borrowed from the women folk would work for head coverings. The rough brown feed sacks would do for the shepherds and Joseph, and Aunt Maggie's baptismal gown would work well for Mary's costume--if Aunt Maggie was agreeable. Other white feed sacks would work for the angels.

Baby Jesus might present a problem, since there was no doll around to play the part, that is until she got hers. Blue was so sure that she was going to get a doll for Christmas that she timidly asked her ma if she might could possibly get her Christmas presents early--with the excuse that they would be so busy with the party and all, that they might be too tired to get up early on Christmas morning to open them. Ma said that was out of the question, in fact, that was the flimsiest reason she had ever heard used to get presents early. Blue gave up then and looked for an alternative.

Come Sunday Blue scooted along the church pew near Pearlie, Mrs. Hackett's daughter-in-law, and whispered that she needed to talk with her. When alone Blue asked her if she thought her nine-month-old baby, Beau, could be quiet enough to play the part of the baby Jesus in their play. Pearlie was delighted at the thought and told Blue she was almost positive the baby would be perfect, since he usually went to sleep around six thirty and noise didn't bother him one bit. *"Great,"* thought Blue, *"Now we only need an innkeeper."* She would have to get an adult for that role, since there were no more kids to play parts.

She later mentioned it to Grandpa Hack, who replied, "Well, what's wrong with me? Do you think your old Grandpa is too simple minded to be in a Christmas play?"

"Oh, that's perfect Grandpa, you'd make the best innkeeper in the world!" and she gave him a big hug. Grandpa Hack couldn't keep the grin off his face. So, Blue's Christmas production was in place. Now to the particulars!

There were two stalls in the barn. The cow could be fastened in one and the other could be used for the inn for Grandpa to stand in. The manger could be placed over to the right in the corner. Blue knew Aunt Maggie would let them borrow her goat, Rosebud, and her cat could be included, which altogether would give an authentic feel to the play. She had a special role for Stout and Bandit. They would act as camels, complete with humps, by tying a pillow on their backs and covering them with tow sacks. A trough that had long ago been used for the goats would be just right for the manger. The short stout legs would mean that Beau would be close to the floor in case of a mishap.

A letter came the next week that Buddy and family greatly appreciated the invitation, and Lord's willing, would arrive on Wednesday, with Christmas being the following Saturday. That suited everyone since the Fancy Knoll school would also dismiss classes on Wednesday. All seemed to be falling into place nicely. The invitations had been handed out to friends from church and school and requests for those providing the music were duly acknowledged and confirmed. Distance and lack of transportation would keep some from coming, but they could still expect a good crowd. The people in the area loved a good party and the Raleigh family and Aunt Maggie were going to do their best to provide that for the community.

In the meantime, all the other Christmas activities were taking place, and Blue was thrilled with everything. The kid's school play was well done and went off without a hitch. The teacher gave them all a small comb and an apple for a gift. The only mishap came when Jackson, one of the shepherds, fell off the end of the stage, but he was unhurt. On Wednesday, school was dismissed with a lot of merry chatter being heard and the excitement was abounding in Fancy Knoll. Blue again reminded everyone that they needed to be at her grandpa's place on Friday evening at around 5:30.

On Wednesday, Buddy arrived just as planned, and the kids and grownups alike had a happy time of getting acquainted. They all liked each other immediately and Buddy and Jolene were thrilled to be involved in the party planning. They had brought a sack of chestnuts and another sack of hard ribbon candy to be shared with everyone. On Thursday, Buddy went hunting and killed a wild turkey, which would be cooked for the two families' dinner on Christmas day. He also got the two squirrels that were needed for the stew.

It was getting late Wednesday when Buddy and the kids headed for the woods. They had great fun looking for the perfect Christmas tree. By necessity it had to be a small one to fit in the sitting room and after agreeing on a beautifully shaped pine, the group headed home with everyone helping with the carrying. Buddy placed it in a bucket filled with rocks and tied the tree to the wall with a rope and a nail. The rest of the decorating was left to the kids.

What a wonderful evening the kids had drawing small stars and bells for decorations and attaching them with bits of string. Miss Lester had let Blue borrow some extra crayons, so after collecting every scrap of paper they could find in the house they cut them in strips, colored them, and put them together with paste made from flour. They then wrapped them around the tree. The adults helped them with the chains, knowing the kids would be up all night otherwise. They then placed angel hair, which Buddy had bought for them in Stewartsville, and placed it on the tree. Their tree was beautiful!

By Thursday afternoon, Ma, Maggie and Jolene had been baking and cooking all day and everyone was so intoxicated with the smells that some declared it was either have a sample or call off the party and just enjoy the goodies all by themselves. The women had already snitched their part, so good naturedly allowed a few samples to be eaten.

Friday morning was spent cleaning the barn, putting the stove in place, gathering wood and placing lanterns around the walls to give light. Every possible item that could be used for chairs was put to use, including upturned buckets, an old car seat and every chair that could be found. Even a few tree stumps were put in place. Aunt Maggie noted smugly, "See! I told you where there's a will, there's a way!"

The tables, made from sawhorses and wide boards, were placed end to end with snowy bleached table spreads placed on each one. Extra eating utensils had been borrowed from Aunt Maggie and a few others, and the job of placing them on the tables was given to the kids to keep them out from underfoot. Apple cider was brought in from the cellar. Coffee and postum--for those who didn't want to be kept awake--was made ready, and hot cocoa was prepared for the children.

People began arriving at around five thirty, with the kids at high fever pitch. The dogs and the cat were free to roam in and out the barn and for all purposes were well behaved. Indeed, they were such a part of the rural homes that they were hardly noticed.

It took quite some time for the greetings to take place, and just seeing old friends was enough to make a memorable evening. It was a very pleasant time for the adults just to visit, while the kids disappeared to get their play parts explained. There were many admonitions from Blue that they must all be very solemn during the play, befitting the occasion.

Finally, Grandpa banged on a pot with a knife and called the group to order. He sincerely welcomed everyone and informed them they would first have a sing-along, and some other entertainment, before they had their supper. A few groans were heard, since some had not eaten at home. It was soon forgotten, however, when the French harp sounded out the first Christmas carol.

Along with the harp, Mr. Cantrell's fiddle and the St.Clair's guitar, the roof was raised in songs like "Joy to the World," and "Hark the Herald Angels Sing." Joe's wife, Mandy, was then called on and sang a beautiful rendition of "It Came Upon a Midnight Clear." She needed no accompaniment! It was awesome! Even the dogs and baby were quiet. After Mandy sat down and thoughts turned back to the present, the fiddler went into his rendition of "Sourwood Mountain" with a good part of the folks either jumping to their feet in dance or clapping from the sidelines. It was a merry time indeed, until Grandpa again called for their attention. He solemnly announced that they would now have a presentation of the birth of Baby Jesus by the youngsters--him included--which made everyone laugh.

The children and Grandpa disappeared behind a makeshift curtain, along with Stout and Bandit. Then Pearlie took baby Beau and a warm quilt and laid him in the manger--sound asleep, just as Pearlie had said it would happen. Buddy brought in the goat from outside and took her behind the curtain. With much laughter and final instructions, the kids got quiet while the audience waited in anticipation.

First appeared Blue in the baptismal gown, bunched up at the waist, as she sat regally on the back of the goat. Joseph walked beside her holding a tight rein on Rosebud. Reaching the stall door, he knocked loudly as a gruff Grandpa opened the gate dressed in his feed sack robe.

Joseph spoke loudly as Blue had instructed. "We need a room tonight because my wife is going to have a baby and we have to hurry."

"Well," growled Grandpa, "I don't have any empty rooms, but she can rest over there in the corner if you want that!"

Joseph pretended to inspect the corner than nodded his head. "That will be five denario please," spoke the innkeeper. Joseph handed him some coins, thanked him and led Mary over to the manger. Pastor Buchanan informed Grandpa later that he had rented out his stable for the approximate worth of around 50 donkeys.

Joseph helped Mary carefully off the goat and she took her place behind the cradle as she looked at her baby adoringly, as befitting Mary. The two shepherds came next with their stout tree branches for staffs and kneeled next to Joseph. Then came the three wise men holding onto their camels--Bandit and Stout--who weren't quite sure about the humps on their backs. Audible giggles could be heard from the audience until Blue said a loud, "shhh!"

The audience stifled their laughter as best they could as the angels slipped in, one on each side of the manger with their arms raised. It was a beautiful sight, especially with the lights from one of the lanterns falling directly on the cradle. The baby continued to sleep peacefully. Then came the time for Clara and Jenny to quietly sing "Away in a Manger," as Clara moved over to stand beside Jenny. All was well until Charlie attempted to move to one side to let Clara by, but found the corner of his tow sack was caught underneath his knee. When he tried to raise himself up, he caused a chain of events that would literally bring down the house.

As Charlie pulled at his costume, he lost his balance and fell against the end of the cradle, tipping it, causing baby Beau to slide over to the floor. Blue leaned forward to grab Beau, but her long baptismal robe got in her way, causing her to fall over the cradle, narrowly missing Beau. That prompted Pearlie to rush over to rescue her baby who was now very much awake and howling. Things at that moment could have been easily set to rights had not a tiny mouse, who had evidently been underneath the cradle, decided to get to safer ground the same time as Pearlie started towards her baby.

Pearlie shrieked and rushed backwards to get to her chair. She took out two of the back chairs as they tried to dodge her rush to get to her seat. Half the folks in front were standing with their seats being shoved, all trying to see the location of the mouse. Ma Lantry, although close to 80 years, had managed to climb onto her chair using Hezekiah's head for something to support herself. Blindly he reached for the chair in front of him to steady himself and grabbed the back of the schoolteacher's chair causing her to fall sideways. The poor mouse was somewhere in the huddle, and so was the cat who had spotted the mouse.

In the meantime, between the screaming of most of the women, the baby crying, Blue begging for them not to hurt the mouse, things were in total chaos. To add to the hubbub, Stout and Bandit decided to get involved and began barking furiously. Only Rosebud and the cow were quiet. Of course, they were both tied. Grandpa as usual was holding his sides and howling with uncontrollable laughter. That Christmas, for many years to come, would be referred to as "the year of the Christmas mouse."

The adults, aware of the kid's probable disappointment--especially Blue's, made sure they complimented all the players on their fine performance and most declared it was one of the best Christmas plays they had ever seen. When things quieted down Grandpa announced it was time to eat. That served to quiet the hilarity down some as the guests made ready for the feast which most had already been anticipating all evening. Pastor Buchanan asked the blessing and baby Beau went back to sleep on his mother's lap and peace was restored to the party.

After everyone was full and getting a bit tired, Grandpa asked Mr. Cantrell if he would close their evening out by playing "Silent Night" on his fiddle. What a lovely way to end the evening. Buddy opened the barn door so that everyone could look out into the beautiful starry night. A hush came over the group as each thought on that holy night so long ago when the Savior of the world had been born. Pastor Buchanan read Luke's account of that night and then asked every person in the barn to join hands as he pronounced the benediction.

Amid many Christmas wishes and thanks to Grandpa and Nettie for the lovely evening and one of the most enjoyable ones they had ever experienced, the families began making their way down Birch Mountain. Their voices could be heard throughout the foothills as each family made their way to their separate homes, still singing the age-old carols of Christmas.

With everyone in bed, Blue could not stand it another minute. She tiptoed quietly into the main room and looked under the Christmas tree. Sure enough, there was a box just the size a doll might be. She tiptoed over and almost squealed at the sight of a beautiful 16-inch doll dressed in pink with white booties and not only that, but a new blanket and several changes of clothing sewed by her ma. What a delight to discover the doll could close her eyes and cry like a real baby. Blue took the doll out of the box, carefully wrapped both she and the doll in a blanket and positioned herself on the couch with her baby in her arms. Being exhausted from the party, she began getting drowsy, her last thought being that she would name her baby, Bluebell. Ma and Grandpa found her a few hours later, sound asleep. Neither had the heart to scold her for getting up so early. It had been a wonderfully busy Christmas for them all.

Nora Learns to Paper Walls

Nora Blandley was without a doubt one of the most creative women in the small community of Fancy Knoll. If any decorations were needed to dress up the church, or an elaborate theme for an important event, Nora was the one to send for. Once when a suitable banner was needed over the schoolhouse door for a Halloween party, she wrote the words "Happy Halloween" and due to the lack of any kind of painted letters, she used dried green beans on a strip of white feed sacks. To add a bit of excitement she made spaghetti like strips of dried red peppers and hung them from the words to indicate it was a bit spooky inside. It was indeed impressive, and the kids loved it.

Although she had very little to work with, she seemed always able to come up with something to dress up the occasion. That included her own house. Being limited on her farmer husband's income, she tried her best to keep their home neat and interesting. Flowers, whenever in bloom, were present in each of the three rooms in their house. Feed sack curtains were changed in the spring and in the fall with suitable colors to match the season. Christmas was a special time for her since she could decorate to her heart's desire. Consequently, throughout the year, she saved scraps of paper, material, dried flowers, pinecones, or anything that might dress up their home at Christmas. Her husband complained that after each Thanksgiving, he was afraid to eat anything, lest he get a piece of tinsel or crepe paper in his mouth.

Nora was especially noted for her love of wallpapering. After she was gone, her daughter, Jessie, and her two brothers had a hilarious time cutting through the layers of wallpaper in their home, just to see how many times their mother had papered through the years. They found several patterns, and even one layer of newspaper from the year 1925. They were able to still make out faded pictures of the comic strip, "Bringing Up Father." The most puzzling layer however, which was in the first bedroom, showed a layer of striped material, not paper, still fastened firmly to the sheet rock wall. Had they not been so young, when their mother had first got acquainted with wallpapering, they would have remembered that that year's papering was one of her greatest achievements, at least in Nora's eyes.

Nora had fallen in love with the modern designs of wallpaper that were being machine produced in the early 1920's. The new pastel designs just suited her fancy and she had set about getting enough money to paper at least one room as her first attempt at papering. Her husband, Herman, had asked her to try painting, instead of papering, if she wanted to change things. His reasoning was that she had enough flowerpots sitting around the house and he was not anxious to look at vines, and such, growing up the bedroom walls. Nora kept quiet and continued her planning. Her problem was how she was going to get the money for the wallpaper.

For starters, Nora already enjoyed a small income by selling her milk and butter in the surrounding area. The primary problem with that, though, was the fact that most folks had their own chickens and cows, so there were few to sell to. Her best option, to that, was to get her goods over to the Fulton Grocery store in Kent which was always willing to take her products. In addition, she also had sold a few garden vegetables in the summer, but all in all, extra income was hard to come by during those post war years. Yet, Nora had used her creativity before to get money and she felt she could do it again.

Her mind wandered a few years back to another time when she was desperate for a few extra dollars. Her first baby, Will, had serious colic for the first six weeks after he was born. She had walked the floor with him for what seemed for hours. In fact, she had been near to a nervous breakdown before her baby finally got relief. Her husband, instead of taking a turn, repeatedly told her to just jiggle him. He remembered that it had worked for his baby brother. It did not work for Will.

The same thing happened when her second baby, Mac, was born. Again, Nora walked the floor. She did fare some better by taking the advice of her mother-in-law by giving him small doses of paregoric. That helped considerably, but she decreed she could not go through another colicky baby by the means of walking the floor.

When she found she was pregnant for a third time, she knew it was time for her to do something. She had noticed a nice rocking chair in the Sears catalog with a padded seat for $4.65 cents and the more she thought on that rocking chair, the more she dreamed of owning that chair before her next baby arrived. The thought of "jiggling" another baby was more than she could handle. However, where to get the money? She prayed earnestly for an answer and much to her surprise the next week, she heard of a gentleman who had recently started a chicken farm and was asking around for women to pluck the chickens and singe their feathers off that he might take them to market. He offered the ladies $1.00 a day but notified the women it would be hard work.

Nora was one of the first ones in line on Monday morning at the gentleman's farm. It was something over a mile's walk, but that did not bother Nora. She as a rule had healthy pregnancies and was used to hard work. For the first couple of days she went home late in the evening humming, smelling like a chicken, with bits of feathers sticking to her clothes, but she was too excited to notice. However, the long hours and continuous plucking began to show the third day and she was hard put to get through the day on Friday. Nevertheless, she went home with a smile on her face and five dollars in her pocket. She had enough to order the chair, and also for the shipping. She felt good. Herman grumbled all weekend over their scanty meals which mostly consisted of beans and cornbread for lunch and cornbread and beans for supper.

Her baby girl, Jessie, was born eight months later, and wouldn't you know it, she never had a smidgen of colic. Nevertheless, both Nora and Jessie loved the chair--as well as most of the ladies in the Knoll area. The younger ones came by now and then to rock their babies to sleep and the older ladies came to simply enjoy the rhythm of the rocker. They sometimes fell asleep.

While musing on the chicken plucking job, Nora searched her mind for some type of employment that would give her enough money for wallpaper. Of course, she would need a nice border paper, also. For the paste she could just use flour and water, to save a few pennies. She got out the Sears catalog and checked the wallpaper samples. She found an attractive pale blue stripe design called the Jeanette. It had a white border and rose cutouts to decorate the border at intervals. She liked that one since Herman couldn't complain about climbing flowers and ivy, which were in several of them. She did her arithmetic and jotted down the 15 cents that a double roll would cost. She figured that 12 rolls would be plenty, with maybe some left over to use in her closet. The price went up to $1.80. Being determined to go all the way she added the border, which was 1 cent a yard, noting that she would need about 10 yards for that. Feeling a bit reckless she added 6 rose cutouts to the list for another 60 cents. Of course, there would also be shipping cost added to that, but a few cents more would not matter. Altogether, it should cost around $2.50 to do the first bedroom. Next year she could work on the other two rooms.

After several sleepless nights, and after going over every conceivable way to make the extra money, Nora just could not come up with anything. That is, until the day her Uncle Claude stopped by for a visit. It had been several months since he had been by and as they talked over old times, Claude mentioned to Nora and Herman that he was now selling Rawleigh products and would they be interested in any ointments or spices? He proceeded to get out a few samples from the large bag that he had carried on arriving. They were duly impressed, but Herman decided they could not afford anything at that present time. After a good meal, Uncle Claude told them he must hurry on since he had a lot of ground to cover. He would need to cover the Fancy knoll area, as well as Kent, before he could return to his home on the Kentucky side. His crops needed tending and he must not dawdle any longer.

Suddenly, a light went on in Nora's head, and before she could think it through, she burst out with, "Uncle Herman, why don't you let me cover this area for you because I need to make $2.50 really bad. Would that be possible?"

Herman sniffed and spit his wad of tobacco off the porch. Uncle Claude scratched his head and almost said no, but sensing how important this was to her, he decided to bargain. "Okay," he finally said, "but you will need to sell quite a few items to make that much profit. I will need a quarter of everything you sell, you know. You understand?"

"Yes, oh yes," shouted Nora. "I can do it. I know I can!" Herman didn't say another word. He knew when Nora said she could, she would. And so, the fast track instructions began; how to fill out order forms, how to present the products, salesmanship tactics, etc. Uncle Claude gave her a few samples on condition that she and Herman buy at least one can of salve for themselves. He could at least say he had sold one thing while in the Fancy Knoll area, in case Nora was unsuccessful. Nora quickly agreed. Herman didn't comment.

The first bedroom wall was as good as papered! But, first, she remembered that according to Uncle Claude she must believe in the product, so she thought of the long scratch on Herman's arm that had caught on a barbed wire fence that day. She had washed it well and bandaged it, but it still looked rather angry. She proceeded to put on the medicated salve from the Rawleigh Company and readied it with a clean cloth. Herman snorted, but nevertheless held still for the procedure. Imagine his surprise when the next morning the redness and soreness had completely disappeared. The salve had worked! Nora now had a personal success story to go along with her sales pitch!

What else could she do to make her product more enticing? Nora's mind went to work, and she knew if she had something to offer along with the salve, she would probably be more likely to make a sale. An idea made its way into her mind. As it has already been said, Nora was quite creative and one of her talents had been in drawing animals. It had always been easy for her since she was a small girl and the walls in the second bedroom had several of the pictures for the children to enjoy. That gave her a great idea. Most of the area homes had little in the way of décor and most walls were bare and empty of any decoration, other than nails for holding clothes or kitchen utensils. Wouldn't the ladies like something pretty to hang on their walls?

A few months back while in the dry goods store, she had noticed several nice clean pieces of cardboard that had been used as cushions for glass fixtures. Nora had asked for them thinking they might make nice backdrops for her drawings. She had taken them home with the intention of experimenting in her artwork for her own satisfaction. She now got them out and realized what nice wall pictures they would make. She went to work. On each one she drew a different animal, and she colored them with her few paints that she had salvaged from an old schoolhouse. What a delight! She thoroughly enjoyed doing the drawings and after a day's work was ready to supplement her salve and flavorings. The pictures would be free, of course.

For two weeks Nora and her children traveled over the knoll and as far out as they could manage the walk. She carried her order blanks, a sample of salves, a few spices, a bottle of vanilla extract and a household cleaner. Best of all, she had the pretty pictures which she knew the ladies would be interested in. It was hard work. Once a dog chased them and at another time an elderly lady slammed the door in her face, thinking they were beggars. However, the people were usually glad for a visit and a chance to sit on the porch and look over the items, even if they couldn't afford them. Nora was a good salesperson and she went home successful on most days with an order or two. The salve was the top seller. At the end of two weeks she could hardly believe she had made a total of 22 orders. She could hardly wait for Uncle Claud. He was as impressed as she thought he would be and offered her a full-time job. Herman glared at Claude so hard that he withdrew his offer. No matter. Nora had had her fill of being a saleslady. She was ready to paper!

She was not only able to order her paper, but also a nice oil cloth for their table. On an impulse, she added a pair of work gloves for Herman. He was somewhat mollified by her gift and things settled down in the household as she waited for the Sears order to come.

The package came on Friday. Her neighbor, George Lantry, brought it over and Nora did nothing all weekend but plan for her new kitchen come Monday morning.

She had so hoped for sunshine on Monday, but on arising the clouds were already rolling in. Undaunted, she began her day with excitement. She hurriedly got the boys off to school, Herman off to work, and began getting her supplies ready. She started her water boiling for her flour paste. She had used it enough times before that she was certain of the right consistency for keeping the paper on the wall. She then unrolled the pale blue striped wallpaper and admired it for a minute or two, before cutting the right lengths. How beautiful it would be!

She decided that she should cut several strips at once and lay them on her large table. That would make it quicker for her to add another one before the paste got too dry, in case of a mistake. Humming she mixed the paste until there was not a lump present and began applying the paste on the first strip of wallpaper. The first one went up beautifully and she started on the second one. Hearing a sound behind her, she turned, and 3-year-old Jessie was standing in the doorway, half dressed, wanting to go to the outhouse. Thankfully, she had not yet put on the paste and so hurried out to take care of Jessie. On returning she was in time to see their cat,

Tabby, headed into the kitchen. Frantic, Nora rushed in only to see the cat on the table evidently thinking the flour mixture was a bowl of gravy. Tabby stood up with the sticky mess clinging to her teeth, yawing and pawing like something wild. On trying to get away the cat's feet were also stuck in the mixture and began clawing at the paper underneath. "Oh no!" yelled Nora which scared Jessie who started crying, grabbing on to Nora's apron. The cat was screeching trying to get away and upended the pot of paste which proceeded to slowly glide down the side of the table where Nora had stored the other rolls of paper for easy reaching.

Nora grabbed for the cat with one hand and Jessie with the other, but her foot slipped in the gooey mess of paste and she slid underneath the table pulling the several sheets of paper with her. She sat in the wrinkled mess, realizing she had just managed to wreck about five rolls of her precious pastel blue wallpaper.

Tabby, finally breaking loose from the glue, and Nora's grip, ran out the door and disappeared. Feeling the pressure of the drying flour and water on their bodies, Nora grabbed the teakettle off the stove, rushed outside, grabbed a cake of Octagon soap and began scrubbing the paste from their bodies. Their hair was the worst part, and if Nora had not been so miserable, she would have laughed at the situation. However, she decided quickly that no one must ever know what a picture that she, the cat, and her baby girl made at that moment. Just then she heard a "Yoo-hoo" and her neighbor, Elsie Lantry, walked out onto her back porch. Elsie did laugh, and then she laughed some more. She could not help it. Finally, Nora joined in until they both became helpless with laughter and Jessie knew that things were going to be all right again.

Being the good neighbor that she was, Elsie began helping and soon the mess was all cleared up. The cat was nowhere to be seen, and the ruined rolls of paper had been well disposed of. On checking, Nora found that she would only have enough paper to finish two of the walls. Her instinct was to have a good cry, thinking of all the work she had put into the papering, but it took about ten minutes of bantering around ideas with Elsie, that Nora's creativity kicked in. She looked at Elsie and nodded her head toward a stack of clean washed feed sacks in the corner. There were several of the same color that she was saving to make new curtains. Elsie, said, "You don't mean…?" "Yep," said, Nora, "Why not?"

And that's what they did. While Elsie stretched the sacks out to full size and ran the iron over them, Nora put on another pot of water for another batch of flour paste. When the paste reached the right consistency, the two worked together to smooth out the wrinkles and to hold the cloth tightly while the paste began to harden. They both did a jig as they saw it was going to work. The rest was pure pleasure and it did not take long to finish two walls as the sacks were a substantial size. Next, they started the white border on the top with the pretty cutout rose decoration scattered every few feet along the ceiling. As Nora had Elsie to help, it seemed no time until they were finished. They sat down exhausted about three o'clock and drank their tea with a great sense of accomplishment. They spotted the cat out the edge of the yard and Nora was relieved to see he was still living.

Herman and the kids came in soon after. Herman knew it would be cold beans probably again, but he would be thankful for that if she had got the room papered. As they came in the house, she smiled at them happily as if she had had nothing but a smooth day behind her. Imagine the male members of the family's surprise at seeing the first bedroom all decked out in its new multicolored walls. They stood for a few minutes with their mouths open, a little afraid to ask Nora how she managed that. After a bit of looking, Herman spoke, "By Jacks, if it don't look downright purty! Nora, you outdone yourself." Nora just looked smug and began to set the table for supper.

Herman changed his mind, some, on going to bed. He opened his eyes to look again and in the half light of the moon realized he was looking straight at what looked like a green vine of ivy climbing up on his side of the bed, with tiny pink rosebuds intertwined. He gave a loud groan and Nora realized what he was looking at. She was too tired to argue and assured him she would change the bed around tomorrow, so he could face the nice blue wall.

The next day, she tugged and pulled until she got their bed fitted in a different corner of their small room. It was inconvenient for her now, for she would either need to get into bed before him, or she would need to go over the foot of the bed to get to her side. She didn't mind. Seeing green ivy vines and pink roses, on awakening, was to her, a lovely sight. She was already planning on doing the kitchen and second bedroom.

No Need for Matchmakers

If a person lives in a community long enough, the result should be a familiarity with the peculiarities of the local citizens. But, although Pastor Amos Buchanan had himself been born and raised in the mountains, he could still be shocked by some of the strange reasonings of the people, especially one Lizzie Gibson.

It seems that Lizzie had grown up in the foothills of Birch mountain and, as far as anyone knew, had never ventured out of the area. That included the larger area of Kent which was only about eight miles away. She had never married and was known to be set in her ways as well as methods of reasoning. That would become quite evident the time her younger brother, Luther, fell in love with a lady from the town of Kent. Lizzie, at 85, being twenty years older than Luther, and the only family member left, felt the need of keeping Luther in line.

Luther predicted that Lizzie would have a hissy fit if he announced that he had found a lady friend in Kent and was thinking of marriage. The first hurdle that came for him would be in his going to Kent to find a wife. That would be unacceptable to Lizzie. Never mind that her brother was 65 years old, and that there was not one eligible prospect for a bride in the area of Fancy Knoll. To Lizzie that was no excuse. According to her he should just stay single. She had remained that way, so why shouldn't he?

Luther had already been single most of his life, due to the lack of eligible ladies in the Fancy Knoll area. Also, he had begun taking care of his elderly parents until their demise the year before, therefore he was unable to go looking for a wife further than Fancy Knoll. He had certainly never regretted that time with his parents, but as time passed, he began to feel the loneliness in his modest little house. One day while working in Kent he met a lady named Hattie Hart at the bank, and on finding she was unmarried and close to his age, he became interested. The friendship soon blossomed into romance and he began to spend considerable time in Kent. Lizzie wondered at Luther's sudden "overtime" hours and became suspicious. Luther, on the other hand, knowing his sister's predictable objections had managed to keep the matter quiet, but things were progressing to the point that he knew he would have to tell Lizzie about his affair.

He wanted to be well prepared, so he ran every possible objection through his mind before he approached her. However, there was one item that he had not foreseen which might be the end of his romance. Hattie had just recently shared with him that she was of the Catholic faith. That was fine with Luther, but according to Lizzie there were no other "religions" other than those that were found in the Fancy Knoll Church. She had had enough problems settling on being a Methodist and now Luther would be giving her another "nomination," as she called it, to get used to.

After a week's worrying, Luther finally felt brave enough to face his sister--especially since he had just installed for her a porch swing that she had "wanted for years." After some forty minutes of clearing the way, by promising that the couple would continue to live in Fancy Knoll and that he would continue to milk Lizzie's cows, Lizzie was softening. He then felt he might as well go all the way, and so casually mentioned that he may be absent from Church at times since he and Hattie would be attending her Catholic church.

Lizzie yelled, "Her WHAT? " Those three words were repeated several times throughout the area of Fancy Knoll before nightfall. "I will not have a Cathlick in my house. Are you out of your mind Luther Gibson? Nobody in our family has ever married a Cathlick,

I will not have it!" At that she slammed the door and disappeared into her parlor.

Luther left the house downhearted and realized his need of someone to intervene for him. He reached the porch of Pastor Amos, called for him to come out, and spilled out the entire conversation. Amos only looked at him, sighed, and then said, Luther, how old are you?" Luther said sheepishly, "sixty-five." Amos let that sink in a moment, then said, "Luther, I was born and raised in these mountains and you and I both know these people's ways. Their reasoning can be mighty far-fetched at times, which means they might not reason like other people do. I'm sure Lizzie will come around after a time."

Amos desperately hoped that those few words would satisfy Luther, but Luther mournfully responded, "But, I want to marry now, not in two years!" After looking longingly back at Cordelia's supper waiting on the table, Amos knew he had no choice. He would have to go talk to Lizzie.

Lizzie was still angry when Amos knocked on her door, but she invited him in and not wanting him to think her inhospitable, offered him a glass of tea. "No thanks, Lizzie. I just came bye to maybe understand as to just what it is that you have against the Catholics?" He knew that Lizzie never left her little bungalow in the foothills, so she could not possibly know anything about the folks over in Kent.

Lizzie turned her back to Amos "Pastor, don't try to change my mind" she huffed, "I have my reasons," Her nose seemed to go up another notch. Amos had decided on the way over that he would appeal to her charitable side, "But Lizzy, I don't understand! You have always been so kind and willing to think well of everybody. What has happened to make you think ill of the Catholic folks?" He then added a few more words that he knew would make a dent in her thinking, "You have been such a great help in my ministry, and I have always counted on you to do the right thing!"

With that remark, Lizzie stood up a bit straighter, sniffed a bit than finally blurted out, "Pastor Amos, I don't take to gossiping--as you well know-- but I've heard some things about them cathlicks that I just can't abide by". Amos knew she had probably never met anyone who was Catholic, so was at a loss as to why she felt so strongly against them. "Well, Lizzie I don't believe it would be counted as gossip since you would be telling me something that, if unsettled, might harm our good relationship with the Kent folks."

Amos waited. Lizzie shifted her feet, wiped her nose and coughed a couple of times. She mulled it over a bit then resolutely turned back to Amos and blurted, "Well If you must know, I'll just come out and tell you. I heard it from a good source that them Cathlicks refuse to eat fish on Friday. Pastor Amos, you know that's Luther's special day to fish, and not only that but Edna told me that their preacher has to wear a robe in church!"

It was Amos's turn to cough and cover his mouth. In fact, he excused himself to go spit. After a moment he recovered and did his best to explain the differences in their way of worship and assured Lizzie that the Catholics were wonderful people and Father Joseph was one of his good friends. And furthermore, Luther probably wouldn't mind at all to change his fishing day, then added a clincher, "And besides, knowing how kind you are, I'm sure you and Hattie will be the best of friends. She might come in real handy at berry picking time and she might even come to one of our singings."

"Well, I'll think on it, but don't ask me to go to that church over there. I don't have any fit robes to wear and I'm not about to buy any!" With that she sat back in her chair and relit her pipe. Amos, making an extreme effort to hold in his laughter, was highly relieved another problem was resolved and hoped he could make it to supper before another emergency arose.

Luther and Hattie did marry and lived many years in Fancy Knoll. However, the eligibility of marriage partners continued to be an issue for the continuation of the community of Fancy Knoll. It certainly affected the marital situation for one Jessie Blandly.

She had lived all of her life in Fancy Knoll. Her mother, Nora, had arrived there when Jessie was but a baby and had carved out for herself a niche in the community, while raising her three children alone. Her husband, Herman, had originally arrived in the area with the family, but one day had left, saying he was going fishing. He never returned, and Nora had watched for him for several months until one day she heard that his "fish" happened to be a young woman who had come up visiting Nora's cousin, Clara. Nora, at length, was able to forgive her husband and went on with her life. She never remarried, deciding that she was content in her situation and would spend all her energy in raising her three children in the best way possible.

Her two boys, Will and Mac, did eventually find mates but Jessie seemed to be content in her single state and Nora never pushed her. There seemed no special reason for Jessie remaining single except for the one most important necessary element--an eligible young man, of which Fancy Knoll was sadly still lacking. The boys who would have been eligible were already married, or determined to leave Fancy Knoll behind and go find work in other areas.

Jessie's mother, Nora, died in 1939 from a heart ailment, but not before she had an opportunity to implore her friends to take care of "her girl." Nora was well loved in the community and consequently most of the women had already decided in their hearts to be a mother to Jessie, as much as possible. It was certainly no chore to love her as she had inherited a good portion of her mother's fun-loving ways and strong determination. Jessie had also inherited Nora's strong Pentecostal faith, which had sustained the family through the years and had given Jessie a love for helping others and contentment with whatever life brought to her. Nevertheless, Nora had been quite anxious that Jessie would have an opportunity to find a good husband and a loving home, since Nora's own had been so hurtful. That was why when the subject of a Lonely Hearts' Club came up at a Fancy Knoll's ladies' meeting, it didn't take long for Jessie's name to come to the forefront. It seemed to occur to several at the same time what a perfect and fun candidate she would be.

After all, that was how Willard and Lucy Raleigh had met, and the ladies remembered how romantic it had been for them and what a good marriage they now enjoyed.

The ladies reasoned that it was perfectly harmless and an exciting way to get a relationship going. Lucy explained the procedure of sending your name and address into a magazine, with a few particulars, and that was all that was required. Only those interested would respond to your letter. On your end, you could screen the letters and choose only those that sounded interesting to you. It could possibly progress to an invitation from you for them to visit so that the two of you could get better acquainted. Jessie was present in the group and just smiled as the women began making all kinds of plans and offers to help her in writing and screening the letters. They could just imagine all the fun they would have reading the responses.

They would all be involved, but only Jessie could make any decisions on an actual visit. Secretly, however, they all had romantic visions of finding Jessie a good husband. After much coercing Jessie gave in, wrote down a few things about herself and left it to Laura to send her qualifications off to the Lonely Heart's organization. Not a whole lot was happening in Fancy Knoll at the time, so the ladies were excited with the idea. Their husbands, on the other hand, took a little different approach and most simply raised their eyebrows. Lutie told Hezekiah he was the most unromantic man she had ever met and wondered why he had bothered marrying her. He let her know that for the most part it was her apple pie. Pastor Amos also suggested it might not be a good idea to delve into Jessies' romantic affairs, but his wife, Cordelia, was in the group and assured him they would be extra careful.

Jessie gave a mundane description of herself for Laura to send: thirty years old; brown hair and blue eyes; not beautiful, but certainly not ugly; love to eat, but not to cook; a good listener and a Christian. That was all she would agree to. However, Laura did omit the comment on cooking considering men's obvious appetites. The women had already agreed to help with the cooking! Two weeks later, five letters were waiting for Jessie at the post office in Kent and almost every day, thereafter, more would arrive. Jessie said it was making her dizzy, so Lutie devised a system of keeping the letters in a box in alphabetical order. In the meantime, the women would help Jessie decide which ones were best to respond to in a return letter. They all faithfully read each one and usually had a hilarious time reading some of them. One gentleman simply wrote on a sheet of paper, "*Dear Jessie, I have never heard of a woman that was a good listener--can't wait to get acquainted.*" Another one wrote that he had six children already and was not against having more, if Jessie was interested.

After a time, as was expected, the ladies decided it might be time for Jessie to think about a visit from one of the gentlemen. Jessie balked, saying she didn't want to rush things. Maggie reminded her that she wasn't getting any younger so why not "take the bull by the horns" and choose one of them to visit. Maggie further doubted that any of them would look like Rudy Vallee, anyway. That invited a round of giggles, so Jessie just invited them to pick one since she couldn't possibly make up her mind. So, with much analyzing and agonizing the ladies decided on a gentleman named Henry Ashley. On paper he sounded good!

The ladies were all willing and eager to help get Jessie ready for her gentleman visitor. Jessie went along with all their preparations with her usual good humor, however a bit tense. Harry was to arrive on Friday afternoon and Hezekiah had agreed to meet him at the fork of the road at the little village of Kent and guide him on to Jessie's house. It had been arranged for Mr. Ashley to stay at Laura and Sam's house, but late that evening Sam had a letter saying that he was to pick up his new plow in Tazewell, which might mean an overnight trip. That being the case, Pastor Buchanan had graciously invited Harry to spend the two nights at his house. His wife, Cordelia, had been called to her sister in Welch to help her with her new baby. Since Cordelia would not return home until the following Wednesday, Harry could stay at the pastor's house and be gone in plenty of time before Cordelia returned home.

With Mr. Ashley's sleeping quarters settled, the ladies began preparing the food to serve Harry. As mentioned before, Jessie did not like to cook, so the ladies had promised to take care of that for her. The pastor mentioned the possibility of the ladies being deceitful, but Cordelia assured him again that a couple of meals should not fall into that category and further arrangements would be made in case of a possible long-term relationship.

On Friday morning Laura washed Jessie's hair with Drene shampoo and pin-curled it with bobby pins. Lutie had chosen Jessie's prettiest blue dress which the ladies thought best matched her eyes and talked her into exchanging her scruffy shoes for her Sunday saddle oxfords. Mandy Thompson suggested Evening in Paris perfume, but Jessie balked at that. Jessie's comment was that "how's he gonna smell Granny's beef stew with that stuff on!" So just a bit of pancake makeup and a bit of lipstick was applied to her face and she was ready.

By the time they heard Hezekiah's horse snorting outside, Jessie and the women were besides themselves with anxiety. Everyone slipped out the back door except Lutie, who could stay for the introductions. She would promptly relate the particulars to the ladies all waiting anxiously at Laura's house.

Jessie's nerves were a mess, but she boldly walked out on the porch to greet her first suitor, determined to act as normal as possible. They shook hands and the message was relayed later that nothing concerning the introduction was noteworthy. The ladies were a bit disappointed but knew that some relationships take a bit of time.

For Jessie, the most important factor was his clean appearance. Everything about him was neat and his manners were very agreeable. Harry, on the other hand, was well pleased to find that Jessie was not as tall as he had feared, aware of his own 5'5" height. She seemed a pleasant lady and unafraid to look him in the eye. Overall, it was not a bad first impression on each of their parts.

After the introduction, the Lantrys left with Hezekiah going back to his fieldwork and Lutie straight to Laura's house. Jessie and Harry went into the kitchen as Jessie, not knowing what else to do, began setting the table for a late lunch. Harry was quite pleased when she also gave his dog some scraps for his lunch. Jessie found the beef stew, made by Granny Dalton, to be delicious and giving each of them a good-sized portion she asked the blessing and began the meal. Due to her nervousness she did not notice that Harry's appetite did not exactly match hers. In fact, he ate more of the chocolate cream pie than anything else.

They soon began to have some difficulty in making polite talk and mostly commented on things they had already shared in letters. That caused the conversation to be a bit over formal, which resulted in lapses in the conversation. After a time, Jessie suggested something else to eat and he suggested that they go for a walk around Fancy Knoll instead. She readily accepted that idea as she knew it would take up a good hour, probably, that she would not have to think of something to do.

She headed out as she normally did with nothing on her head and due to the mistiness in the air, her curls soon disappeared and most of Laura's morning work became undone. In addition, the dirt roads presented a problem, especially when someone is trying to make a good impression. The damp earth soon began to cling to their feet and Harry felt the need to stop often to remove the mud from his otherwise immaculate shoes. The walk went smoothly otherwise except for the fact that every woman in the neighborhood seemed to be also taking a walk. Any of the local men could have advised Harry as to what was going on, but he innocently thought it was nothing out of the ordinary, although a bit weird. Usually most folks stayed in on misty days, but these Fancy Knoll people went for walks regardless of the weather.

A bit of excitement happened when one of the Hackett children caught everyone's attention by falling in the roadside ditch. Jessie didn't hesitate as she flew to the little girl's rescue pulling her quickly out of the water. That resulted in both getting covered with mud and more water, but seeing there was no real damage, Jessie kissed the little girl and handed her over to her ma.

By this time Jessie was a mess but continued the walk on as if nothing were amiss. Later, Harry looked at her muddy clothes as well as her calm manner and commented, "Jessie, you are quite a lady!" Getting compliments from a gentleman was new to her, so she just shrugged and went to get a cloth for Harry to wipe his shoes.

Jessie was relieved to be home in her warm kitchen although looking a bit worse for the wear, while Harry remained as neat as ever. She again offered him something to eat, but he replied that he was still full of the late lunch, so would settle for another piece of pie if she didn't mind. She didn't, so while he ate pie, she ate another bowl of stew. He started to comment but remembered that in her description of herself she had mentioned that she liked food.

After having a rather stilted conservation, Harry mentioned a little before seven that he thought it best that he retire early to Pastor Buchanan's house, especially since he had been up since four that morning. Jessie agreed that it was a good idea and they parted amicably with just a good night.

He and his dog made their way over to the pastor's house while he wondered just how long he should prolong his visit just to be polite. It was obvious that there would not likely be a future to his and Jessie's relationship, but he felt that maybe he ought to give it another day. He was a bit disappointed that they had not hit it off but had known it was a risk for them both from the beginning.

On arriving at the pastor's house, however, he enjoyed his visit with him and wished he had come over a bit earlier. Pastor Amos, having been alone for a week was also quite happy for someone to converse with and the two spent a most pleasant evening until about ten when Harry mentioned he might retire. He had shared with the pastor that he did not feel he and Jessie would have a future together.

Pastor Buchanan showed him to his room, which was his and Cordelia's room. It was their nicest one, so the pastor changed the sheets and took himself to the small back bedroom to sleep. Harry was unable to sleep for some time as he pondered how to bow out politely and end his visit with Jessie. He would certainly not want to hurt her feelings, not knowing that Jessie was having much of the same thoughts as she too retired for the night. Harry helped himself to a glass of water,

Pastor Amos was having his evening devotions, when he suddenly remembered that perhaps his visitor's dog had not been fed. He surmised that Harry had already enjoyed a big supper at Jessie's place, so he went into the kitchen, retrieved some dry dog food, added a bit of milk for moisture and some left-over corn and potatoes. He stirred it all together and placed in one of the kitchen bowls, intending to place it out on the porch for the dog. However, at that moment the next-door neighbor pecked on the back door asking to borrow some flashlight batteries. They chatted a while and on returning to the kitchen Pastor Amos noticed the bowl was now empty and realized Harry had already fed the dog. Therefore, he returned the bowl to the kitchen sink for washing the next morning and retired for the night.

The house became quiet with only a few snores being evidenced of the house's occupancy. Around three, the kitchen door quietly opened as Cordelia came in, so very grateful to be safe in her warm home again after an overnight drive from Charleston. She knew Amos would be delighted that she had been able to catch a ride with Mr. Foster, enabling her to arrive home early.

As the reader can guess, both she and Mr. Ashley were about to receive the surprise of their life. She never turned the light on but quietly put on her nightgown and slipped into bed. How good it felt just to lie down! She decided not to wake Amos and just let him find her beside him come daylight.

With tenderness, she reached over and laid her hand lightly on his shoulder knowing what a sound sleeper her husband was. However, that was one thing Harry was not, and the inevitable happened. On feeling a hand on his shoulder, Mr. Ashley jumped up, throwing out his arms to block whatever creature it was that was trying to attack him. Cordelia screamed when she realized it was not her husband and her main thought was that if Amos was not here, then where was he? "*Had he been murdered?* She wondered later at her reaction and as to how so many scenarios could possibly run through one's mind in such a short span of time.

By this time, Pastor had made it into the bedroom and reached to grab Cordelia just as she let fly with her fist and caught the pastor, instead of Harry, smack in the eye. He was blinded at first, but after several minutes managed to get her quiet enough to ask what she was doing home at this time of the night. Finally realizing it was her husband who was holding her, she grew quiet and began to tell him of her unexpected ride back to Fancy Knoll with Mr. Foster, who was a cousin of her brother-in-law. Pastor Amos in return then explained their mysterious visitor and the reasons behind his presence in their bed, when suddenly the truth of the situation hit him, "Oh my! What must that poor man think? Cordelia you attacked him!" He ran back into his bedroom to get his pants so that he could try to explain.

At that moment they heard the back door quietly close and before they could get their thoughts together, a horse was heard galloping away from the house with a dog barking close behind. Pastor knew what had happened! He entered Harry's room and found a hastily scribbled note lying on the pillow of the neatly made up bed.

"Pastor Buchanan, I realize what must have happened and I am truly sorry, however, I think it best that I go ahead and leave. As I told you last evening, Jessie and I did not hit it off as I had hoped, so I think it is best that I just go, seeing it so close to daybreak. Please pass along my sincere apologies to your wife--that was your wife, wasn't it? PS. Thanks so much for the stew. Jessie fixed stew yesterday afternoon, also, but it was too salty to eat. She seemed to enjoy it so much herself, I didn't want to tell her I'm not allowed. To be honest, yours was much better! Sincerely, Harry Ashley"

It then dawned on Pastor Amos that Harry had eaten the dog's food. He truly tried to be sorry about the whole affair, but instead he dissolved into helpless laughter. He wished no humiliation on anyone, but he was overcome with laughter. In fact, he laughed so long, he decided to call it a night. He gave Cordelia a big hug, assuring her he was delighted to have her home and got up to go into his study. He wrote a long note apologizing profusely to Mr. Ashley for the misunderstanding. He thought it best to keep silent about the stew. He instead invited him back for a future visit and a sample of his wife's stew, which he assured Mr. Ashley, was even more excellent than his.

Shortly after eight, Pastor Amos made his way to Jessie's house. He dreaded telling her of the departure of Mr. Ashley, not knowing if she would be hurt, or pleased. He and Jessie were good friends, in addition to his being her pastor, so he wanted to be up front in everything. And so, he told her plainly that Mr. Ashley had headed back to Kent after deciding that they had really very little in common and he did not want to further waste her time. On seeing Jessie's smile, he knew she was feeling the same way. He thought it best not to cause any further harm to Mr. Ashley's reputation, so revealed nothing further concerning Mr. Ashley's visit, to the disappointment of some of the ladies.

Suitors aren't for Everyone

Pearlie happened to be at the post office at the same time as Jessie the following Tuesday and duly noted that four letters were handed to Jessie by the postmistress. She and Jessie looked at each other and read each other's eyes. Jessie groaned, "*Not again!*" Pearlie spoke, "Ah, come on Jessie. Try just one more time. You never know what good might come of it." Jessie sighed knowing she was in for another visit. She knew her friends well enough to know they would not give up easily.

That evening she got the box from under the bed. This time she chose. She pointed a finger at the paper and on opening her eyes saw she pointed to number three. She hesitated, but then got out her pen.

On her way home from the post office the next morning Jessie stopped at the gate to Laura's house just long enough to yell that the next lucky suitor would be one Horace Farley and that she would let them know the day. After all, she thought, why try to keep it a secret when most of the community knew more about the men than she did!

Within two weeks, Mr. Farley arrived to greet a very pretty Jessie, looking rather noncommittal--at first--and then she looked twice at Mr. Farley and decided she liked his looks very much. He was well built, handsome with a beautiful head of dark hair. He appeared very sure of himself and Jessie began to think he might have possibilities.

Lutie noted the change in Jessie's expression and soon happily made her way to Laura's house. Again, the women had cooked a fine supper of fried chicken, potato salad, green beans, fried okra, and a wonderful sweet potato pie. Horace's mouth began to water before they even sat down. He told Jessie it smelled heavenly. That prompted her to think perhaps she might try a bit of Evening in Paris later in the evening.

Since the two had not been writing as long, as she and Harry, it seemed that their conversation went along more smoothly. Especially since he appeared to be quite interested in the neighborhood and its origin. They also went for a walk, which this time happened to be a nice day. Again, the neighborhood women chose that time to take their walks--which hadn't happened since the occasion of Jessie's last visitor.

Later as Jessie thought back over her afternoon, she was quite pleased with the outcome. Although she had noted that Horace tended to frequently smooth back his hair, even though there was no noticeable wind, he still was very personable and seemed to have a great sense of humor. She anticipated that they would talk well into the night.

However, about six thirty a note came from Pastor and Cordelia that they would not be able to keep Horace as planned due to an emergency with one of their parishioners. Jessie almost panicked since she, the Bennett family and the pastor were the only ones who had an extra bedroom for company. Jessie ran next door to alert Lutie to come up with something in a hurry.

Lutie hurried to the Bennetts and found that their daughter and children were in for a visit and would not be able to house Mr. Farley. After talking it over with Hezekiah it was decided there was nothing to do but have Lutie spend the night with Jessie. The two women would give Mr. Farley the downstairs room and they would sleep together in the upstairs room. Both Lutie and Jessie had unquestionable reputations, so Hezekiah was unconcerned about neighborhood gossip. Besides that, Lutie would bring their dog, Bandit, and post him in the living room while she and Jessie would be sure to keep their bedroom door locked. If an emergency came up Lutie needed only to yell out the window and wake Hezekiah who was a light sleeper. Tomorrow the Buchanans would return and that would take care of tomorrow night's stay for Horace.

Lutie came over at eight, did the dishes and let Jessie and Horace occupy the living room to continue their lively discussion on the coal mining industry in the area. At ten o'clock Lutie went to bed and Jessie, feeling bad about staying up later, excused herself also. She gave Horace instructions to make himself at home and she also retired. She shared with Lutie that she was looking forward to spending more time talking with Horace and before going to sleep she and Lutie decided what Lutie would be fixing for breakfast

Jessie had still not dropped off to sleep at one o'clock when suddenly she heard a horrific crash from her downstairs bedroom. She leaped up to find the flashlight as Lutie, being startled, screamed at her asking if someone was shooting at the house. Jessie grabbed for the flashlight, dropped the key to the door and, bending over to retrieve it, hit her head on the dresser. The dog in the meantime began barking loudly. After a full minute Jessie was able to find the key, get the door opened and bound down the steps. Never in her life had she entered a man's bedroom, but this night she did. She later decided it probably had not been the wisest decision, especially with her head throbbing the way it was, but she was always one quick to help in time of danger. She at last got Mr. Farley's door open, which was also locked, and which luckily required the same key. The question crossed her mind as to why he would want to lock the door. Surely, he didn't feel the need to lock it from her and Lutie?

On entering, she was in shock as only Mr. Farley's backside was showing with his head somewhere down near the floor. Later she and Lutie howled with laughter as they agreed how thankful they were that he was a city gentleman, otherwise, he probably would not have been wearing pajamas.

But at that moment Horace was yelling, "stay back, stay back" in a garbled speech. Both women stopped short as he stood up silhouetted in the bright moonlight, and lo and behold it was not Horace Farley! It was a bald man who talked in a foreign language! They both screeched and turned to run out the door.

The dog barking and the ladies' screams had alerted Hezekiah who came running with his shotgun sure that the women had been molested but found instead a man frantically trying to wrestle with a broken bed and two women trying to get through the door at the same time. Unable to hear above the dog's barking he pulled Lutie and Jessie toward the upstairs and told them to stay there and lock the door until he could find out who it was in Mr. Farley's room.

The two women sat huddled on the bed imagining all kinds of horrid thoughts until Hezekiah came and told them all was well. He explained that the bed had fallen and that they were in no danger. He assured them that the moonlight had made it appear that Mr. Farley was someone else.

A lone figure was seen in the early morning hours as Jessie's second suitor walked down the road, suitcase in hand, and surprisingly looking as normal as ever. Jessie and Lutie bounded over to Lutie's house as soon as daylight came to question Hezekiah. He shared with them how truly sorry he felt for Mr. Farley as the two men struggled on the bedroom floor trying to move the mattress out of the way to get to Mr. Farley's toupee. His strange speech was explained when he had finally found his dentures safe behind the side table. Hezekiah had then made him as comfortable on the floor--on the mattress--as possible and left him in peace.

Hezekiah shared with them that Mr. Farley was accustomed to taking off his hairpiece at night as well as taking out his dentures, hence the locked door. He had rightly been concerned when the bed fell that his hairpiece would be ruined, and his teeth broken. Mr. Farley had apologized to Hezekiah and said to tell Jessie he had found her to be a beautiful woman. She was sad at first at the outcome of his visit, but soon her sense of humor returned, and she decided the well-learned lesson was that it doesn't pay to be something you aren't.

Jessie never spoke of him after that except to reprimand anyone who referred to him as the "bald eagle." She had never been called beautiful before and the thought gave her a warm feeling for a long time. A few years later, after becoming a professional counselor in Charleston, she ran into Mr. Farley, with no toupee. He was bald! Although he seemed a bit embarrassed, Jessie pretended not to notice, and he shared that he now had a wonderful wife and hoped that Jessie had found someone worthy of her. She just smiled and told him she was indeed happy. On leaving she leaned near to him and whispered. "You are still a fine-looking man!" His smile could have lit up the room.

After Horace left, Jessie had advised the ladies that she was burning all her letters from her perspective beaus--no more box under the bed, but the ladies weren't quite ready yet to give up. They felt that the first two suitors had not had a reasonable chance to get acquainted and it really had not been fair to either Jessie, or them. Consequently, they all pleaded for one more visit, "the third time's a charm," they told Jessie. It was important to them to have tried everything for Nora's sake to find Jessie a good husband. If this last choice didn't work the ladies all promised to drop any further correspondence between Jessie and the prospective suitors. They solemnly declared to keep hands off!

Sighing, Jessie once more closed her eyes, moved her finger down the page and stopped at number nine, one Charlie Blake from just over in Stormville--a staunch Baptist and a Democrat. At first, she laughed and was going to choose someone else because Charlie Blake was twenty years older than she was and from his first letter, one could tell immediately that he was not looking for a new wife--he was looking for his recently deceased wife, Emma.

Ordinarily he was the last on the list that she would have chosen but then it popped into Jessie's mind, "*Wait a minute! Charlie is perfect! He really has no interest in me and so it will be just a short visit. My friends will keep their word and I can get on with my life.*"

She wrote the next day and invited him to come, if he so chose, on August 13. He replied in short order that he would indeed be there. Jessie let Laura know that this time she was going to be herself. She had learned her lesson from Horace Farley, and she would meet Mr. Blake just as she was--no frills, no makeup. It was not really what the ladies wanted, but knowing Jessie had reached her limit, agreed to just do the cooking and leave the rest up to Jessie and Charlie.

Charlie arrived early in the morning in his clean bib overalls and baseball cap. Jessie stood quietly on the porch in her best everyday dress with her hair pulled back with a pink ribbon. They shook hands solemnly and sat on the porch getting acquainted. The ladies of the community had to settle for waving from the road, or just thinking up something they needed to borrow from Jessie.

During the first hour her visitor had already called Jessie by the name of Emma three times, reinforcing what Jessie already knew that Charlie was still grieving the loss of his wife. He shifted topics and asked her about her church affiliation. Charlie sit up a bit straighter than necessary when Jessie announced their Fancy Knoll church was interdenominational, but her leaning was toward the Pentecostal way of worship. "You have heard of the Pentecostal beliefs haven't you, Mr. Blake?"

"Of course," he sputtered, "do you mean to tell me you can... you know...speak in tongues?"

"Yes, I do, Mr. Blake and I also raise my hands in worship and have been known to even shout hallelujah now and then. That's perfectly okay in our church."

"But," ventured Charlie, "Don't you feel uh...feel a little disrespectful uh... making all that noise?"

"Of course not! Charlie, tell me something, did you love Emma?"

"Of course!" he huffed, sounding offended that Jessie would even mention such a thing.

"Well how did you let her know that you loved her?"

Charlie's eyes got misty as he thought about that. "I guess I told her a lot that I loved her--but she knew I did anyway. I bought her gifts sometimes and hugged her every chance I got." Jessie could see Charlie's thoughts trailing off as he sat remembering.

"Charlie, those are some of the same things I do when I want to praise God. Sometimes I just want to hug Him and tell Him so. I don't think He minds if I get a little lively."

"But it's so noisy! Do you folks think God is hard of hearing?"

That tickled Jessie's funny bone and she couldn't resist saying, "Well, Heaven is a long way up you know!"

Charlie couldn't help but chuckle at that and shortly thereafter, the conversation turned back to Emma.

"I tell you what, Charlie" Jessie said, "Why don't you tell me about Emma. I truly would like to know her better."

Charlie's eyes lit up and for the next hour he talked his heart out about his beloved wife. How good it felt! Both he and Jessie were teary eyed when he finished, but they were healing tears. Jessie gently told Charlie that what he needed to do was to go back home and give himself time to say goodbye to Emma and perhaps in time the Lord would send him another wife, if that was His will for him.

They had a nice day talking and rather early in the evening they both retired for the night--Charlie next door at the Lantry's and Jessie to her newly repaired bed. Jessie let Charlie know his delicious supper had been sent over by her friends Maggie and Nettie, and that their early morning breakfast would be prepared by Mandy Thompson.

Jessie was delighted that at last, one of her suitors had made it through the night with a good night's rest. When Charlie left the next morning, he thanked her profusely for her understanding and he did something which shocked her speechless--and that wasn't easy to do to Jessie. He leaned over and kissed her squarely on the lips. She stood speechless as he said, "Now, Jessie, let me give you some advice. You need to leave this little knoll and go get you some more education. The Lord has given you the gift of listening, and that's exactly what a lot of people in this world needs!"

She watched him walk down the road. Just before he turned at the forks of the road, he turned back and looked at her one last time. They waved to each other and he passed out of sight.

In the evening hours Jessie sat for a long time in the porch swing musing about her episodes with the Lonely Hearts' Club. She was relieved it was over. She was not angry with any of her friends for orchestrating the events. She knew they all wanted her best, but Charlie's words had triggered something in her heart. Somehow his words felt right. Each of the three men had given her a touch of the romance that she had never had, and she was content with that. Harry had called her a lady. Horace had told her she was beautiful, and she had received her first kiss from Charlie. It was enough! Charlie had given her more than he knew, though. He had made her aware of a purpose in life!

A Time with Grandma

Cousins were rare in Fancy Knoll for the most part; there just weren't that many families related enough to have a number of cousins. However, the Gulley family that moved into the area one summer day was the exception, but they were there for such a short time that no one really became acquainted with them. Pastor Buchanan had visited the house a couple of times and a few of the women went by, but beyond that the family was gone before much else could be known about them.

The community did note that the grandma spent a lot of time outside with her grandchildren, mostly looking for mountain tea, picking berries or fishing and swimming in the creek. They noted that Grandma sat on the bank while keeping a close eye on her four grandkids. The one impression the kids had made on the Knoll was that they were a "wild bunch," loud and rambunctious. The local folks at first thought the four youngsters were siblings, however a few were privy to the fact that they were cousins--from three different sisters.

Although it was not uncommon for an extended family to live together in those days, having four youngsters from three sister's households living with a grandmother was a bit unique. However, that was not the only oddity concerning the children; it was also their names that were such a curiosity to the Fancy Knoll residents. To everyone's puzzlement, their names were Wink, Nink, Joe and Mink. It was found that Joe and Mink were brother and sister with

Wink and Nink being offspring from two other aunts. Of course, these were only family nicknames, but still a puzzle to the Fanch Knoll community.

It was such an oddity that a few of the women took unscheduled walks by the rented house just to see if they could strike up a conversation. Nothing came of it so, ultimately, a rumor had spread that the kids might have been snatched from their homes by force, and the old woman had "done away with the parents." Evidently there was no truth in that since it was quite evident that the lone adult adored the kids despite their rowdy ways, and they in turn loved her. Once Maggie Snow had stopped for a visit and was witness to an incident which settled her mind about how much they loved their grandmother.

When Maggie neared the house, the woman was sitting in a cane backed chair underneath a tree. The rowdy children were in an argument as to who loved "granny" the most. They fairly ignored Maggie as they sought a way to prove their devotion. There was no other chair in sight, and since the grandmother didn't offer an alternative, Maggie propped her back against the tree, waiting for an opportunity to engage Granny in a chat.

She was prepared for a wait as to the conversation, because the kids were in the process of determining which of them loved Granny the most. The kids had somehow come up with the idea of testing each other's bravery and love for her by approaching the neighbors' cranky goose and staying close by till the count of ten, before running back to Grandma. They all had been leery of that goose, after seeing it chase another goose, and Joe noticing it at the edge of their field thought it would be a great idea for their contest.

Nink and Mink weren't so sure of the test but agreed to it if Joe would go first. Wink was all for it, being the tomboy that she was. Grandma was a bit skeptical but had her cane ready by her side in case the goose might chase the children.

Joe, the Conqueror, readied himself for battle. He first hitched up his pants ln order to be free to run in case of pursuit. He then looked around for a sword--well, a stick would have to do in his case. He decided on a piece of cardboard for a shield and proceeded to stuff that in his shirt. That made things a little bulky, but it did boost his confidence. He was ready! He would prove who loved grandma more!

The young fighter swaggered the few hundred yards and drew near the enemy. His bravery went up a notch when the enemy turned tail and walked away. Since his cousins had already counted to ten, he evidently wanted to show just how brave he was, so he leaned forward and tapped the tail of the goose. That did it. The outraged goose turned on Joe honking, with wings spread wide, and they both headed straight for grandma. Joe made it to about 3 feet from her before leaping headlong into her lap. His momentum took granny, chair and all backwards with the goose close behind. Joe's shield had fallen around his hips as well as his pants and he had no idea where his sword had landed. Luckily, the goose took flight over them both and headed back to his own side of the field.

The other three cousins were crying hysterically from the safety of the porch when they saw their grandmother shaking on the ground with her apron covering her face. Maggie had her back turned to them, also shaking. They were both convulsive with laughter.

Joe gave a shriek thinking Granny was crying. That prompted the other three to descend on their grandma, pleading for her to speak to them. She finally got them away from her and when things settled down, asked them why they were crying. They replied, "but we thought you were crying!"

As they quietened, Granny explained that she loved them alike so that meant they must love her alike. That suited them, and soon they went on with their play, making sure they kept to their side of the fence

That incident seemed to clear the air between Granny and Maggie, and Maggie had not needed to employ any of her usual tactics to get information. Grandma readily explained to her that the children's parents and her own husband was in another part of the state, building homes for each of the families. It seemed that Grandpa Gully was a builder who preferred having his family living in close approximation, so he had bought a large tract of land in a small town farther south. While his daughters and their husbands all shared in getting the new dwellings built, Grandpa had rented a place there in Fancy Knoll from his old friend, Milton St. Clair, and moved Grandma and the four youngest grandchildren in until the houses were completed. He would then return and move them back down to their new homes.

There were also older children of the sisters, all male, but none was living at home. Most were working away from home. Of course, they were also loved by their grandma, but there were two, however, who had been thorns in their grandma's side for a long while and she was happy to get away for a vacation, as she called it.

Those two were a bit adverse to work and usually lived wherever they could get a free meal and bed. Grandma Gully had had her share of their company and though she never complained she did find ways to limit their desire to take up permanent residence in her home. For example, one grandson and wife came to visit and after a prolonged stay Grandma Gully devised a plan to encourage them to move on. She found that neither of them liked boiled cabbage, so she conveniently began cooking cabbage almost every noontime with leftovers for supper. Thankfully, she liked cabbage but since her grandson did not, he and his wife soon moved on to another location. She was a wise woman.

Another grandson moved in on a more permanent basis. He was a pleasant fellow, howbeit a bit lazy, who did not like getting up early, which continually interfered with his work ethics. One morning after calling him a good amount of time, with no results, Grandma poured cold water over him, bed and all. He got up for work.

There were several local opinions of these two, none very flattering, but all would have to admit they led a colorful life. The story is told that sometimes for need of drinking money they would go into a bar pretending to be coal mine owners and recruit workers for their mines. After speaking rather loudly about their failed efforts for getting men willing to work, they would soon have several drinks from those wanting to get on the good side of their potential employers. Another story was related that once on getting picked up by a state trooper while hitchhiking, the two related to the trooper that usually once a year they would take to the road in memory of their earlier days before they reached success and just bum around the countryside. The trooper swallowed the story and one of the two ended up hiring the trooper and gave him a time and place to show up for work if he was interested. The trooper assured them he would be there and that was the last any of them saw each other.

Therefore, to have a break from these two older grandsons, Grandma Gully was most thankful for this respite with her four youngest grandchildren. When Grandpa had put his plan into action to build each of his daughters a home, she was delighted that she had been given this opportunity.

The children were very distinctive in looks. Mink's blond head was in sharp contrast to her brother Joe's red hair, although Nink declared her cousin's hair to be more orange than red. Nink considered her own color to be muddy blond, while she thought Wink's wavy sandy colored hair was much prettier. One day, Nink decided she was tired of hearing the nice comments about her cousins' hair with nothing being said about hers, so she began begging Grandma Gully to let her get a store bought permanent. She thought that perhaps at least folks would comment on her curly hair. She promised to fill Grandma's pipe for her every day and help her wash the clothes. That was no small chore since Grandma was having to wash the clothes on a washboard.

However, Grandma Gully was a woman of sensitivity and seeing the longing in Nink's eyes to have curly hair she set about making a way for that to happen. She picked blackberries with the youngsters and sold eggs to get enough cash to pay for Nink's permanent. It would be expensive, costing around three dollars, but it would be worth it to see Nink feeling good about herself. The big day came, and Grandma and the four kids flagged down the big Consolidated Bus to ride over to Kent, which was the nearest place to boast a beauty parlor.

If Wink, Joe, and Mink were jealous they never let on, probably because they were so curious as to what Nink was getting herself into, plus the fact that they had not been outside of Fancy knoll for the two months they had been there. They were also allowed to go on the condition that they behave themselves. Of course, there was no one to watch the rowdy youngsters, anyway, and Grandma would never have thought of asking for help.

On arriving at the Cut and Curl Beauty Parlor, the curious group of kids climbed up into the chairs and got ready to watch the proceedings. Nink, losing some of her bravado, nevertheless climbed bravely up to the shampoo bowl to have her hair washed. She started to complain to the hair lady that Grandma had already rubbed her head raw that morning, but a look from Grandma stopped her. After the washing was complete the lady began to roll her hair on rollers and then wrapped each curl in a smelly soaked pad. Each curler was then attached to a clamp, which was attached to electrical wires, which in turn hung down from a hood like contraption. All in all, it was a strange looking sight when finished. The heat was then turned on which would hopefully cause the hair to curl tightly. However, the outcome could be very unpredictable.

It was necessary for the operator to watch closely for any sign of burning of the skin, which was likely to happen. A paper fan could be used, or some operators would even blow on the heated areas to give more comfort to the one being permed. In Nink's case, Grandma Gully was right there with a folded-up newspaper to not only to fan, but also to blow on the hot spots.

Wink, Joe, and Mink were hysterical after about five minutes. They just could not contain their laughter at seeing Nink with the long wires leading up from her hair to the electric perm machine. They howled and hooted with Grandma threatening to take them all straight home. Of course, she couldn't leave Nink in her situation, so they continued until the entire beauty shop was either laughing with them or wishing they would all go back to Fancy Knoll. Nink was quiet except for complaining about the red spots, which were showing up around her neck and head. Unknown to the others she had already decided she would never ever have another permanent. She would rather die with straight muddy colored hair.

The ordeal did finally come to an end and the hateful curlers taken out of her hair. No one was saying anything as if all were holding their breath. Nink looked in the mirror and let out a happy screech-she was beautiful! Her three cousins just looked a bit amazed and for once that afternoon they were quiet. It was like looking at a different person. Nink had changed. She even acted different and talked excitedly all the way back home. For once Grandma did not have to comment to her that, "beauty is only skin deep!"

Her glamour lasted exactly two days, after which Grandma Gulley grew tired of the smell and washed out the mass of curls thinking nothing would change in the appearance of the hair. Nink took one look at the mass of fuzzy mousy hair and proceeded to cry the rest of the afternoon. Grandma forbade Wink, Joe, or Mink to say one word to her about her permed hair. Of course, after a couple of weeks her hair settled down and she began to like herself again.

And so, the days and weeks went quickly by. The children spent most of their days out in the fields and woods and especially in the nearby cemetery. It was exciting for them to make trails around the graves and memorize the names on the tombstones. They were always careful to not step on anyone's grave and could be heard at times apologizing to "Martha," or "Thomas" or "Mr. Turnbill." They were ever on the lookout in fear of getting caught and banned from the cemetery.

Being careful paid off when one day Joe spotted a black car driving up the dirt road straight at them. The four children scattered like roaches and hid in the thick evergreens on the north side of the cemetery. They were petrified of getting caught but being kids felt a delicious excitement at being privy to the actions of an outsider.

A nicely dressed woman got out of the car and walked to a grave not far from where the children lay and placed a large wreath of beautiful flowers on the grave. The kids were close enough to see the tears, which ran down the woman's face. They heard her say, "Momma, I'm so glad you're here in this peaceful place where no one can ever hurt you again." She proceeded to carry on a conversation with "momma" and later as the kids discussed her words with Grandma, they surmised that her ma had not been welcome to be buried in some other cemetery and the daughter, by necessity had brought her here for her final resting place.

Grandma Gully told them it was probably because of her race that she had been refused burial in other cemeteries. Of course, Grandma used that time to again instill in her grandchildren the fact of God's love for all people and that it was her desire that her grandchildren must never ever feel themselves better than any others of God's creatures. "He loves us all alike, you know," were her final words.

The next day the children again were in the cemetery and Wink got the great idea of sharing some of the flowers with Grandma Gully. Their time in the rented house was almost up and she felt they should give Grandma something nice as a gift. What better thing than a bunch of pretty flowers. And so, they did. They carefully chose a bouquet from the wreath using several colors--careful not to mar the arrangement and proceeded to take them to Grandma. She knew immediately, of course, where the flowers came from, but being the wise woman that she was, she would not openly condemn the children. She knew it was an act of love on their part.

Instead, she sat down with them and gently shared with them that she understood why they had taken the flowers and she loved them all for it, but that it had not been right since the flowers were bought for another person that was loved just as much as she. As she placed them in the Ball canning jar on her kitchen table, she told the cousins they must think of a way to make up for taking them. The four of them hashed around several ideas and it was Mink who came up with the notion that they should give the unknown woman some other kind of flowers in return. Grandma reminded them that there were no flowers around their little house, so they would need to decide what kind of wildflowers they could put on the grave. Wink wanted the pretty blue violets they had found out in the woods the day before and the others agreed. Nink got the idea of planting them instead of just laying them on the grave, and Joe offered to dig a bed for them at the graveside.

The next morning Grandma and the kids carefully dug up a blanket of violets and carried them to the gravesite. They sat to the side in the shade while Joe dug out an oblong bed for the flowers and they then all helped place the violets along the edge of the grave. After watering them, Wink thought it appropriate to ask pardon from the lady for taking the flowers and they left the cemetery feeling much better. Grandma thought it strange but for the rest of their time on the Knoll the children never again played in the cemetery, except to check on their violets. It seemed that they now had a personal interest in the quiet resting place of the dead.

Grandpa Gully sent a letter that he was coming for them on the fifteenth of the month and things seemed changed for them all. Nothing real noticeable; just an undertone of melancholy. The kids were less rambunctious, and each seemed to want to be closer to Grandma anytime she happened to be sitting.

Grandma too felt something letting go in their lives. She knew they would never be in a situation like this again and wanted to prepare the children as well as she could for the coming years when she would no longer be with them. From the pain in her body she was now experiencing she was certain her time would not be long with any of them.

On their last night in the rented house, Grandma fixed the meal of each one's choice of food. She found some wild rhubarb to make a pie, especially for Mink. Wink was happy with a big pan of gravy to go along with Grandma's biscuits. Nink asked for wilted lettuce and green onions with hot bacon grease poured over the top and for

Joe, she just made sure the peanut butter jar was on the table. She made sure there was lots of laughter and fun. They played dominos and old maid and she told them stories about her childhood. When she saw they were getting sleepy she gathered Mink up on her lap and as the other three gathered around her feet she spoke to them some last words that she hoped they would remember in the years to come. She knew there was a possibility that some of these sweet grandkids would face some hard things in their life, so had asked the Lord to help her speak of things that would be of benefit for them. She held their rapt attention.

"Children, I have loved having you with me these months but now you must go back to your parent's home and I hope you will always be good obedient children, as best you can. It is possible you will be hurt by others somewhere along the way. I want you to remember to always treat others, as you want them to treat you. That way if they don't treat you nice in return, it is not your fault." Grandma Gully paused and repeated her last sentence as if it were important that they agree with her.

She continued, "If others mistreat you, the burden is on their shoulders. In the years to come, just remember that your Grandma loved you and has prayed for you--even though I will no longer be with you in person, our good Lord will not forget my prayers." They looked at her questionably, but she just hugged each of them close knowing they could not possibly understand the burden she carried for each of them. She would leave them in His whose hands were stronger and mightier than hers.

Early the next morning she made a big pan of biscuits, enough to take on their journey with them and tried to keep her mind on good things--pure things, like the Bible said. She was so relieved that the children were looking forward to seeing their new homes and therefore looking forward to returning to their parents. Each one skipped out to the car when they heard Grandpa's car coming down the road. Grandma Gully walked from the house more slowly, looking back only once. The group left Fancy Knoll as quietly as they had arrived with no one realizing they were gone until the smoke came no more from the kitchen chimney.

Two weeks later the long black car visited the cemetery in Fancy Knoll once again. The lone woman got out and was surprised as she approached the grave to see a mass of pale blue violets covering the side of the gravesite. Seeing a sheet of paper stuck into the dirt with a stick at the head of the gravestone, she picked it up and read the words:

"we feel bad cause we took your ma's flares we wanted them for our grandma, and we could not find any more we put some purple violets in the ground and hope they grow good we are sure sorry bout your ma. we are cousins"

The woman's face lit up with a smile and she determined to find the children so that she might thank them, but after asking around no one could tell her where they had gone. However, the violets gave her a sense of closure knowing that someone else had cared and knew the spot where her mother lay. Years would pass, and the violets would one day cover the grave. The cousins would grow up and as Grandma Gully had predicted some would indeed endure some hard times, but only time would tell if they would remember and benefit from the outcome of their grandma's prayers.

Pride for The Hills

The year of 1941 brought only a few changes to Fancy knoll. However, three new families had moved into the area and a few automobiles could be seen on occasion driving on the local dirt roads. A small grocery store had opened near the town of Berryville, which meant the Fancy Knoll folks would no longer need to travel the twenty miles to Tazewell for their food staples.

Sally Lester had returned to the Fancy Knoll School for the second term and community gossip arrived with her, concerning a possible marriage proposal. The pupils were concerned, of course, because that usually meant that they would lose their teacher. Although the prospect of a wedding was exciting, most of them were hoping for a broken engagement.

By September, battery operated radio sales were on the increase, due to the threatening signs of war, which were taking place. A feeling of dread was being experienced by most of the grownups, but the schoolchildren were mostly unconcerned, never having experienced going through one. However, several older residents still remembered the First World War which had ended in 1918. That was especially true of one of the newcomers to Fancy Knoll, named Mr. Jarvis, and he was always willing to share his knowledge of the war with anyone caring to listen.

He had moved into the old Shinn place in the summer of 1940 and it did not take the community long to discover that he had a strong pride in his country as well as the state of West Virginia.

Patriotism was a strong subject to him and he was committed to promoting it to his fellow citizens. That is what gave Miss Sally the idea of asking Mr. Jarvis to speak to her school pupils. She was always on the lookout for things to interest her students and since history was her weak subject, she knew she would benefit, as well as her pupils if Mr. Jarvis would agree to speak to them. He did so immediately!

Mr. Jarvis came to the school in mid-September and at first the kids looked at him rather doubtful, but with a stern look from Miss Sally, they settled down obediently to hear his presentation. Surprisingly, he had his listener's full attention five minutes into his talk. He first reminded the children of the freedom that our country enjoys, and then he shared some of his war experiences that he had privy to in the trenches of France in the year 1918. He had come home with his left hand missing, which served to keep the schoolchildren interested.

The boys especially liked his stories about seeing the big land-based guns, called Big Berthas, that weighed tons. He also brought along a gas mask to illustrate stories of how they were used in the trenches to protect them from the deadly gas used by the German Army. Both boys and girls loved the stories about the pigeons being used by his outfit to carry messages back to the American lines. He told of one such pigeon, called Cher Ami, who once saved 194 soldiers trapped behind the German lines, by carrying a message twenty miles back to them.

His eyes held them riveted as he proudly alleged, "We don't know what will happen in the next few months, but if we again are drawn into war, I would gladly go again. My country means a great deal to me as I pray it will for you. Though you are just schoolchildren, you can still help in the event of war. Learn to love your country and make a firm stand in what you believe in!"

All eyes were on his as they felt the earnestness in his words. The kids went home that day with a greater knowledge of the meaning of war, and in addition, more than one declared they were going to be patriots of Fancy Knoll as soon as they could figure out how to go about it. Most couldn't wait to get home to share with their families about Mr. Jarvis. Miss Sally was more than pleased with Mr. Jarvis's talk and invited him back again the next week.

The next week he came back, and the kids were in their seats and quiet before he could remove his coat and hang it in the cloakroom. He then began talking about the state of West Virginia. He evidently felt just as strongly about West Virginia as he did the entire country. Shortly into his talk, the kids were made aware of his all-time hero, Stonewall Jackson.

"Children! Stonewall was born right here in our great state of West Virginia--in Clarksburg, on January 24, 1824. He was a great confederate general who fought in the Civil War, but was also strong in his faith and strong in what he believed in." Mr. Jarvis waited while Miss Sally brought out the map of West Virginia and asked Joe Compton to locate Clarksburg, which he quickly located in the northern part of the state. Mr. Jarvis congratulated Joe on finding it so quickly and then he seemed to speak directly to each individual pupil as he thundered, "Know this state of yours! Stand up for it! Do all you can to defend it!"

At least two hands immediately went up wanting to know how they would go about defending it, so he first began to talk to them of the beauty of the state and the top priority of keeping the countryside clean. He declared proudly, "Ours is a great beautiful region with hills, hollows, rivers, caves and coal fields. Let's do all that's possible to preserve those!" He reminded them that they had a responsibility to help keep the landscape clean of debris, both in the creeks and on land. They should respect the wildlife, trap and hunt only those animals needed for food. Most of all, they must learn about their state so that they might later be able to elect the best leaders for the state's interests.

Mr. Jarvis's intensity had already fired their enthusiasm to the point of taking some type of action. He, of course, recognized this and knew it would be beneficial for them to be involved in some worthwhile activities.

He went on, "Children, some people think ill of our state. They seem to think our state is less desirable or progressive than some others. Don't you believe it for a moment! There is a great potential here for some of you to become state representatives, or members of the Congress or who knows maybe even the president. It is possible!" Some of the kids could already picture themselves behind a big desk. He went on, "The worth of a state is in the minds of the people! Think highly of citizenship and you will be a good citizen. Stonewall Jackson fought for what he believed in during the Civil War as I did in the Great War--and now if I need to fight again, I will!"

The children, as well as Miss Sally, were mesmerized by his words and felt ready to go out to do battle that very day. The older boys were ready to don their uniforms. The teacher was prompted to ask him to meet with her later and discuss some further activities for the kids. She knew from experience that her Fancy Knoll kids liked to put actions to their convictions.

Miss Sally and Mr. Jarvis met together the next evening to put together some ideas to promote patriotism in the minds of the children by adding a civics class to their regular history class. It would be structured as not to interfere with her normal lesson plans and in fact would be more of an extracurricular activity. She had to admit that Mr. Jarvis knew a lot more about both subjects than she did and felt it would do the kids a great benefit.

Mr. Jarvis was willing to come every two weeks, check up on the kids' assigned projects and give them an hour of storytelling with time to ask questions. The school board was happy for more additional teaching from someone "in the know."

During the next month, Mr. Jarvis mulled over ideas of how to make the learning of so many facts more possible and fun for the kids. After all, learning about history, government and state statistics took quite a bit of memorizing. He devised a plan. His hour with the kids would include a drill, which he could manipulate from week to week with the hope that the kids would be learning almost without being aware of it. Miss Sally loved the idea.

From that week, a strange sight could be seen along Huckleberry Road as the Fancy Knoll School kids marched down the road behind Mr. Jarvis. With Miss Sally in the rear they were taught to walk quietly, looking straight ahead and always to show respect for anyone they happened to meet. Once a friend came to visit Mr. Jarvis who had been an officer in the Great War with him, and Mr. Jarvis thought of a fun thing to do with the kids. He purposely had them walk by his house on their trek that day, since he knew his friend would be sitting on the porch. Mr. Jarvis had already told the kids about his friend's visit and the fact of him being a former army officer, so as the troop approached, Mr. Jarvis ordered the kids to stop, turn towards his visitor and salute him, as his due. The children were delighted when the old gentleman stood and returned their salute. They continued with their drill which went something like this, but with changes and repetition both being a part of each drill. Mr. Jarvis would yell,

"Who's our president?"

The children would answer,

"Franklin D. Roosevelt!"

"Our 18th president?"

"Ulysses S, Grant!"

"Our state governor?"

"Homer A Colt!"

"Year West Virginia became a state?"

"1863!"

"How did we become a state?"

"By proclamation of Abraham Lincoln!"

"Our state flower?" And so the questions went.

Mr. Jarvis interchanged his questions and it did not take long before the entire class was reciting historical facts without even thinking. He constantly reminded them of the visions of our founding fathers, and of course being the active kids that they were, they clamored for more. They wanted to exhibit actual "deeds" to show their patriotism.

The sessions continued to be an adventure for the kids--they learned history and a love for the land through the exploits of others. One day Daniel Boone was the subject of the class. The kids, especially the boys, were thrilled at Daniel's adventures and his love for hunting and trapping--that was stuff they knew about. Mr. Jarvis explained that after the Revolutionary War, Daniel had at one time been a surveyor in the state of West Virginia; in fact, he made his last survey in Charleston in 1798. He then settled in Missouri, hunted, and trapped until he was 83 years old. Blue couldn't wait to share that with Grandpa Hack. He had been feeling puny lately so maybe that would help cheer him up and get him out in the woods again!

Mr. Jarvis told them about Daniel being captured and adopted by a Shawnee chief, but loving his fellow countrymen, escaped and went back to defend his fort from a surprise attack. For several days, the boys swaggered around with their Red Ryder air rifles hoping they might spot an Indian.

On another week, it was a story about Paul Revere. My, how they loved that story! For days, the boys were seen practicing on their horses out in pastures--and on the road when they were permitted--in case they would ever be needed to warn Fancy Knoll of any incoming army. They spent considerable time deciding what route to take in case one of them would be called upon. They were hearing talk every day about the possibility of the United States being drawn into war, and they felt they needed to be ready.

Soon the girls began to complain that they had nothing to do. They wanted to get involved in something patriotic also, so Miss Sally gave a lesson on Betsy Ross and gave the girls a project of designing a flag for Fancy Knoll area, "in case it would ever be needed." The girls were delighted and spent several weeks working on their flag and even got some of the local women involved. It was a great learning experience for them all.

While listening to the radio one evening, Mr. Jarvis heard the plea for all listeners to go out and look for multiple types of scrap materials to be collected to be sent to defense plants for use in making weapons of war. "*That would just suit my Fancy knoll school kids!*" he thought. He jotted down several things, listing old tires, scrap metal, car bodies, old bed springs, stove parts, wheels and even old rags and placed it with his notes to share with the kids in the next session.

The Unrest Begins

In the meantime, Mr. Jarvis and Miss Lester put their heads together and decided on having a contest between the children that would further encourage good citizenship and a better understanding of a country's preparation for war. After several days of brainstorming the two came up with the idea of Mr. Jarvis providing a contest for the boys and Miss Sally would get the girls involved in something suitable for them. That separation of the sexes seemed to be necessary, due to the difference in the two groups' interests and abilities.

On Monday morning the day went as normal, as the class of students were not informed of the contest until just before the close of school. That was due to the high level of excitement the boys were able to accomplish in a short period of time. As Miss Lester had anticipated, the announcement of a contest and the unscheduled appearance of Mr. Jarvis took them all by surprise and they were hardly able to contain their excitement long enough to hear the rules. For that reason, Miss Sally had carefully prepared written instructions for each boy to take home to his parents.

Mr. Jarvis explained his contest. It would consist of two groups of boys who would collect scrap metal. He explained the government's need for any sort of scrap metal available to be used in the making of weapons in the defense plants. Of course, that quickly fired them all up, and their minds were already seeing things they could collect. All the boys under 13 years old would make up one group and those above 13 would comprise the other group. The latter group had fewer boys, which made it a fairer number. A time limit was decided upon for the scrap gathering and then each pile of metal would be weighed on Mr. Thompson's farm scales.

Mr. Jarvis announced that the winning group would get to accompany him to the small city of Welch in mid-December to attend the annual meeting at the World War I Memorial building for the Great War veterans. It was the highlight of his year and he thought the boys would enjoy attending and being privy to all the stories that usually circulated during the gathering. Mr. Jarvis reminded them that it was a special honor to attend because the building was the very first memorial building erected to honor World War I veterans and that was "right here in our state of West Virginia!" It had been dedicated in 1923, and Mr. Jarvis had attended almost every meeting. The boys thought that would be a wonderful trip and would work hard to win the prize.

The girls were content to stay out of the contests. Only Blue Raleigh showed any interest in the contests, but that was only because of her fondness for Tag Lantry. The two usually were teamed up in most activities in their classroom. Still, the girls needed to be equally involved to keep their recent enthusiasm going forward.

Miss Lester knew that the sale of defense bonds was being encouraged from all quarters and decided that would be a good thing for the girls to work on. Although none of the girls could buy even the smallest bonds, which were sold as low as $18.75, but they could possibly buy 10-cent savings stamps and put them in a booklet until they would have enough for a full bond. That would be a good project, especially for Blue and Clara, since Blue had been hunting ginseng roots since she was a small child. The roots should bring in enough to buy a good number of the 10-cent stamps and it would keep the girls busy for a while. Others of the girls could work in the harvesting of fruits and vegetables to earn dimes with which to buy the stamps.

In addition, most of the girls in the community were happily involved in their Ovaltine Clubs. Mrs. Thompson had allowed the girls to gather at her house to listen to Little Orphan Annie on her radio, which was sponsored by the chocolate drink company called Ovaltine. The company provided its club members with badges, decoder rings and other paraphernalia, which would be sent, in exchange for proof-of-purchase labels. The girls loved to play pretending to be office workers and secretaries. Lola Shinn kept track of everything and did the ordering that was necessary. She loved keeping records of their radio premiums and such, so when approached by Miss Lester about collecting the defense stamps all the girls pooled their efforts and added that to their "office" work. In later years, a couple of the girls did indeed become secretaries for one of the large mining companies in western West Virginia. Lola became a bank stenographer.

For the boys it was a different story. The competition was in high gear from the word go. With everyone knowing the older boys had a slight edge over the younger group, the smaller boys did get an extra piece of metal thrown their way, now and then. And so, it happened that Mr. Giles up on Crane Creek even got involved. He was not well known in the community since he had kept to himself through the years, but it was also due to his living further into the foothills. He had always been friendly enough to the community, but he just seemed to be one of those people who enjoyed living out their lives alone and the people had allowed him to do that.

It happened that he had an old Ford Coupe chassis sitting outside his barn, which had been stripped of most of its parts. It had broken down on a visiting relative, years back, and out of the blue, the cousin had offered the vehicle to Mr. Giles for $35 dollars, "and it's yours!"

Mr. Giles had bought it on the spot; however, it kept losing its parts to other machinery until it finally rested out behind the barn, giving in to the rust and weather. At the makeshift post office one day Mr. Giles overheard some of the men folk talking about helping the younger kids a bit "just to keep things even" and he came up with a dandy idea. He would drag the old car body to the end of his field and then think of a way to make the younger boys aware of it--and just let nature take its course. It would help the kids out and get rid of the eye sore.

On Tuesday, Mr. Giles waited on the outside bench of the small grocery store since he knew that a couple of the younger schoolboys passed by there on their way home. Pastor Amos also happened along about the same time, and that suited Mr. Giles' purpose well. He engaged the pastor in a conversation and asked him to visit a while with him. This was very unusual, but the pastor was more than happy for a chance to get better acquainted with the somewhat solitary Mr. Giles.

A short time into the conversation Tag, and his friend, were seen approaching, so Mr. Giles winked at the Pastor and began to tell him about an old chassis that was in his back field and he wished that one of the school boys would find it and haul it off. He raised his voice a bit but pretended to pay no attention to the boys. Out of the corner of his eye he could see the boys' faces light up as they speeded up to a run and was soon out of sight.

The two men had a good laugh, as they knew there was going to be some activity at Mr. Giles place. The two boys were already making plans for a big metal haul the minute they left the men's presence. They had to act fast before the older team of boys could get wind of it.

The two men remained on the bench a while longer as the pastor and Mr. Giles had their first meaningful conversation ever. It was a nice time for both, and they found they truly liked each other. So was to begin a friendship that would last for several years to come.

The two boys could not wait to get to Joe and Cecil's house after supper. They all huddled in the back bedroom, fearful less someone overheard the conversation and the secret might get back to some of the older boys. Of course, none of the older boys were within half a mile from the younger ones, but they felt they could not be too careful.

In the meantime, three of the older boys, Russell Thompson

and the Henry twins, Bill and Will, went out that evening looking for scrap. Being older, they were able to scout out farther--plus they knew the younger boys were being given a little help, so they needed to search every possible place. They made their way further up into the foothills, not expecting much, but still wanting to cover every area possible. Imagine their delight in finding a full body chassis in the lower end of Mr. Giles' back field! Being concerned that they might get caught, considering Mr. Giles's reputation in the community, they went back towards their homes to make their plans as how to somehow get that car chassis back to Mr. Thompson's barn without getting caught. They reasoned that once the car body was in their team's pile of metal, Mr. Giles would be too embarrassed to ask for it back.

Since it was getting late, they headed for home to re-group with their other three members who made up their team to plan their strategy. The younger boys were just getting ready for their move. On hearing his parent's soft snores each boy had quietly exited his house and hurried to meet up with the others at the big oak tree by the community cemetery. It had been their playground for years and they felt quite comfortable there at any time of the day, or night. They were all respectful of the graves, but also found them to be dandy scouting trails in an Indian attack. Charlie arrived first and took that time to eat one of his ma's biscuits, which he had hurriedly stuffed into his pocket on leaving the house.

Soon the other boys arrived and the six of them set off for Mr. Giles's field. They already had his permission--or they felt they had--so went with a clear conscience to hijack his car chassis. They arrived in the field without incident and nothing was stirring. They had made sure their dogs were fenced in, but it seemed like those dogs could smell adventure. Within a short time, both Tag's dog, Stout, and Cecil's big boxer, Jolo, came bounding into the cemetery. "Rats!" said Tag, "let's hope they keep quiet or we are all sunk." The two dogs looked apologetic but content to be back with the boys again sat waiting to see what was coming next.

The boys looked around the area glad to see the car body was sitting at the very end of the field on the top of a steep bank. "Great!" said Charlie, "if we can just get it started over the bank we can take off!" They each circled it finding a good place to hang on too and checked out the weight. "Whew!" said Cecil. "We are going to need help with this bugger!" They all tugged as hard as they could but could only budge it a few feet.

"I've got an idea. Let's see if the dogs can help," said Cecil, as he unwound the rope he had tied around his waist before leaving home. He had carried one with him ever since Mr. Jarvis had shown them some rope uses, he had learned during the Great War.

So, along with the leverage of the two dogs, especially the big boxer being tugged forward by Tag, and the other boys' strength, the chassis inched to the edge and over. Once on the slick dewy grass the Ford Coupe went down the hill at a good pace. Once at the bottom, however, they could get it no further.

"We can't give up!" puffed Tag. "We have got to think of something!" It was Charlie who came up with a solution. "I bet Pa would let us borrow that cart he hauls fertilizer in. He won't tell on us and I will explain about hearing Mr. Giles saying it was okay with him." And so, the boys had to be content that they had at least been able to move it down the hill. They went home damp and exhausted, slipped back into bed and finished the night out in sleep.

Meanwhile the older group of boys had made some plans of their own and knew they also needed to test out the weight of the car before making their actual move. One can imagine their surprise when they approached the area from down the road and saw the car chassis was not sitting on top of the bank of Mr. Giles hill. "*What in the world*?" They pretended to walk nonchalantly up the road toward Mr. Giles' house, in case he was looking out. But soon, to their relief, they saw the chassis sitting at the foot of the hill. Unknown to them, Mr. Giles had earlier also been surprised to look out his window to see the car so soon gone.

The older boys in the meantime, being completely out of sight of Mr. Giles' house at the bottom of the hill, took their time trying out its weight to see if they could move it. They soon surmised they were also going to have to get more help if they were going to get the car moved any distance. They left still wondering who, or what, had gotten the car that far down the hill.

Charlie explained to his dad the next morning the younger boys' dilemma in not being able to move the chassis further and pleaded with his dad to just help them get the car onto the wagon and they could do the rest. Mr. Bennett would only agree to help get it onto the cart, but to no more. Charlie was elated as he and his team sneaked back again in the evening with rope, fertilizer cart and Tag's horse. With the help of Charlie's dad, they were able to turn the chassis on its side and back the wagon up underneath it enough to tip it onto the wagon. With the rope secured as well as possible, the kids were instructed to get on home as soon as they could and if the car body fell off, they were just going to have to leave it until the next day.

The boys agreed, with four of them walking beside the wagon to steady the cart and the other two guiding the horse. Things went well until they started to cross Crane's Creek and a wheel hit a rock about half-way across. That resulted in knocking the chassis off the side into the mud. Remembering what Charlie's dad has said and that Tag had to have the horse back, the boys were forced to untie the rope, leave the car body and go home. They were wet, tired and discouraged as they fell into bed for a second night's fitful sleep.

The next morning, being Saturday, found the older team of boys hurrying out to Mr. Giles' place determined to get the car moved at least to Russell's pa's field where they could have more time to get it to the weigh-in site. "Oh no!" yelled Will. "The car is gone again. What in the world is going on?" They began scouting the area for tracks and again much to their surprise found the car in Crane's Creek, half buried in the mud. It took a good part of the morning for the boys to extract the car from the mud and get it back up onto the bank. Having to do chores at home on Saturday afternoons the boys decided to come back at night and see what was going on. Evidently, whoever was moving the car was doing it at night and they had been doing it by day. They would try to get to the site before whoever it was who was moving it, if possible, because time was running out.

Tag in the meantime had talked to his dad and explained the situation and asked him to see if he could please help them get the car up onto the cart and then they should be able to get the car body the rest of the way without a problem. Hezekiah agreed if they would wait until evening after the milking then he would go help them at least put the car back up on the cart if they could get it out of the mud. He was the more concerned about the time involved in doing that, than he was in getting it the rest of the way.

The group set off well before dark and the boys were delighted to find the car already sitting upon the bank. They didn't stop to question; they just wanted to get it on the cart again. Mr. Bennett had also come along and with both dads to help, the chassis was soon sitting on top of the fertilizer wagon secured well with rope. The men left, having enjoyed sharing in the boys' adventure.

Soon after, the older group of boys had skirted the main road going above the area and came down the road behind the Crane's Creek crossing just in time to see their younger counterparts headed back into the long lane towards Mr. Thompson's weigh-in place. They had been outsmarted! The five younger boys too busy to notice, were busy pounding each other on the back in congratulations.

The stacks of scrap metal continued to build throughout the next two weeks. At the end of November, the weigh-in was declared to be too close to call and almost the entire community came out for the celebration and to congratulate the boys. However, none ever got to make the promised trip to Welch to visit the War World I Memorial. On December 7, the country of Japan attacked Pearl Harbor and America was forced into war. Fancy Knoll would somehow never be the same after that. What had only been made-believe before, would soon become a reality. For some on all fronts, a war was happening before they were ready, but at least the Fancy Knoll kids had some idea, thanks to Mr. Jarvis.

As for the surrounding area, only a few would be eligible to enter the Armed Forces any time soon, but all farmers were called on to increase their food production. Victory gardens sprang up and rationing came into being. President Roosevelt's, "Do Your Part!" slogans were posted everywhere as the people indeed rallied to do what they could.

Mr. Jarvis himself only lived through May of 1943. On one of his last visits to the school, he quoted his hero, Stonewall Jackson, as he mourned the fact that he would not be accepted into the Army because of his age. He solemnly repeated the words of his hero one final time, "My religious belief teaches me to feel as safe in battle as in bed. God has fixed the time for my death. I do not concern myself about that, but to be always ready, no matter when it may overtake me...that is the way all men should live, then all men would be equally brave."

Serenading is not for Sissies

On some days, the Fancy Knoll school kids were just simply lethargic, especially after the holidays were over. By early in 1942, the kids had grown accustomed to hearing war news as the main topic of most adults, but it seemed far away to them--almost as far away as summer vacation. The older population were engrossed in increasing their spring planting as the president had asked them to; garden seeds were being poured over, canning supplies were being readied and new fields were being plowed. Those were important projects for them, but for the younger ones the days seemed to drag bye and any new happening got their attention in a hurry. Even though Mr. Jarvis worked hard to keep them interested in what was happening in other countries, the geography of Japan and Germany was still just too far away to capture their attention for any length of time.

On one of those "nothing going on" days, the schoolteacher, Sally Lester, announced to her pupils that she was engaged to a city gentleman from Ohio named Harman Gentry and they planned to be married soon. That caused quite a stir even though it had been a subject of gossip since the beginning of the school year. Some of the schoolchildren felt put out that Miss Sally had not told them before about her sweetheart, but she explained that the wedding date had only recently been decided on, and she had not wanted to speak too soon. In addition, the wedding details had just been finalized. They had thought earlier she might go to his place in Ohio for the wedding, but due to the declaration of war, Harman had registered for the draft and the couple had upped the date to spend as much time as possible together. After some finagling, things had worked out for Harman to come to West Virginia for the ceremony.

Early in April, a tired Harman arrived one Wednesday afternoon to the relief of the entire community. He had taken the bus to Kent and due to a break-down he was three hours late. Mr. Jarvis, who was to meet him there, had finally decided he must not be coming and had come home without him. Miss Sally was beside herself until she saw Harman walking down the dusty road carrying his two suitcases. Most of the community had been watching all day for his arrival and those who had not been watching for him were keeping a close eye on Miss Sally. If he had not arrived soon, they were making plans as to how to locate him, but now that he had arrived safely, he would be looked over carefully as to his treatment of her.

None should have worried, however, as the two seemed delighted to see each other and their feelings for each other was obvious to the welcoming committee. After a good meal and a short rest, Harman was ready to face the community. Since he had arrived on Wednesday, he was able to get acquainted with most of the folks at the evening services on Huckleberry Rd. He seemed especially attentive to the schoolchildren, as was expected, since it was of importance that he might win them over to his good side. The adults seemed to approve of him, also, and Miss Sally looked extremely pleased at his reception by the community.

The Fancy Knoll folks made plans to provide their schoolteacher with as nice a wedding as possible. They had not only provided a place for the groom to stay before the wedding, but also made ready a small cottage for their honeymoon. In addition, the local ladies had prepared a week's worth of food. Miss Sally would have to wait until later to show off her cooking skills for her new husband.

The cottage, which belonged to the Raleigh family, had been offered for the week's stay with an option for them to rent if they wanted to stay longer. Originally, the couple had planned to marry after school was dismissed for the summer, but like the plans of so many others, the threatening war took priority over all else. Miss Sally had secretly hoped her teaching contract would be renewed for another year and that she and Harman could continue to live in this pleasant community. Neither could have guessed that come September there would no longer be a Fancy Knoll school, and Harman would be far away in the South Pacific.

However, the present things were most important now and the wedding preparations were put into action. The honeymoon house was descended upon by the community women who seemed determined that no speck of dust would survive their onslaught. Scatter rugs were beaten and hung out in the warm spring breeze, as well as the bed linens. With floors freshly waxed, walls scrubbed down, dishes and kitchen utensils made ready, the cottage was finally declared to be ready for the honeymoon couple. On the wedding day, fresh flowers would be placed throughout the house. The school kids made a large sign welcoming the new bride and groom and placed it near the steps by the porch. Fancy Knoll wanted to make sure their schoolteacher and new husband would feel loved and proud to be a part of their community!

In addition to a spotless house, the grass had been trimmed and flowerbeds cleaned out. The children would be given the job of gathering armloads of the area honey locusts to deck the trellis leading up to the cottage porch on Friday. The roses had not yet bloomed so the trellis would work for the locusts. In addition, there was an abundance of wild honeysuckle and early apple blossoms gathered to decorate the area around the banquet tables. It was an exciting day for the women and children. Most of the men responded, as usual, with a simple raise of the eyebrows.

While the wedding day plans were being finalized, plans for an evening chivaree, or "serenading," as local folks called it, was also in progress. Most local couples were serenaded on their wedding night, or soon after, with many of the community taking part. Everyone was invited with the stipulation that they bring something that would make a noise; pots, whistles, metal against metal, anything that would make a loud noise. The revelers would either march around the house, or simply just stand in the yard where the married couple was staying and make as much noise as they possibly could until the couple would make an appearance, usually on the porch. The couple would be congratulated yet again and usually would not be left alone until they gave each other a kiss before the crowd would go back to their own homes and leave the couple in peace. At times, the serenades might be offered some sort of refreshments, but it was not required. It was usually a lot of entertainment for the well-wishers and a bit embarrassing for the newlyweds.

This introduction into married life was a must for Miss Sally and Harman according to some of the older boys, as they began to plan in earnest for a rousing chivaree. The main instigators were Jack Thompson, Charlie Bennett and the twin boys Will and Bill. These boys were the oldest teens in the community and loved nothing better than getting into mischief of some kind. They rarely caused any real havoc but had come close several times.

First, they decided on their noisemakers. Bill said he would sneak their ma's canning pot out of the house, which was sure to make a lot of noise. Jack was going to bring his ma's washtub and a hammer to beat it with. Will had an old rusty trumpet that still made a loud noise, although off key. Altogether, with everyone else's noisemakers, there should be plenty of noise for the serenading. However, just making noise was not going to be enough for this chivaree; a bit more excitement needed to be planned by the group.

Since Harman had been staying with Jack's family the couple of days before the wedding, Jack had helped him to take his clothes to the honeymoon cottage and later helped him dress for the wedding. He took note that Harman stowed his suitcase on the enclosed back porch, so as not to mess up the clean house. He told Jack he would unpack later after he and Miss Sally moved in. That gave Jack the idea to get the couple on the front porch during the chivaree and he would sneak round the back way and grab the groom's clothes for the night. Of course, the plan was to bring back the clothes the next day.

Will came up with the idea of catching a couple of frogs to place in the living room and hope the frogs would stay hidden long enough to scare the wits out of the couple. To complete the boy's pranks, Charlie thought a bucket of sand tossed throughout the couple's bed would be hilarious if it could be done. So much would depend on timing and access to the inside of the house.

All those attending the chivaree were duly notified to meet at Jack's parent's home at seven and proceed from there after the wedding festivities were over. There were local stories of other serenades where the groom would be ridden on a fence rail, but after seeing Harman's size, the boys thought it best to forgo that particular feat.

On Friday noon, classes were dismissed as the wedding reception preparations got underway. The couple would soon leave for Tazewell for the actual ceremony. They were to ride over in Mr. Jarvis's 1939 Plymouth convertible and would apply at the courthouse for their license before being sent close by to where a suggested preacher would marry them. The ceremony could have been done in the Fancy Knoll church, but it would have required a blood test and a three-day wait which was not feasible with the groom coming from such a distance.

The groom looked handsome in his navy-blue suit and his black hair perfectly smoothed down with Brilliantine, but it was the bride who took everyone's fancy. Miss Sally had gone straight to Laura's house from school where several of the women waited to help her dress. She had brought her wedding clothes with her at the beginning of the school year, just in case, but had kept them well concealed. She had chosen a belted pale blue dress with a white wing collar and trimmed in white buttons the length of the dress. She wore a small pillbox hat with veil and white opera pumps. With her cornflower blue eyes and mid shoulder blond hair, she was declared to be as "pretty as a picture." The younger girls could hardly be away from her presence and some had asked if they could go with her to Tazewell.

To get them out from underfoot, Lutie Lantry sent them out into the field to gather wildflowers. That delighted the children and they gathered several bunches, mostly blue violets and white star chickweed, which they considered the most beautiful. The bride knew the flowers would not likely make the trip but nevertheless bragged on and on about her pretty bridal bouquet.

It was reported later by Mr. Jarvis and Jessie Blandly, who went along as witnesses, that the wedding ceremony was very lovely and went smoothly. Both the bride and groom arrived "without a hair out of place," according to them. Mr. Jarvis was happy to report, however, that they were able to put the top down on his convertible on the way back.

On arriving back in Fancy Knoll around five o'clock, the reception quickly got under way. Several tables were laid out with food for the wedding supper, which was taking place in the cleared area outside the church. Each family was responsible for bringing their own chairs or blankets that would be placed underneath the several shade trees. The newlyweds had their own private table which was decorated to the hilt with lilacs. That did not last long, however, since Harman seemed to be allergic to the smell of lilacs and they were removed in hopes of stopping his sneezing--which it did. Of course, that gave the older boys an idea for something else to torment the couple with on their wedding night. They would make sure that all the lilac bushes around were minus their blooms by late that evening, ready to be placed in the bedroom of the honeymoon cottage.

It was a wonderful evening for the community. There was visiting, storytelling, square dancing, musical talents exhibited and in general a feeling of good will and jollity. The children had prepared a skit projecting what Harman and Miss Sally might look like when they grew old. Tag Lantry stole the show when he swaggered out in a pair of bib overalls, powdered hair and a beard fashioned from loose chicken feathers glued onto a piece of paper. Since Tag was very slim and Harman was quite a robust gentleman, Tag had placed a couple of folded towels inside his overalls to add some padding. The result was hilarious.

Sarah Bennett, as Miss Sally, wore a headscarf tied under her chin, her mother's apron and her Grandma's walking cane for support. Tag smoked a make-believe pipe and pretended to be hard of hearing. The other smaller children pretended to be their many grandchildren walking behind them.

The audience was hardly able to suppress their laughter and hilarity until Tag and Sarah stopped directly in front of the married couple and Tag opened his mouth to sing. Tag, never the bashful one, had been practicing for days on a couple of verses from the old song "When You and I were Young, Maggie," changing the name in the song from Maggie to Sally. As he began the song, the gathering became quiet and it mattered not that he started a bit high, the audience was his as he sang in a loud clear voice. *"They say we are aged and grey, Sally, As spray by the white breakers flung, But to me you're as fair as you were, Sally, when you and I were young. And now we are aged and grey, Sally, The trials of life nearly done. Let us sing of the days that are gone, Sally When you and I were young."*

The crowd went wild in applause while most of the ladies dabbed at their eyes. Even Harman was a bit teary eyed. Hearty congratulations were given to all the kids, especially to Tag for his song. After the good nights and many well wishes for the bridal couple, the folks gathered their dishes in preparation for going home. The final grounds clean up could wait as it was getting late and would be dark soon.

In the meantime, the older boys had been a busy group. The two frogs had been caught and were safe in a small cage at Will's house. Bill had collected a milk bucket of sand and the boys had talked Jackson and Tag into gathering up all the lilac blooms they could find in the immediate neighborhood--without getting caught, of course. Noting the sky was showing some dark clouds coming in, the group felt the need to get organized in a hurry. A flurry of activity erupted as everyone began gathering pots, buckets and what have you to be used for serenading. They were to meet at the gate to the Thompson place and would walk together to the honeymoon cottage that sat at the lower end of the Knoll. They needed only to wait until it was dark enough.

Jack and Charlie went ahead to look over things and make sure nothing went wrong. Mr. Jarvis had left about an hour before to take the couple to their new home. All was quiet when the two boys arrived, so they stayed out of sight as well as they could and began their preparations. They discovered that the only way they could get into the back door without being spotted was to first climb over the fence into the field behind the house. Once there, they would need to climb over the second fence that enclosed the backyard. The fence surrounded the house for good reason. For part of the year, at least, a bull belonging to Lawrence Raleigh made his home in the back field and it was a well-known fact that he did not take to strangers in his area. The second fence had been added to keep the bull from intruding into the back yard and those inside safe from his intrusion. Jack and Charlie weren't afraid, however, since it should not take but a few moments to get over the two fences plus the fact that it would also be dark. In addition, the bull usually stayed back of the pasture for his evening feeding time.

Back on the Knoll, however, things started going wrong for the boys from the very beginning. Granny Dalton happened to be making one last trip to the outhouse for the night and caught Jackson breaking off her lilacs. She was furious and grabbed her cane, which she proceeded to shake at him, threatening his very life. Poor Jackson knew he could outrun Granny but knew also that he would have to answer to his own parents later.

In the meantime, the rather large group waiting at Jack's house started down the road to go to the chivaree. Then to everyone's dismay, after about ten minutes into their walk, there came a horrific downpour that quickly soaked every member of the group. Amidst the shouting and shoving, they practically fell over each other trying to get back to shelter. The soaked group was upset, but good naturedly waited out the rain and most decided to go on despite being soaking wet. Of course, being called "sissies" also helped to get them on the road again.

This time they made it to the cottage where a likewise drenched and an impatient Jack and Charlie waited under a chestnut tree. So far, there had been no sign of the bull and on seeing one lone light in the living room Jack reported he thought the two were sitting on the couch and seemed to be just talking to one another. He cautioned the crowd again about being quiet and shared his plan with them. He, with Charlie's help, would get into the house from the back, but it would be necessary for Jack to climb over the pasture fence to get to the fenced back yard. He thought he would only need a short time to turn the frogs loose in the living room, toss the sand underneath the sheets, spread the lilacs around and grab Harman's suitcase off the back porch. All that needed to be done after the couple had come out on the front porch to welcome the rowdy group. Speed was important, so Jack cautioned the group to keep the couple on the porch for several minutes if they could.

Jack warned in a loud whisper, "Do not start before the signal! Charlie is gonna hoot like an owl, then you all start making noise as loud as you can, so I can get over the fence and onto the porch. As soon as they come out stop the banging, so I'll know they're out. I'll get back around here as fast as I can. Has everybody got it?" He heard a bunch of whispered affirmations.

He and Charlie hurried towards the back of the house. After checking any movement from the bull, Jack went over the first fence into Lawrence's field. It took a few minutes to transfer the frogs and sand and lilacs over the fence, especially since the lid kept coming off the bucket of sand. Jack scooped up what he could as Charlie stood at the fence and watched for the bull. It was dark as midnight and on hearing nothing, Charlie raised his white shirt and waved it to signal all was well. No one had ever told him that waving a piece of cloth was the number one way to get a bull's attention!

That was exactly what happened! The waving of the shirt caught the bull's eye and he came charging through the field at full gallop. If one can scream while whispering, Charlie screamed for Jack to get over the fence in a hurry. Jack indeed had heard the snorting and made it in one leap, but the barbed wire caught his best dress pants, from knee down, in a long tear and he wasn't sure where the bucket of sand landed but it was no longer in his hand. He got down on his knees to collect as much as he could sweep up in his hands hoping Charlie would hold off on his owl hoot to give him more time. Just at that moment there came a "who, who," but unknown to the crowd in front, it came from an actual owl who had been watching from the field's fence.

That prompted the most awful sounds and shouting from the front of the house as the serenaders thought it to be the signal from Charlie. Jack grabbed what sand that he could in his shirt tail and sprinted for the back door. He needed to be inside quickly, as he knew it was possible the couple might not stay out front but a short time. He made it in the back door and onto the porch and quietly re-closed the door. He checked his leg, which had bled some onto his pants. Seeing it was slight, he disregarded the cut, but was unable to get rid of the sand which seemed to be clinging to every part of his wet body, including his hair. He was a miserable mess and was now more determined than ever to make thing miserable for Harman and Sally.

He waited for the quiet which would indicate the married couple had gone out on the porch to welcome the serenaders. After what seemed to be several minutes of noise, it did become quiet and he slipped over to the door, which opened into the kitchen, and to his dismay found the door locked. *"Cat hairs and chicken feathers!"* he thought to himself, being the closest words, he could think of to express his disgust and aggravation. Now he couldn't get into the house with anything and was left with a bunch of lilacs and two bullfrogs. He looked around for Harman's suitcase, he could at least take that--but no clothes of Harman's were in sight. "*Rats!*" Everything was going wrong. He turned to go back to the yard and to his dismay found that the latch on the outside of the door had fallen in place locking him in. "Well, that's just dandy"! He couldn't get out and neither could he get back in! Everything in him wanted to scream.

Noting an end window, he began trying to get that raised when the clamor started again with the same shouting, banging and singing, then total silence. Finally, he heard a loud whisper from the fence corner, "Jack! Come on out. They're not coming out! We'll get them another night." He yelled back, "I'm locked in. Get me out of here" then added, "Where's that bull? My Ma is going to kill me."

And that was how the evening ended except for another downpour, which again soaked the revelers who couldn't imagine how such a nice evening could end so wretchedly. Will and Bill went down the fence line to where the bull had retired and did the owl thing to signal Jack and Charlie that the way was clear. Charlie hurried over the fences, unlocked the door and the four wet and tired boys were more than happy to go home for the night. So were the other serenaders.

Saturday was a quiet day. All the school pupils had been sufficiently warned to stay clear of the honeymoon cottage, although the newlywed couple was spotted once carrying bunches of lilacs over to the next field. Most folks were pleased when they showed up in church the next morning with Miss Sally smiling sweetly to everyone. Some of the older boys were uncomfortable to say the least and wondered that the couple had no shame since they had not had the decency to at least stick their heads out for the folks who were serenading them. The little girls swarmed around them once again wanting to be near their teacher. It was up to Blue to ask the inevitable question and she asked just as everyone was hoping. She put her hands on her hips and said it right out, "Why didn't you come out on the porch! Everybody was waitin' for you!"

Sally responded innocently, “Right out where? When?”

“Friday night,” spoke several of the children at once.

Looking as puzzled and innocent as possible, Harman replied. “But we couldn’t come out! We weren’t here Friday night. We went back to Beckley, so that I could pick up Sally’s wedding ring I had left there to be sized.”

With a collective groan, the older boys slunk down into their seats, while Mr. Jarvis sat in the back bursting with laughter. He had truly been able to pull one over on the boys! Knowing that the newlyweds wanted to return as soon as possible for the ring, he had suggested that they keep quiet about the trip and as a wedding gift he paid for them a night’s stay in a nice motel. He had further suggested that the couple prop up some pillows on the couch to fool the revelers into thinking someone was in the house. Mr. Jarvis had grown fond of Miss Sally throughout the school year and felt she deserved an evening away from the community. He had driven them back to Tazewell soon after the wedding while everyone was busy getting ready for the chiveree and he and the couple had enjoyed a good laugh imagining what was going on back at their cottage.

Harman and Sally were not told until sometime later, however, who it was that had placed a pair of frogs, a scattered bucket of sand and an arm load of purple lilacs on the back porch of their cottage. Granny decided not to tell on Jackson, once she had enjoyed hearing about the botched chivaree. She knew Jackson had been persuaded to get involved by that ornery Jack. Jack’s ma was the most furious of all on seeing the long tear in Jack’s Sunday pants and the amount of sand in her Monday wash water.

People remembered a few years later that was the last serenading they could remember in that area. The changes that were coming meant that many of the local customs would disappear along with the dwindling population of Fancy Knoll.

The Last Hurrah

By the end of April, Harman, the new husband of Miss Sally, knew he would likely be drafted soon. Things seemed to be moving much too fast and the couple's future plans had to be put on hold. Sally had been officially notified that the Fancy Knoll School would be closed for the next school year, causing the few children that were left to be bussed over to the Kent school. That would mean her future plans had to be changed drastically. She had so hoped to live in this peaceful place for years to come, teaching the kids she had learned to love so much. Now, it seemed she most likely would for sure go to live with Harman's parents in Ohio until Harman could return home from the army. It was a sad time for her and her new husband--as it was for many young couples in love.

In March, Pearlie Hackett's husband, Jude, and Lenny Thompson both had been drafted and had gone into boot camp. Pastor Amos said on Sunday morning, through tears, that he wished that he could stop the clock. It seemed everyone was leaving. The Thomas family had already moved back to North Carolina to take care of Clara's elderly parents and much to Lutie Lantry's dismay, her close friend Laura and husband, Sam, were returning to Arkansas to help farm the home place, since Sam's younger brothers had been drafted into service.

The heart of Fancy Knoll seemed to be fading away, with no one left to restore it. There was such a feeling of unrest. Not only were the changes caused by war, but also the very life of the community seemed to be ebbing away. The Bennett's and Joe and Mandy Thompson were already making plans to move to Michigan to work in the defense plants. Even the older schoolboys would most likely soon be called into service.

In the latter part of April, when the dogwoods began blooming, some of the folks met together and made plans to have one last big get-together at the end of school. It would be a happy time, hopefully, for celebrating the memories of a once close-knit thriving community. They planned to contact everyone possible that had ever been related to Fancy Knoll. That next week many letters went out from the post office over in Kent. Everyone was thrilled when they heard that Jude Hackett was getting to come home on a three-day pass before he would be shipped out overseas--just in time for the picnic.

Arrangements were made to bring Grandpa Hack off the mountain, as well as making sure Josie, Rosie and Granny Moore were also transported safely to the event. This would be one day that everyone possible would have the opportunity to be together for what perhaps might be one last time.

Considering the dwindling population, it would be both a homecoming and a farewell party for the community, although no one wanted to talk much about the farewell. One of the St Clair family had contacted a singing group from the local radio station to come and provide the entertainment. Of course, the residents would also provide music and the church quartet would share in the special singing. It was by collective agreement among the planning committee that every effort would be made to make it a happy day with as few tears shed as possible. They would have this one last day of enjoyment even if, according to Maggie, "we have to order some from the Sears catalog."

School was to close on May 22, so the plans were made for the big hurrah to coincide with the last day of school. For the first time in several months, something besides war occupied the older folk's minds as they prepared for the big day. All seemed determined to make it the most pleasant time possible. A mountain of food was prepared with several jugs of lemonade in evidence. The Rudd twins, Josie and Rosie, brought beautiful decorated cakes, but their usual fruit juices were nowhere in sight. Mr. Jarvis had asked the school kids to come sporting as many red white and blue items they could get their hands on. Blue saw that Grandpa Hack wore his red suspenders and the dogs, Stout, Bandit and Jolo came wearing ribbons of the three colors around their necks. The platform for the musicians was also decorated with flowers and ribbons.

Fortunately, the weather was beautiful for the outing, however a little cool. The women made sure there were plenty of blankets for the older folks. They had wanted to bring Grandpa Lantry over from the nursing home, but he was having a bad day and it was not advisable. Hezekiah had promised to go over later and share with him all the day's happenings.

It was to be a good day! The horseshoe stakes were placed in a nice level spot and the diamond for the inevitable baseball game was prepared. The people came from all directions--the people of Fancy Knoll.

The horseshoe competition began immediately among the older men, which at times could get quite rowdy. They seldom could take the time off from their work to enjoy a game of horseshoes, so they didn't waste time getting started. The older boys and girls got a baseball game going while the younger kids gathered to mark off their hopscotch squares. It would be some time before they needed to ready the food, so the women took the time to visit among themselves.

The older folks were seated on the sidelines and hard put as to which activity to watch. There was a lot of banter and laughter for them to take in and most of them simply enjoyed the happiness of the community--and remembered. Granny Moore chose her own activity by closing her eyes and taking a nice long nap. They awakened her for the food, of course.

Later in the afternoon things quieted down a bit and all those, who were so inclined, were invited to share any stories they had about the people, or events of the earlier days of Fancy Knoll. Several people responded. Some stories were hilarious, and some were sad, but the sad ones were quickly followed by another one before anyone could get teary-eyed. Granny Shinn told of hearing one time of an old man on Crane Creek who died and before they could take him over to the cemetery to bury him, a heavy rain came up, followed by a flash flood. She related that as they were trying to get him across the creek to bury him, "he fell right out that coffin into the water and that was that!" Granny sat back, and it grew quiet. "Well, what happened, for crying out loud?" yelled out Granny Honaker. "Well, how am I to know?" Granny Shinn said crossly, "that's the last anyone ever saw of him!"

Grandpa Hack spoke up and said he had a story to tell about a man named Silas that lived on Fancy Knoll a long time ago. Everyone loved Hack's stories, so it became quiet, so that everyone could listen.

"Once this very handsome middle-aged man moved into Fancy Knoll and told around that he was on his fifth marriage. According to him, his first wife had died of dropsy and the second one had put ground-up glass in his cracklings and tried to kill him, so he had run her off. The third wife wouldn't cook, so he divorced her. Then came the fourth one who one day put castor oil in his collard greens, thinking it was vinegar. He related he had never been able to get over that, even if she did have poor eyesight. He got rid of her. The fifth and present one, according to him, he was keeping locked in the cellar. He hastened to explain that he treated her very well, but she sometimes got homesick and would run away if not kept in a secure place. He further let the folks know that if one day they found him dead, they would find the key to the cellar on top of the kitchen cabinet."

Of course, by this time Grandpa Hack had everyone's attention as they all strained to hear the end of the tale. Much to everyone's aggravation, he took time to re-light his pipe and get settled deeper into his rocker. Finally, he continued, "Well, the old man died in 1898 and it was a sorry sight to see how the people rushed to his house--not to see him--but to see what the wife in the cellar looked like. No one could wait to look for the key, so they just busted through the door with a crowbar and what a great shocker it was when they found the cellar was empty! Most of the folks crowding the doorway just stood there in amazement, realizing they had been taken in by an old liar. If Mr. Fox hadn't spotted a piece of paper pinned to the wall, we never would have found out why he told such a lie."

Here Grandpa paused again. "Well, what did the paper say?" called out several in their frustration. Grandpa held up a napkin and pretended to be reading from a piece of paper, "*My dear friends of Fancy Knoll, I know you are all here to see my poor wife. I'm sorry to disappoint you but I have none. I did it to protect myself. After four wives, I got the idea I was so pleasing that women would just not leave me alone. So, if they thought I had a wife, no women would come around looking for a husband. Be assured I have had the most peaceful two years that I have had since my first wedding day. You have all been good friends to me and I thank you. Silas J. Thornton.*"

When Grandpa finished his story, most of the Fancy Knoll had a good laugh, including Grandpa Hack, while others saw nothing funny about his story. Grandma Honaker whispered to Lutie that the twins, Josie and Rosie, who were young at that time, had not taken the news well. Several felt that they had cast an eye on Mr. Thornton themselves.

One of the highlights of the day came when a car drove up and Jude Hackett got out in full uniform with Pearlie hanging onto him as if she would never let him go. He had baby Beau on his other arm. Everyone present broke into a big cheer as if he belonged to them all. In a way, he did! To them, he represented all the hometown boys and men who were being sent away to fight on the other side of the sea. All the people gathered around him as if they just wanted to touch him and wish him Godspeed.

All in all, everyone seemed to have a wonderful time that day, and as the gathering still lingered into the evening, no one seemed willing to go home. However, it had begun to cool down a bit, so after a few speeches inside the schoolhouse and a beautiful homemade quilt was presented as a parting gift to Miss Sally, the people filed out and left for their individual homes.

Only a few looked back at the now empty forlorn school. Mr. Jarvis could hardly contain his tears, but they were mostly unseen. Preacher Buchanan noticed the torn screen flapping against the side of the door thinking it needed fixing but turned away realizing the futility. Cordelia pulled him toward home. Miss Sally dared not look back, saving her tears for the privacy of her small honeymoon cottage. She felt a shiver pass through her body. It felt like the soul of the community had just slipped into the shadows.

While starting up Birch Mountain, Maggie and Blue hung back from the entourage that was helping get Grandpa Hack back to the cabin. It was growing dark and the two turned back toward Fancy Knoll where they could see clearly the outline of the schoolhouse silhouetted against the darkening sky. In tears Maggie held Blue close as Blue waved Stout's ragged red ribbon towards the school in one final goodbye. Maggie knew in her spirit the door was closing on the happiest days of her life. The winds of change were racing toward her mountain. The two turned homeward as the lonesome sound of a troop train could be heard as it passed through the lower valley.

Epilog

And that's the end of my stories. Most folks can look back to some place in their memories that they call the "home place" and regardless if the image is of happy times, or sorrowful times, it is imprinted into their minds. For me that place will forever be Fancy Knoll, although I was past thirty before I ever laid eyes on it.

It no longer exists as a community, having long ago given way to a world of concrete and modern factories, but I can still feel the heartbeat of that community. The geographical place never grew enough to exist on a map, but it would nevertheless forever exist in the hearts of the people who lived there. Only a few are left, though, who remember it as home. In my mind's eye, it reminds me of a chain link fence with one link at a time being removed from the whole. As the chain became shorter, I made up my mind to keep these memories alive by some means and now my writing of the stories has given me that pleasure.

Sometimes in late evening, I can imagine I hear the laughter of Grandpa Hack from his rocker here on the mountain, or the voices raised in praise from the church on Huckleberry road, or dear Mr. Jarvis proclaiming his allegiance to the state of West Virginia. Again, in my mind I share the joy of Cordelia Buchanan after the conversion of her husband, Amos, and that sweet Jessie Blandly finding such fulfillment in helping others as a counselor.

Most of all, though, I can hear the laughter of dozens of folks who called themselves Fancy Knoll residents. A man once said, "The most wasted day is that in which we have not laughed." Oh, my! How we folks laughed! When I think back, it usually involved the youngsters though--those kids who have somehow now grown old.

I guess laughter was our balm of Gilead. It could get us through anything! I remember when Stout died, with all our hearts breaking for Blue, she insisted on what she called a Christian funeral for that dog. We all gathered one cold morning at a spot near the timberline and stood there, teeth chattering, singing "You are my Sunshine," Blue's favorite song. Most of us were smiling through our tears.

Then there was the wake of Granny Dalton. We all loved her dearly and mourned her passing but when someone sat down a bowl of very sour buttermilk by mistake and her cat got the milk all over his long whiskers, he had us all rolling in laughter as he tried to clean himself, detesting the taste of the buttermilk. I have never laughed so much at a wake.

The tears come when I realize that never again will we laugh together. Never again will the children fall in line at the old schoolhouse with their hands over their hearts, to pledge allegiance to our flag and sing about our West Virginia hills. No longer will folks gather on the banks of Crane Creek to witness a baptism in its clear cold water. Those days are gone forever.

I alone am still on the mountain. I have watched as one by one of the folks who made up Fancy Knoll have left. As long as I am here though, those people will still be here also--that is in my heart. My happiest moments have been here on the mountain. Many years ago, I learned about my heavenly Father from a curious little girl named Blue. She brought light into my life at a time when I no longer cared for anyone. One day she held my hand and told me that I was loved. We remain friends and she comes with her children--and now a grandchild--to see me and we laugh and talk of old times.

Some folks think I am crazy and maybe I am, but I am satisfied here on Birch Mountain. During the day, I refuse to look in the direction where Fancy Knoll used to be. It is nothing now but a big industrial park. I can hear the activity there, the whistles and see the smoke, but I refuse to acknowledge it. I wait until the evening hours when the factory people have gone home and as I look through the mist, I see instead, the people of Fancy Knoll moving about on the dirt road, calling out to each other or gathering for evening worship. Of course, I know it's in my imagination, but it is those images that keep me sane up here on this lonely mountain.

Some time ago, Blue told me laughingly that someone over at that park called me crazy. That was because late one evening they came up on the mountain and saw me standing out on the porch in my petticoat singing the Great Speckled Bird at the top of my voice. I loved that song!

That reminds me, Blue has promised to try and find me a picture of Roy Acuff. I've wondered all these years what he looked like--a man that could write a song that pretty--he must have been a wonderful feller.

You probably wonder what happened to folks who lived in Fancy Knoll. Well, all the old ones are gone--the Lantrys, Nettie, Grandpa, most of the Thompson family, Nora Blandly, Mr. Jarvis; just about everyone except a few of the younger generation. One of the Compton boys never came home from the war, Joe on the other hand became a druggist over in Charleston. Charlie Bennett went into acting, but never made it farther than in small acting groups. Beau became a minister over in Kent. Blue, after her marriage to Tag, became a science teacher. Tag went into the lumber business and Jackson became an honest lawyer. I am so proud of him!

Mr. Jarvis would be the happiest of all if he knew that two of his students, Will and Cecil, went into politics, both for the state of West Virginia, under Governor Okey Patterson. They helped lobby for that fancy turnpike going over to Charleston.

In a sense they were all my children, but Blue is my pick of the litter--wouldn't she love being called that! That makes me think of Blessing, Tag's big hog. I don't guess I ever told this to a soul, but after I heard that story about the boys giving her chamomile tea to save her life, I slipped down there late one evening just to get a look at that sow. I had never in my life heard of a hog getting a stay of execution. I stood in the shadows that night and got my curiosity satisfied. I then got back up the mountain as fast as I could.

Folks would have thought me crazy if they could have seen me sneaking around the Lantry pigpen. They would have taken me on to the asylum, for sure. I laughed all the way back up the mountain. Somehow, though, I feel a kinship with Blessing. She was always a boon to others and that's what I hope has turned out in my life. That's a right nice way to be remembered.

Sincerely, Maggie Snow

About the Author

This book is a collection of simple stories written in the vernacular of the Appalachian region during the late 1930's and the early 1940's. Although written as fiction, every chapter has a person or event reminiscent of the author's own life. The author was raised in West Virginia and now, as a widow, she lives a quiet life in Idaho near four of her six children. The years have taken her many places away from the hills of her home state. She was born with a desire for learning new things, but the fulfillment of that desire came only at fifty years of age--and after the birth of 7 children. She became a nurse and later attended Bible college. In 1998, after a seven year stay in the Philippines as a Baptist missionary, she returned to Indiana for a time before a desire to return to the hills became irresistible. On her return to the Appalachian area she continued to work and live in the same community she grew up in. However, due to her age, and an opportunity for a home in Idaho, she left the area of her childhood for good and settled into, perhaps, her last move. She continues to call West Virginia home, however, and states that her early years in the hills were the most endearing and uncomplicated times of her life, plus a remarkable era to be born into. Her enjoyment of her early years is greatly contributed to the church as being the center of most communities and the sharing of the same values-- if not the same preferences. She states that the memories of those days are like shadows who hide from the sun, trailing her wherever she turns. "I both lived them and sometimes I long for them."

Printed in the United States
By Bookmasters